# Obstruction

*by Sylvie Grayson*

other books by Sylvie Grayson

**Suspended Animation**

**Earth Quake**

*"...Interesting characters, family conflicts and divided loyalties make this a book that kept me up half the night..."*
Amazon reviewer

*Legal Obstruction* is a work of fiction. Names, characters, places and incidents are products of the author's imagination or are used fictitiously. Any resemblance to actual events or locales or persons, living or dead, is entirely coincidental.

Except for use in any review, the reproduction or utilization of this work in whole or in part in any form by any electronic, mechanical or other means, now known or hereafter invented, including xerography, photocopying and recording, or in any information storage or retrieval system, is forbidden without the written permission of the author or publisher.

GREAT WESTERN PUBLISHING
220 Bay Street, Victoria, British Columbia, Canada
Copyright © 2014 by Sylvie Grayson
Excerpt from *Earth Quake* copyright ©2014 by Sylvie Grayson
All rights reserved.

For information contact
sylviegraysonauthor@gmail.com
www.sylviegrayson.com

ISBN: 978-0-9938288-3-6
Great Western Publishing is a registered trademark of Sylvie Grayson.

Cover art by Steven Novak    novakillustration@gmail.com

# DEDICATION

I am blessed with wonderful support that has enabled me to write. To my husband, who leaves me alone when I need to work but is always ready to listen, read and lend a hand with difficult passages. To my children who had faith in me and helped with their support and practical suggestions.

To my critique group:
Anna Markland, author of *Hearts and Crowns* and other medieval romances,
Helena Korin,
Reggi Allder, author of *Money, Power and Poison*
and Jacquie Biggar, author of *Tidal Falls*
who all supported me to polish the words for publication, my many thanks.

Any errors or omissions are mine alone.

**Sylvie Grayson**
**www.sylviegrayson.com**

.

# LEGAL

# OBSTRUCTION

## CHAPTER ONE

The dog barked sharply, then once more and Joe put down his coffee cup. "That must be them now," he said, heading for the door, his long legs covering the carpet in swift strides. Geoff came more slowly, setting his cup on the fireplace mantle, pausing to adjust his shirt collar and check his image in the mirror on the hallstand before following his older brother down the granite steps to the front drive.

Joe was already at the car, hand on the door, the sheepdog bustling about his legs and whining anxiously. He joshed through the window with Dubuy about being late, getting lost the minute he left the city, too much of a tenderfoot to follow perfectly straightforward directions. The older man levered himself out of the driver's seat and turned to grasp Joe's hand in a firm shake, a wide grin on his face.

Geoff watched with undisguised interest as the passenger door opened and a young blonde woman stepped onto the pavement of the drive, adjusting the jacket of her suit and leaning back to take a briefcase from behind the seat. As she straightened, the sunlight glowed on her hair. Not blonde, more honey brown, pinned up in a roll on the nape of her neck. Geoff grinned, watching the look on Joe's face as he caught sight of her. Stunned, that's how he looked, momentarily lost for words. His jaw went slack and eyes widened as he stood holding André Dubuy's hand forgotten in his own big fist.

To his credit he recovered quickly enough. His mouth snapped shut in a grim line and his eyelids drooped to that guarded look that Geoff had seen so often in the last couple of years.

The woman walked around the back of the car toward them. She wore a well-cut light grey suit, the short skirt showing off fantastic legs, the fitted jacket very conservative. Medium heeled shoes, black. Briefcase held with confidence. Under her jacket she wore a charcoal grey sweater with a cowl neck, just enough to soften the businesslike effect of the suit, frame her face and hide her chest. Good move. She obviously meant business, in a well-bred and competent way.

"Joe," said Dubuy, taking the woman by the elbow and bringing her forward, "I'd like you to meet Emily Drury. Emily, this is Joe Tanner, president of *Tanner Enterprises*. And this is Geoffrey Tanner, his brother. Geoffrey, Emily Drury."

Joe had taken her hand and held it for the required moment, giving her a hard level look that would have had Geoff running for cover if he'd been this woman coming north to talk about taking a position with the company. He sometimes wondered if his brother knew or cared what effect he could have on people with his tough aggressive stance.

Geoff elbowed him out of the way and stepped between, extending his hand. "Welcome, Miss Drury. Come on in and let's get comfortable. I know this is your first time here, but André has visited before. He knows we don't stand on ceremony." He tucked her hand in the crook of his arm, pushed past a frowning Joe and led her into the house.

"This house was built by our grandfather, another Joe Tanner, when he first came to Vancouver Island and began to farm here. I guess they thought they'd have a lot of kids, because he went crazy on size, but in the end they only had two children. The main floor is made entirely from stone taken right off the farm from a quarry at the other end of the land. It's quite unique. When they added the second story, they went to the post and beam style."

Geoff knew he was rambling but he was comfortable with the topic and felt an obligation to fill in the gap and ease this woman's position. If he left it to Joe, she'd be running for the hills after the first few minutes of forced face to face interrogation.

She smiled gratefully at him and it transformed her face. She was quite a heart stopper, younger than he'd first thought. Too bad he was already engaged. No, not too bad, he loved Vanessa with all his heart. But she sure was easy to look at. Joe was going to have a hard time with this situation if she decided to come and work with them.

"It's a lovely house, Mr. Tanner. You must be very proud to live in a home your grandfather built."

He shrugged good-naturedly. "Oh, I don't live here, Joe does. I live in town, much more civilized. Now, the offices of *Tanner Enterprises* are in the left wing of the house, down that hall. Joe likes to keep things close to home." Geoff gave a warm chuckle and shot a glance over his shoulder at his older brother.

"I'm not the one you need to be talking to; I only hold a small interest in *Tanner Enterprises*. It's primarily Joe's baby, but he felt there might be things you could do for me as well, if we decide to go ahead with this idea of hiring in-house legal counsel. I have a couple of hardware stores in town, with Dad as a minority shareholder. We like to work together, Joe, Dad and I, keep it in the family. It saves resources."

He led her to the family room and gazed happily around. The room was spacious and comfortable, big old sofas ranged around the perimeter with side and end tables standing in a haphazard but charming fashion within arm's reach. He seated her in the big firm overstuffed chair that was customarily Joe's domain. That should put a burr in his shorts if there wasn't one there already.

"Sit here," he said with a welcoming grin. "I'll get you some coffee. Do you take anything in it?"

"Just black, thanks." Emily smiled at him and settled herself, briefcase at her side. As she looked around the room André Dubuy and Joe came down the hall. Geoff took coffee orders as they arrived.

A huge fieldstone fireplace big enough to roast an ox took up most of one wall. Double glass doors led through the back to a red brick patio where they often relaxed in summer. Planters were grouped at one end, empty this time of year, some dead dried plants still hanging over the sides and blowing stiffly in the intermittent breeze. Mum would be out to plant them in the spring. Aspens formed a type of windbreak down one side of the field behind the house, waving leafless branches in the chill winter wind.

André took a seat near Emily and he saw him reach to give her hand a reassuring squeeze before he settled back to adjust his jacket. Then he turned to address the others. "You've discussed several times hiring legal counsel in house, especially given your present rate of growth and plans for the future. And since I'll be retiring shortly and not able to take care of business for you much longer, time seems to be of the essence. Did you know I've sold the law firm?" His bushy brows waggled with the excitement of his announcement.

"Did you now, you old fox?" Joe replied. "I knew you were planning on making a move. I didn't think it would be this quick."

"Well, I'll be seventy in the spring, so it seemed to be time. That's one advantage to being self-employed, eh, boy? You can work as long as you like. Of course, the opposite isn't always true. No early retirement package, is there? Not unless the bottom line is damn good and healthy!" They all laughed.

"Yes, so," André continued, his voice smooth and flowing like aged brandy.

It was one of the keys to his success in the courtroom, Geoff thought. What jury could resist that full-bodied voice with its reassuring, confident flow of words?

"I sold the firm, amalgamated really but I'll get paid out, nice lump sum up front along with continuing payments over a ten year period. All confidential, of course." Emily snickered and André grinned at her. With lawyers, Geoff thought, everything was confidential.

"My partner Sam is going to head up the new firm and Emily has the option of staying on with them. They want her very badly for her courtroom experience. They're rather lean in that department. But you and I had talked and Emily has some interest in pursuing the matter. So, here we are." He sat back and beamed like a fond father on his beloved children.

Geoff wasn't fooled for a minute. He detected the familiar sharp glint in his eye even if the others didn't.

Joe took the proffered coffee from his brother as his piercing hooded gaze swung to Emily. What an impact that gaze could have. Did he understand how unfriendly he looked? "You have some interest in this idea. How much?" he demanded.

The colour in her cheeks came and faded again but she held her gaze steady. "Some, Mr. Tanner, as André said. The amount of interest I have depends on what kind of position we're talking about, what kind of working conditions, your expectations, the remuneration package."

She paused to take a sip from her cup. "André mentioned accommodations being part of the package. I'd need to see them, decide whether it would be better for me to stay onsite or live in Bonnie and drive out. I have a household of three, so these are all things to consider. Perhaps you could begin by telling me what you had in mind and what your own expectations are."

Geoff mentally clapped his hands. He'd seen Joe make grown men squirm with that flat look and abrupt manner. Emily hadn't blinked an eye. He snuck a look at Dubuy and saw his small smile of satisfaction as he settled into the cushions and drank his coffee. Dubuy was no fool, he knew what he was doing.

Joe's face relaxed a little as it always did when he talked about the business, and he began to discuss his plans for expansion. He talked about the goals of the company, the recent growth of the import part of the business, his hopes for expanding the export side.

As he continued he spoke more and more to Emily. She met him head on, questioning him where he was vague, asking for details and explanations until it seemed they were unaware of the other two people in the room.

Gracefully she brought the conversation to a close, reaching for her briefcase. Extracting a folder, she opened it on her knee. "It's getting late and we don't want to take up more of your time than is necessary. Here's a copy of my curriculum vitae. I'm sorry, Geoff, I only brought one copy. I hadn't realized two would be more appropriate. I hope you have an opportunity to read it."

She flashed him a brief look and he felt the warmth of that impact. She knew enough to take her allies where she could find them, she seemed to be saying.

"This is a breakdown of the type of work I've concentrated on, files I've handled since beginning practice with Dubuy, Jefferson three years ago. You'll note, Joe, that over the last year I've done ninety percent of *Tanner Enterprises* work, under André's supervision of course."

She slanted a smile at André that softened her gaze and captured Joe's attention, but reverted to a more sober expression as she swung back to continue addressing them. "I conducted most of the Chambers work for the firm. Sam Jefferson is a solicitor and prefers not to go to court. Any actual Supreme Court trials were conducted by André and me, with André as lead counsel."

She handed the papers over and rose. "I'd like to see the offices before we go, Joe, if you don't mind. And the accommodation. Would we be staying in the house?"

Geoff leaped to his feet when she stood. He felt like cheering. She'd essentially run the meeting once André sat back and relinquished the reins to her. And now she was elegantly bringing it to a close. Instead, he took her hand and held it, smiling into her face and ignoring Joe as he rose from his chair. "There's a second house on the property not far from here. I'll show you," he said.

~~~

Joe stalked back into the living room and glared down at his brother. Geoff had cracked himself a beer and sat in his brother's chair, feet propped on a nearby stool. He frowned. "That's my chair, you hound. First you put Emily in it, then take it for yourself."

Geoff barked a laugh and his brother had to smile. He went to the kitchen to get his own beer and cuffed him on the back of the head as he went by. "Well, what do you think?"

Throwing himself down onto the nearest sofa, he landed his shoes on the armrest. "Does she know what she's doing? Will she do a good job for us? Will she *stay*? I don't want to get them all moved out here just to have her change her mind." He sounded decidedly disgruntled at the thought.

Geoff was amused. "Who is in her 'three person family', may I ask?" he countered. "Could it be a loving husband and maybe a child?"

"I asked her that already." Joe waved his beer airily. "I didn't want a commune out here. I questioned whether her husband is coming. She said no, her son and his nanny."

Geoff's jaw dropped. "You're joking. So it's not *Miss* Drury, it's *Mrs*. Drury."

"Nope, I asked that too. She prefers Ms. Drury, thank you very much."

"Whew, she doesn't look like she has a kid. Too young looking. I don't know." He shrugged at Joe's acerbic expression. "I couldn't tell if she liked the house or not."

Joe lifted his brows. "Neither could I. She plays it pretty close to the chest, doesn't let her expression give her away."

"Speaking of the chest. When she took her jacket off, I couldn't help but notice…"

Joe froze him with a look. "You're an engaged man, you

ass! What do you think Vanessa would make of that comment?"

"What? I can't look? I was just admiring the scenery. I noticed your eyes were riveted somewhere in that general vicinity, big brother."

Joe dismissed him with a sharp glance. "Well, we'll hear from her Tuesday, so we need to make up our minds before then. She seemed competent. She asked all the right questions. She even had me rethinking my decisions a few times."

"Face it, Joe, old man Dubuy's a pretty sharp cookie. If she was his right hand man, so to speak, it's because she knows her stuff not because she's got a great pair of legs. Although that doesn't hurt, from my point of view."

Joe sat up irritably on the couch and glared at his brother. "God, you never quit, do you? Vanessa better get you to the altar before you change your mind." Sighing he sank back against the cushions. "I think you're right though. She's sharp as a tack. So why is she interested in moving out of the city to this backwater town of Bonnie and working exclusively for us? Something's not right."

Geoff felt himself bristle. His big hardware stores were thriving in this 'backwater town' as his brother so inelegantly put it. "Maybe she's had enough of the big city hustle. She's got a child. Her husband's dead or they've divorced and she's on her own. Maybe she hopes for a better quality of life in Bonnie for her little family. Who knows? It's a sure bet that she isn't going to make her decision lightly. And if she does decide to take the job, she won't be quitting in a hurry to move her child again. So from that point of view, she's probably a good bet." There was a pause as both men contemplated the situation. "On the other hand," he added, "good thing you changed your mind about her office."

Joe looked startled, then their eyes met and they both burst into bellows of laughter. When Joe finally caught his breath, he gave in to a final chuckle. "That's for sure. I honestly never gave it any thought, but when she said she wanted to see the offices, I started to panic."

Geoff rolled his eyes. "No kidding. I was thinking, where's Joe going to put her? The only vacant room is that little cramped space at the back."

Joe snickered and shook his head. "The deal would have been finished before it started if I'd shown her that. Well, Dad can just take what he wants from that room and we'll clear out the rest. He hasn't used it for years, anyway."

"No," said Geoff, "but I can hear the howls of protest already." They both chuckled again then lapsed into companionable silence.

He roused himself again. "What are you going to do about Shirley?"

Joe looked blank. "Shirley? What about her?"

"She's an old battle-ax, that's what. She's been working for you for years and thinks she owns you, lock, stock and barrel. She worked for Dad and you just took the easy road and kept her on. Half the time even *I* can't get to speak to you because you're *busy* or *in a meeting.*"

Joe frowned. "She does the job. What more can you ask?"

"She gets in the way, and doesn't add a whole lot. Her computer skills are next to nil. And she's going to resent the hell out of any newcomer. You know how she is every time you get a new girlfriend. What are you going to do about her?"

Joe moved his shoulders in a disgruntled twitch. "Hell, I don't know. And I've only had one girlfriend." He thrust his hand through his thick dark hair and it fell forward again, hanging over his forehead. "I know she's a bit protective but sometimes that's a blessing. I don't get a whole lot of work done if I have to answer every phone call that comes in. And she doesn't seem to mind the long hours. All I really need her to do is answer the phone, type a few letters and keep the office open. Surely to God they can work together!"

"Joe, you're a wonder." There was amazement in Geoff's voice. How could his brother be so obtuse? "You know damn well Shirley will try to eat that girl for breakfast, first of all because she's young and good-looking and second because she'll have access to you and your office without having to get her permission. She won't want to share you. It's a recipe for disaster."

Joe rose to his feet and moved restlessly around the living room, finally stopping at the glass doors to stare moodily out at the bleak landscape. The evergreens at the end of the lower field were black conical shapes in the gloom of oncoming evening. The arbutus grove down by the ocean's edge glowed a lighter green with their shiny leaves reflecting the late sun. Their peeling red trunks were the only spot of colour down there, picked up and reflected back by the old red of the bricks in the patio.

Geoff watched his tense shoulders and wondered what it would take to pry Shirley out of the *Tanner Enterprises* office. Joe just didn't like to deal with change. He'd had enough of it with his marriage and then divorce, his battles with their father. He never took on a new scuffle now unless he had absolutely no alternative. His money was on Shirley staying.

"Well," Joe said, turning back to the room, "we don't even know if Emily's going to accept yet. One thing at a time, here. We'll deal with it when we get there."

Geoff snorted.

## CHAPTER TWO

Emily was silent for so long that André had turned the car onto the Malahat Highway heading for the outskirts of greater Victoria and home before she spoke. "Thank you for arranging that, André, I appreciate it. You really went out of your way."

Dubuy turned his face to her briefly, a fond smile on his lips, before looking back at the road. He reached down to flick on the headlights to pierce the winter gloom. "You're welcome. It was no favour, however. If you take that job, they'll get a very competent lawyer on staff who'll be able to handle just about anything that comes at them. The only things you might need support on are Court of Appeal work, and maybe contracts that are across more than two countries. They couldn't afford a lawyer on staff who has enough experience to do those on their own, anyway."

She was silent for a minute, knowing he was waiting to hear her reaction to the afternoon. "I don't think he liked me much. Joe, I mean. I can work for clients who don't particularly like me, but I don't want to put myself at the full-time mercy of an employer like that. I'm really not interested in that scenario. It spells disaster."

André mused for a minute, his lips pursed. "Well, I've known Joe Tanner for a few years, must be five or six now.

And you've worked enough on his file in the last while to know how his company has come along. He started out pretty small with his line of exports and it has grown by leaps and bounds. Now they want to branch out in a different direction for imports, going into Europe. So he's decided to focus on the southern countries, Portugal, Spain, Italy and Greece. He even has designs on products from Turkey once they get a foot-hold in the European Union.

"Right now he's negotiating with a company in Portugal and hoping that will start to open up parts of the European Common Market. He has big plans. And he needs you. He's a smart man, Emily, so he knows someone with your skill in business and contracts is needed. Maybe give him a chance."

Emily was silent, pondering his words.

André glanced over at her, then back at the road. "There's also his personal life," he added. "He was newly married when I first met him."

Emily turned to him with interest. Joe Tanner hadn't struck her as a man who would be interested in any long term relationship.

"The marriage didn't last long. She was from eastern Canada, family had lots of money. I think she saw him as an example of the rugged western male or something. Kind of turned her on for a while. And he saw her as a diamond, something to be cherished, maybe a little beyond his reach.

"Suffice it to say, they weren't happy. Ended in divorce within a couple of years. Joe is very close-mouthed about anything personal but Geoff mentioned one time that he was badly hurt by it, hadn't really formed another close relationship since. But deep down, I think he's a good man, a fair man. He might take a little time adjusting to the fact that his lawyer's a woman, then he'll be fine. And so will you."

Emily studied André's profile in the dim light. His face was starting to show its age, becoming jowly, a little heavier. His white hair had receded back from his forehead, the scalp shining through on the crown. Thick brows hung low over dark eyes that snapped and sparkled when he was animated.

She'd always loved his eyes. When she was a child, he'd look at her with those twinkling eyes and waggle his brows, she'd laugh and run to him for a hug. It was such a good feeling. She'd always known that he loved her.

This man was very dear, like a father. He'd been a great friend of her own father's and the two families had spent a lot of time together when she was small. Angeline Dubuy was a big woman, taller than André and mother of his five children. What a brood they'd been, all quite a bit older than Emily and her brother John. But their children had been a steady source of baby-sitters for her parents. When she was tiny she'd called him Old Guy, which was her child's rendition of his name Dubuy. And she'd called him that with affection ever since.

She often thought it was her association with Old Guy and Mrs. Dubuy that had sustained her during some difficult years. She was sure she wouldn't have been able to complete her schooling without their help and support, constant faith and love that had kept her going through very dark times.

Now she studied André's face to see what he really thought, but was unable to discern anything more than what had just been said. "I might make another appointment, then," she ventured. "Go back up to look around the city of Bonnie, get a feel for it. I'll talk to Joe again too, in the middle of next week maybe. I can discuss what kind of contract I want, what kind of remuneration package. The salary he mentioned isn't enough, I feel. And that house, well it's nice, but it's as much a convenience for him to have me close as it is a savings for me to live on the property instead of renting my own place."

André laughed, and patted her knee. "Atta girl, you tackle him. He doesn't need to get a bargain here, just good legal counsel. Why don't you talk to him about shares in the corporation?"

Emily's eyes narrowed as she studied him. "What do you mean, Old Guy, a share of *Tanner Enterprises?*"

"Sure, why not? If you're going to be working there full time, helping him build his company into something much bigger and more profitable than it is now, why not get a piece of the action? Ask to see the financial statements." He grinned and waggled his brows at her.

She gave an answering grin.

"Think about it, Emily. You've been under a lot of strain over a long period of time. You've lost both your parents, gone through law school, articled and had a baby. You're showing signs of exhaustion. We both know it'd be a mistake to go with Sam and work for the new firm. They're workaholics. No one matters but the partners, the associates will carry the whole load like they do in any big law office. They're in there nights, weekends, vacations, you name it. Not a very healthy lifestyle, right? Especially for you right now with your own issues to consider.

"There's Andrew to think about. I know you have Mrs. Morrison, but you still take the main responsibility for the baby and she needs her own time. So this may be the perfect solution. The work should be interesting, it's been fascinating working with Tanner in the past as he's branched out. You like international law and you're the best there is at contracts, which are mainly what the job consists of, contracts and negotiations. And the hours will be less than you work now. Of course, there'll be times when there's a push on. You know that as well as I do, but if it gets to be too much, you just tell Joe you have to have a junior lawyer in for a few weeks to get everything done. He won't blink an eye. Or you can keep Sam on as consulting counsel and use him for help on the really big stuff.

"And if you can get some shares in the corporation as part of your compensation package that would be another source of income. You may even get to the point where you don't have to work full time. You have some money left from your parent's estate, don't you? Something put by? Think of it as a future retirement package or a chance to build a lump sum of equity."

Emily nodded, then realized he couldn't see her in the dark. "Yes, that makes sense. And I do have some money left. I put most of it into the down payment for the house. Other than that, I'm afraid to touch it in case I really need it one day. I think if I take the job, I'll keep the house in Victoria and just find some renters. I don't want to cut off my access back into the Victoria market if this doesn't work out as well as I'd like."

They were passing through Thetis Lake Park now, and the high rocks and giant cedar trees on either side of the highway made it very dark along the road. Rain sliced against the windshield, the trees towering above them blowing and bending in the wind. André slowed the car and moved forward steadily, following a line of tail lights barely visible on the highway ahead.

"Well, there you go," he said. "If you can get some shares in Joe Tanner's company, you're well on your way to becoming more independent. Maybe ask for Vice President, you want to be able to act for the company with authority, so might as well get the title that goes with it.

"Then there's that other issue just rearing its head." He gave her a pointed look but went back to his original argument. "You have to think of all the angles, Em. What do you want to put on your curriculum vitae, things like shareholder of the corporation, past Vice President and so forth. You won't be there forever. Look out for yourself, no one else will. So, go back, meet with Joe Tanner and see what you can wring out of him."

~~~

In the reception office, Shirley answered the phone with a song in her voice. *"Tanner Enterprises."*

She listened for a moment to a low female voice asking for Joe, then replied, "I'm sorry. He's in a meeting. Can I have him return your call?" Another pause while the woman spoke again. "Who may I say is calling?" she asked.

Just then Joe marched out of his office. "Who is it?" he mouthed at her. She wrote 'Emily Drury' on the little pink message slip but Joe's hand covered the pad to get her attention.

"I'll talk to her," he said low.

Shirley shook her iron-grey hair in its tight perm and hung up the receiver. "She's already gone. She said she'll be in her office until six, if you want to call back."

"I said I'd take it! Why in hell did you say I was in a meeting?"

She looked up at him in astonishment and he backed up a step, lowering his voice.

"I was in there working at my desk. Why not ask me if I want to take the call, or simply put it through to me? Come on, Shirley, I'll tell you when I need to have my calls screened. I always do. Otherwise put them through!" He stomped back to his office, slamming the door behind him.

Her lipsticked mouth remained open in an O of surprise for a minute, then she automatically grabbed for the message slip to see who this woman was that Joe was so anxious to talk to. He'd ripped the slip off and left with it clutched in his fingers.

Well, definitely the first name was Emily. She tried to read the next page, tilting it to the light to see if she had left enough of an impression with the tip of her pen to decipher what it said but couldn't make it out it.

She sat for a minute, deep in thought. This certainly put a different light on things. Who was Emily? Obviously someone Joe wanted very badly to talk to. Did this mean that woman from Toronto, that Margaret Shaw was on the way out? Perhaps he was finished with her and moving on. That was fast.

Huh. Shirley had never thought much of her. Joe hadn't seemed all that interested in her either, truth be told, but she would pursue him, oh yes. Flying into Vancouver for the weekend, phoning and insisting Joe go over there to see her, spending the weekend with him. Sometimes she'd had the nerve to come over to the island. Once that she was aware, Margaret had even stayed at the house. Stayed three days.

Shirley snorted. Good riddance to that one! Thin as a stick she was, her nose a mile high. Thought she was really something and Bonnie was a little no account city that wasn't quite good enough for her.

But then she sobered. This could be a new threat, this Emily. She didn't remember Joe ever losing his temper over a phone call before, not even from Margaret Shaw. She'd have to keep her eyes open. There was definitely something new in the wind.

## CHAPTER THREE

Joe sat in his office and pulled at his hair with both hands. Emily was on another line taking a call and he'd had to leave a message with her secretary. He'd been waiting all day to hear from her. She said she'd call Tuesday and he'd been afraid to leave his office.

He'd thought long and hard about taking her on in the company and decided he'd be a fool not to. He'd talked it over with Geoff and his father to get more perspective. They both agreed with him that it made sense, for a myriad of reasons. Dad thought it would improve the image and prestige of the company. Dad's opinion should always be taken with a grain of salt. But Geoff thought it was a great idea and Geoff was a serious businessman with excellent judgment, even if he was his younger brother.

Emily knew the legal affairs of the company better than anyone, he'd pointed out. Better than André Dubuy probably, that old fox. He'd obviously passed on most of the legal work to her, at least over the last year. Well, that's how it was done and they all knew it, the work was moved along to the lowest common denominator, and in that firm for André it had been Emily. She had enough experience to do everything they needed, not just for *Tanner Enterprises* but also for Geoff's businesses, their family land holdings and anything their younger brother Jon might need for his store.

Plus she'd run that interview as if she were the one doing the hiring, which from her perspective might have been true. But it had been impressive to behold, once he recovered from the shock of it. To have her working like that on behalf of the company wouldn't be half bad. It would be great to have someone else in his corner, someone capable and professional.

Geoff had certainly enjoyed watching her in action. She'd warmed up to him on the spot, of course. That was his brother for you. He liked people, had an easy-going friendly manner that wasn't threatening, and they liked him right back. In Joe's opinion, that didn't always make him a terrific businessman when the negotiations got tense. But he had a hidden streak in him that was as tough as any in Joe. He just didn't show it that often, kept it hidden behind his 'Mr. Geniality' facade.

Apart from that, Joe couldn't deny even to himself that he was interested in Emily in a more personal way. He'd only been thinking about her non-stop since the weekend when he'd watched Dubuy's car drive away. Yes, he'd noticed when she took her jacket off at the other house while they were showing her around. Geoff needn't think he was made of stone or that he'd been stricken blind suddenly. Her chest looked nothing short of magnificent. And her legs had certainly held his attention as he walked behind her to the car, talking to Dubuy.

Feeling suddenly hot, he ran a hand around the inside of his shirt collar. He'd missed her phone call. What if she decided she didn't want to come? What more could he offer to entice her up here?

This place was a little remote for a young woman like her. Not the town itself, Bonnie was a great little city, but the *Tanner Enterprises* establishment. They were far enough out of the city that it was an effort to get into Bonnie and be social, go shopping and do things women liked to do. She'd have to take the time to make the trip. If she was used to living in a bigger city then she was likely going to be concerned about that.

And she had a child. What was the story there, anyway? Dubuy had been very close-mouthed, simply confirming what Emily had said, that the husband would not be moving up with her. Just Emily, her child and the nanny. If she came at all.

What was Shirley thinking? Actually, Geoff was probably right, although he'd never really paid much attention before. She did run the office as if she were a mother bear and each caller was a threat to her cub. He grimaced.

He hadn't minded till now. Sometimes he'd even appreciated it. She kept the salesmen away, the advertising people and all those others who tried to make a buck selling him something that he didn't need or want and wasted his time while they did it.

But the secretary could be a pain in the neck. Like right now. Or during the time when he'd been breaking up with Marie. His wife was the one who'd left, she was the one who made the decision to sue for divorce. But when she called so they could arrange those things that needed arranging, negotiate a settlement between the two of them, Shirley had refused to put her calls through. Always, she took a message and then took her own sweet time about giving it to Joe, sometimes not until the next day.

Joe had been hurt and angry in those tough days and didn't care that Marie had waited to hear from him. But later, when time had passed and he was calmer, less volatile, he'd realized those foolish tactics had contributed to the fact that he'd been dragged literally to the courthouse steps before they settled their differences. Marie eventually got tired of the brush-off and lost her patience, going straight for the jugular. His jugular.

He sighed. He knew he'd have to do something about Shirley, he couldn't let her run his business office on such personal whims. If *Tanner Enterprises* was going to grow the way he envisioned, thrive in the import-export market, he'd need to brush up their image including how the first contact at the office was handled.

Suddenly the phone shrilled and he dove for it. He heard the secretary snatch for it as well, but he got there first.

"*Tanner Enterprises,*" he barked into the mouthpiece.

There was a moment's hesitation, then Emily's low melodic voice, "Joe Tanner, please."

"This is Joe." To his chagrin, his voice had mellowed considerably between the first sentence and the second.

She chuckled. "This is Emily Drury."

"I know." Joe grimaced at how unfriendly he sounded, but was suddenly lost for words as he listened to her warm laugh.

"Oh." Another moment of silence. "Well, I told you I'd call today, and so I am. Thank you for returning my call. I was just in with a client. But, to get back to our meeting last week, I've given the position you're offering a lot of thought and I still have a few questions. I'd like to come back up to Bonnie, meet with you again and perhaps iron out some of the details we didn't cover last time. I feel we need to sort out specifics before either of us can make a decision, don't you?"

"Well, I thought it was pretty clear. But maybe I'm being short-sighted. It might only be clear to me because I'm familiar with the needs of the company. I'm more than willing to meet again, and sort out whatever we need to sort out. When would you like to get together? I'm free most of the week." He frowned darkly at his calendar glowing on the computer screen in front of him, wondering exactly what she meant by ironing out *details*.

"I'm free later Thursday afternoon, I could be there by four. How does that sound?"

Joe scrolled down and his eye leaped to an appointment in Vancouver on Thursday afternoon with Ray Gaines, his warehouse manager, and a date with Margaret Shaw that evening. Margaret was flying in Thursday morning from Toronto for a consultation with a client and leaving the next day. He hadn't seen her in more than two weeks.

He only hesitated for a second. "That's fine. I'm clear

then, too. I'll see you here at the office at four. Can you find your way to Arbutus Bay from Victoria on your own, or do you want directions?"

"Oh, I think André can fill me in and I have GPS."

"I'll email you a map. André's vague about these things and the GPS has you turning off the highway on the wrong road."

Laughing again, she said, "Okay, I'll watch for the map. See you Thursday."

Joe hung up, a feeling of relief and sudden anxiety warring in his gut. Relieved she'd called, he was anxious that the details she referred to might not allow her to take the job. He'd have to do some work on the offer *Tanner Enterprises* was making, see if he could sweeten the pot and make it more attractive. What was she looking for?

He dialed his secretary on the intercom. "Shirley, get hold of Ray. Tell him I can't make it to Vancouver on Thursday and reschedule for Friday afternoon, same time. And Shirley. Let the phone ring twice. If I want to get it, I will. Don't pick it up till the third ring. Then I want to know who's on the line before you tell them I can't talk to them. Unless I say that you're to hold my calls. Got it?"

Ignoring the stunned silence at the other end of the line, he clicked off and jabbed an outline to call Toronto.

~~~

The lighting was dim in the restaurant, the music soft classical, low and unobtrusive. Joe leaned back in his cushioned chair, hand on his coffee cup and looked around the comfortable room. The restaurant was familiar ground. He'd eaten here a hundred times over the years, and could swear it hadn't had a lick of redecoration in all that time. The walls were still covered with the same muted fuzzy wallpaper, the heavy faded carpet was an indeterminate rose and green blending with the decor. The chairs were a soft lemon yellow in dated patterned upholstery that rolled easily beneath the diners on solid brass casters.

In sharp contrast, the food was excellent. The menu had

kept up with the times, substituting some of the heavier meat dishes of previous years for lighter fish and pasta selections. Although in this town where logging still held sway in many quarters, a lot of men felt they hadn't eaten unless they'd had their chunk of blood red steak accompanied by fried mushrooms swimming in butter and a baked potato sinking under its cargo of bacon and sour cream.

The owner of the place was absent most of the year, leaving the establishment in the more than capable hands of Hubert, the maître d'. He would swear Hubert had been born in the restaurant and would probably die here. He worked every night the restaurant was open, directing operations and waiting personally on select tables.

Joe knew a lot of the patrons, closeted off at privately spaced tables, primarily involved in discussing business. They'd nod or signal to him as they entered and left the restaurant, several stopping by the table to exchange a word or two. Some were local retailers or manufacturers, many of whom did business with *Tanner Enterprises*, and more than a few were owners or operators of logging and lumber companies. He saw the president of an island saw mill across the way, deep in conversation with the head of a hardware and building materials buying group. They had both nodded to him as they entered.

This restaurant was really the best the city of Bonnie had to offer. There were other more exotic eating establishments further up town, catering to the business and traveler trade. The Italian restaurant across the street was pretty good and there were several ethnic offerings in the downtown - Vietnamese, Mexican, Japanese, even Turkish. And along the highway Chinese food restaurants and some local grills specialized in breakfast and burgers.

Joe thought about the woman who'd be returning to the table shortly to conclude their discussions before she drove home, back to the big city where she lived and worked. And he couldn't help but wonder. What was Emily Drury after?

He didn't see this position, in-house legal counsel to a

medium sized firm, as a step up the corporate hierarchy for a lawyer of three years' experience with so much contract and courtroom work under her belt. It seemed like something a guy who was winding down his career would be interested in, who'd climbed the ladder and found it wanting, or had just never made it to the top.

Emily should be moving on with Sam Jefferson, Dubuy's partner, competing for the big files and important clients, looking to make partner in a few years. Shouldn't she? He shook his head, staring blankly at the tablecloth.

That issue aside, she drove a hard bargain, he'd discovered to his chagrin. He grinned into his coffee, then swallowed the last of it and motioned to the waiter for a refill. The afternoon had been entertaining to say the least. She'd certainly had his attention from the moment she walked through his office door.

She'd arrived promptly at four o'clock and made her way unannounced into the reception area. Joe had given Shirley the afternoon off. He didn't want any fireworks or untoward comments to put Emily on her guard before he had a chance to get her committed. So he made sure the secretary was out of the way. She'd been happy at first to have the unexpected free time but then her antennae shot straight up, her face a study in suspicion at his motives for giving it to her.

Joe sighed in weary surrender. She was going to be a problem, no doubt about it. Geoff was right, though he hated to admit it. Likely all he had to do was have a talk with her, explain what he needed and what her responsibilities were. He'd take care of that at the next opportunity. Leaving it up to the employee to create her own job description was negligent on his part. Too distracted, he'd been happy as long as things got done that he needed done.

So Emily had arrived to a quiet office that afternoon, no Shirley, no calls. Joe left his phone to the answering service and settled in to discuss her *details*. They'd taken him by surprise. A higher pay hadn't alarmed him. He'd been expecting something along those lines. After all, he never thought he'd get someone of her calibre at the salary he first floated. But the position of vice president and an option on shares in the corporation, that had been a bit of a jolt. But by the time she finished explaining her view of the role she'd play, he'd come around to understanding her point of view.

Now that he'd had time to mull it over he was a little more comfortable. He was getting more than he'd originally bargained for. She was going to be his right hand 'man', just like she'd been for Dubuy. She'd be another capable executive in the company. The whole thing wouldn't rest on his shoulders. He found the idea to be a surprising relief. Within a couple of months she'd probably be making decisions that wouldn't have to land on his desk first.

And she'd do a good job, he'd bet money on it. He laughed shortly. Actually that's exactly what he was doing. Because he'd given her what she wanted. Slightly red in the face, slightly damp under the arms, he'd given her what she asked for. She'd had to work hard for it. But he'd listened, discussed, negotiated determinedly and conceded a higher salary and options on shares. The options could be exercised after one year, if she lasted that long, and more options for the following year if she got there as well. And she'd be Vice President of *Tanner Enterprises* from the day she started work with them.

He felt flushed and slightly off balance. It went against his personal style to make snap decisions. He tended to define his goals carefully, search out and explore his options, consider all the angles before coming to a carefully balanced and considered verdict. Once the choice was made, he didn't revisit it again unless something happened that forced him to. That's how a good businessman should operate he'd always maintained and he'd stuck by that principle through high pressure and difficult times. Now here he was making decisions that would have far reaching effects on the future of his company, and making them at the snap of the fingers. Emily's fingers.

Geoff would squawk. Joe cringed inwardly. Not because

he disagreed, but because Joe was always riding his ass for making a judgment call before he'd considered all the factors with weighty precision. And Joe Sr would have something to say about it as well, he always did. Neither Geoff nor Dad held enough shares to block his actions but they'd always run the company with consensus in mind.

Joe's watchful gaze caught Emily re-entering the dining room and wending her way between the tables toward him. She was an eyeful. He couldn't help but notice, to his amusement, the heads turning and conversations stalling as she walked past other tables toward his own.

She was wearing a prim little dress with high lace collar, long sleeves, wide belt and hem nearly down to her ankles, with high heeled shoes and a matching clutch bag. On someone else it might look like a spinster's outfit, reserved and tidy. But somehow on Emily it only seemed to accentuate her womanliness, her curves, highlighted by her thick gleaming hair held back with glittering combs anchored behind her ears. Her sparkling earrings winked back the reflected light.

He stood as she approached their table and leaned over to hold the chair for her. She gave him a guarded look but the colour came high in her cheeks at the courtesy as she sat. She settled herself under his steady gaze, pressing her lips firmly together with their fresh coating of lipstick.

So it's settled, Joe thought, watching her. She's coming to work for me. His heart suddenly lifted with relief. He'd been heavily burdened these last few years with expansion going on in so many directions at once, and no one within his organization capable of taking some of the load off his shoulders.

It lifted with thankfulness to Dubuy. André had known what he was doing when he'd suggested Joe needed in-house counsel and proposed Emily for the position. It lifted in anticipation of working with this enigmatic woman, finding her capabilities, using her as a sounding board when he was uncertain about a decision or just to knock ideas around.

And if he were totally honest with himself, his heart was lifting with something else, excitement at the prospect of having her in his office. She was stimulating, exotic, and he already enjoyed her immensely, even though she still looked at him as if he were the cat watching the mouse hole and she was the mouse.

Dinner had been entertaining. She was a lively guest and clever conversationalist. And it certainly didn't hurt to look at her. Except he knew no more about her now than when they'd started. She'd skillfully steered talk to work-related topics, throwing in some current affairs and local politics.

Well, so she was cautious. That was good, wasn't it? She wouldn't presume on his personal life either. And her caution would naturally wear off. She'd learn to relax, trust the relationship, trust him and he'd find out all he needed to know about her.

"Well, Emily, did you get what you wanted today? Did you accomplish what you came up here for?" He smiled, mostly at his own expense.

Her smile in reply was open and warm. "Yes, essentially. I'm quite happy with the agreement. Are you comfortable with it?"

At his nod, she gathered her things together. "Well then, thank you very much for the lovely dinner and great company. I enjoyed it. I'll say good-bye as it's a long drive home."

It was clear that business was concluded and dinner was business, therefore it was concluded as well. Joe grimaced as she continued, "My start date will be in about a month, maybe a week or two longer. I'll confirm with André and let you know the exact time. If there's anything urgent that needs to be looked after before that, you can let me know. I'm sure I could fit it in while I'm still in Victoria."

Joe raised his brows at the offer. Well, why not? She already had his whole file. She knew more than he did about most legal aspects of the company, and probably even more than André.

"I'll be drawing up an employment contract for your signature, Joe. You'll need to get independent legal advice before you sign. We should have all those details pinned down in the next week or two." An employment contract, huh? Okay. It made sense, so he'd sign an employment contract. He grinned to himself.

Joe followed her through the door and into the foyer. He knew every other male eye in the room was on her, watching the subtle sway of her hair as she moved, the swing of her dress. He felt like he'd had his eyes glued to her all afternoon, if not to her face than her backside or her legs when she was heading away from him. And her breasts. But he hoped he hadn't been too blatant, that she hadn't noticed.

Once she started working for him, would he get eyestrain? Maybe he'd have to start wearing glasses. Grinning at the thought, he quickly sobered and wiped the smirk from his lips as they arrived at her car. Reaching down, he opened her door.

She certainly didn't spend a lot on transportation. There was a baby's car seat in the back of the older model sedan and he did a double take, suddenly aware of Emily as something other than a lawyer or a great looking woman. She was a mother. An alien being in his personal world. He'd never had much to do with young mothers, other than his sister Natalie. What might it mean in terms of her working for him? He was frowning again as he watched her taillights grow dim and disappear into the dark.

## CHAPTER FOUR

Joe hustled the cell phone out of his pocket and checked for messages. One from Geoff, probably to see how the meeting with Emily Drury had gone. Nothing from Margaret.

He placed another call to her hotel in Vancouver, hoping for some damage control in that quarter. He'd rather abruptly broken their date for this evening and knew he was going to be made to pay. It was too late to fly over to see her now and she hadn't been happy. She was leaving for home in Toronto tomorrow morning, and there wouldn't be time for him to get over to Vancouver to see her before she flew out.

But there was no answer from her hotel room when they rang him through. Margaret must be out. He left another message for her to call at whatever time she got in, but he slept through to morning with no interruptions.

Early next day he caught her on her hotel room phone. "Sorry, Joe," she said, "I can't talk, the taxi's waiting to take me to the airport." Her voice was brisk, her enunciation precise and cutting.

Whoops. "Well," he soothed, "I just wanted to say again that I'm sorry I couldn't get over to see you this trip. Did you have a good time last night?"

There was a moment's hesitation, then her voice came

sharply over the line. "I had a wonderful time. Met up with some old friends, and made a rather intriguing new one. I hope your evening was as enjoyable. Who is your new woman, by the way? Shirley told me about her."

Shirley? What did she have to do with this? Joe's gut clenched. He was wary and at the same time livid. Just wait until she got into the office this morning. There was going to be hell to pay! That woman was definitely stepping out of line.

"I don't have a new woman, Margaret." His voice, he hoped, sounded reasonable and calm. "I don't do things that way. You know that. I was interviewing. We're going to hire a new person in the company, executive level, and we were on the second interview. Shirley's never even laid eyes on her." And for good reason, but he neglected to voice his opinion. That was another matter entirely.

"Oh. Well, she needs to have that explained to her. I suggest you sort that out, Joe. She was most explicit yesterday morning when I called, suggesting you weren't able to speak to me because you were getting ready to see Emily."

Joe was dumbfounded. He tried to placate Margaret, promising to get to Toronto as soon as he could, and hung up. Things looked rocky there. He'd have to make a big effort to fly out to see her, send flowers, do something.

And he had to deal with Shirley. This had obviously been coming for a while and he'd ignored it with his usual ability to walk past anything that wasn't right under his nose, screaming for attention. He was a single-minded bastard when it came to business. He'd be the first to admit it and Geoff was never hesitant about pointing it out. Sometimes, like now, it could cost him dearly.

~~~

In the open kitchen, Emily hugged Andrew to her, nuzzling the crease in his neck and breathing in his baby scent of powder, soap, and soft skin. He smelled of banana. He had just finished a snack, leaving the dregs mashed into the tray of his highchair. He wriggled in her arms and she set him on his feet, taking a last swipe at his hands with a damp cloth.

He bounded free of her, jogging through the archway into the living room on his tiptoes, blond curls bouncing as he bumped along. The cat ran ahead of him, stopping every few feet to make sure he was still coming, then racing on again. A beautiful grey tabby, Kitty had been with them ever since Emily had found her as a tiny thing lurking in the bushes outside their front door, big-eyed, lost and hungry. She'd taken her in, fed her and cleaned her up and Kitty had been her shadow ever since.

Until Andrew was born, that is. Then Kitty became his self-appointed guardian. Wherever Andrew crawled, walked, loped, Kitty followed. She sat under his highchair and cleaned up the crumbs that fell her way, as if it was her right and duty to do so. When Andrew played in the yard, Kitty played as well, exploring plants, batting at Andrew's toys, digging in corners, dozing in the sun. They had a symbiotic relationship. They worked off one another, supplied companionship and joy.

She hoped Kitty would take well to the move. She'd borrowed an animal travel case and was determined to keep her in the house for a full week once they got up to Bonnie before she even got a whiff of the outdoors.

Her roving gaze picked up the outline of the paper snowflakes she and Andrew had taped on the windows at Christmas. She'd taken down most things but left those up until just before the movers came.

She sighed. Christmas had been nice. Quiet but nice. A few friends had dropped by Christmas Eve, people from law school. She'd spent the next morning at home with Andrew. Suzanne, a longtime friend who lived in the city had been there for a while. Then she and her son had gone to the Dubuys' for Christmas dinner. It had been a little lonely, leaving the noisy, overflowing Dubuy household and going home to put the baby to bed.

She'd stood in her living room staring out the window,

watching the rain slanting down in the glow of the street lamps. Then she shook free of her melancholy, unplugged the tree lights and went down into the basement to check for water leaks. If it was going to flood, it seemed to happen at Christmas.

Now Emily looked thoughtfully at Verna Morrison, Andrew's nanny, as she put away the food from lunch. Verna was no spring chicken. She wouldn't be moving furniture on this trip. But she could be useful just being there when the movers were loading and she could direct traffic like a cop.

"Verna," she said, "it might work out better if Andrew stayed with Suzanne during the move. There are two trucks transporting our stuff. One of us needs to be here, supervising the loading and to lock up the house. And the other needs to be up at the other house directing where everything is to go. What do you think?"

Mrs. Morrison sat down and poured herself a cup of tea. Emily smiled to herself. Verna thought a cup of tea solved everything. And sometimes she wished it did. She plunked down across from her and reached for her own cup.

"I've already seen the other house," Emily continued. "I can pretty well decide where things should go. We can mark the boxes as we pack." Emily sipped her tea and watched Andrew play with the cat's tail and then scream with laughter.

Kitty was the strangest animal. She would put up with Andrew's teasing endlessly. Although the cat had trained him early on. She'd set her own boundaries about what she'd put up with and had bared her claws a few times to warn him when she'd reached that limit. Several occasions had seen Emily nursing Andrew's sore hand where Kitty had inflicted a tiny scratch. And so Andrew had learned not to be rough, and Kitty seemed to enjoy the play as much he did.

Verna finished her cup of tea and rose to clear the table. "I think that would be best. If Andrew were taken care of, I'd stay here until the movers have emptied the house. Then I could come over to let the cleaners in the next morning and hand off the keys to the tenants when they arrive. I'd pick

Andrew and Kitty up on my way to the new house. I'm going to stay at my daughter's place, did I tell you?" she added. "She's anxious to have me come. She thinks she'll see more of me after we move, because when I come to Victoria on my days off, I'll stay with her."

"Oh, dear. Is this going to be an inconvenience for you, Verna, this move out of town?" She watched Mrs. Morrison anxiously, worry clouding the back of her mind. Mrs. Morrison had been with them since Andrew was six months old. She'd come in answer to an advertisement for a nanny, the first applicant to appear at her door. Emily had been nervous about contemplating leaving her baby to go back to work. She'd been sure she'd never find a single person who was careful enough, capable enough, caring enough to take her place.

But Mrs. Morrison had walked in and disarmed her totally. She was a big woman, heavy and slow moving, with a quick sense of humour and a warm smile. She'd seemed as down to earth and organized as Emily could wish for. In some ways she reminded her of Angeline, André's wife, and she'd relaxed in her company immediately.

Verna Morrison had been living with her daughter since her first grandchild was born, but now there was a new baby and the daughter was staying home to look after both children. Mrs. Morrison wanted something to keep busy.

She hardly caused a ripple of change in the workings of their household and yet suddenly everything seemed possible and ran more smoothly. She'd grown to rely not only on her services to look after Andrew but also her common-sense advice and level-headed approach to life. Now she worried she might lose her dearest ally.

"Not at all, my dear. Don't worry, you can't get rid of me that easily. I won't be deterred by a little move up island. Mr. Morrison and I lived for years on a farm near Kamloops in the interior of BC and I loved every minute of it. I don't have to milk two dozen cows every morning on this move so I'll be more relaxed." Emily burst into laughter at her expression, standing there with arms akimbo, fists at her ample waist and her eyes wrinkled up in mock apprehension.

The baby's head turned at the sound. He laughed, too, clapping his hands and running in to join them. Emily scooped him onto her lap and hugged him tight. "You scamp," she scolded, still laughing, "You are the nosiest little boy I've ever seen. You just have to see what's going on, don't you?" He giggled at the movement of her fingers on his belly, then slid down to the floor again.

"Well, that's good. We'll do it that way." Emily's voice reflected her satisfaction. "The move is next weekend, you realize. We'll have to get busy on the rest of the packing. I only have a few files left to finish at work, so I'll have a couple of days off and the movers are delivering more boxes and packing tape tomorrow. I should junk out the cupboards while we're at it. I haven't done it in a long time. That'll cut down on what we have to drag up there. And then there are all Andrew's things that he's outgrown. I can box the clothes up and pass them on."

Verna pursed her lips. "Why don't you leave that to me? Really, what we should be doing is sorting it by size and just packing it away. Andrew isn't going to be the last child you ever have and it sounds like there's room for storage there."

Emily levelled a look at her. "I'm not going to be having another child any time in the near future, Verna. Believe me, it's fine to pass it on. Someone else can be using it." She rose to pull Andrew's fist out of the cat food.

Mrs. Morrison put on her stubborn look but then suddenly acquiesced. "Very well, I'll take care of it. You look after the kitchen, because I don't know what you want to keep and what to get rid of. Just don't throw out that brown betty teapot. It makes the best cup of tea."

Emily laughed and helped her gather the serving bowls from the table. As she started to fill the sink with soapy water, she thought of the dishwasher in the house at Arbutus Bay and began to hum to herself. This move wasn't all bad, not by any means.

And if she had to leave her home, she'd the best send off.

~~~

Suzanne Masters had started it, wanting to see everyone while they were in town for the Christmas holidays. And if Emily was leaving, all the more reason to party. She began calling old friends and word quickly spread about the gathering at Emily's house.

Emily invited the Dubuys but they declined. Instead, Angeline offered to take Andrew for the night so she could really enjoy herself.

The Mid-Winter Bash, as Suzanne dubbed it, started out as a drop-in with wine and appetizers and ended as an all-out house party. Emily didn't know how many people came through her front door. She tossed coats on the sofa in the front room until she couldn't even see it anymore.

Her friend Don was in town with an entourage of theatre people that he worked with, and they brought music, including their own equipment. He informed her she wouldn't want her own stuff abused this way so it was best to just let them have a free hand in setting it up. It was certainly loud, but it got people dancing.

Emily pressed her way through the throng to the kitchen looking for a glass of wine. There were no more wine glasses but she found a clean coffee mug in the back of the cupboard. Then Tami, a friend from law school appeared behind her with two guys in tow.

"I had to come in the back way," she shouted. "The front steps are jammed with people. Do your neighbours call the cops?"

Emily laughed. "I don't know. I don't think I've ever had a party this big. I guess we'll find out."

Tami leaned close to speak in her ear. "I brought a couple of friends." She indicated the men behind her. "This is Bill and that's Ryan." Emily waved at them. She'd met Tami's boyfriend before. The second man, Ryan, put out his hand to shake. He was only a few inches taller than her but when she took his hand she was startled by the size and strength of it.

He smiled at her and hefted a bag under his arm.

"I've got wine, can I pour you some?" She found another coffee mug and turned to see Tami and Bill disappear into the crowd. Suzanne and Jake forced their way through to the kitchen and chatted for a while, then Emily was called into the next room to settle an argument about who had taught Torts class in second year law. She'd finished her wine and was looking around for more when she felt a warm hand on her hip.

"Do you want to dance?" Ryan said in her ear.

She turned to smile at him. He had a nice square solid-looking face, with warm crinkles around his dark brown eyes. "Okay, but I'm thirsty." He handed her his cup and she took a drink.

Dancing with him was nice. His body was solid muscle and he pulled her in snug against him. She knew her breasts were slightly flattened against his chest and she didn't even mind. Ryan didn't seem to mind either. His hand slid from her waist to rest on her hip and hold her a little more firmly. She slanted a look at him and he smiled back.

The music was so loud they didn't talk, but he bent and whispered in her ear, "Okay?" She considered for a second, then nodded. She was okay, this was fun. When the dance was over, Emily pulled back and curtsied. "Thank you, sir."

He laughed, his gaze pinned to her face.

She was pulled away to say goodbye to a few friends who were leaving. When she returned, the lights had been lowered and the music was even louder. Someone drew her into a group dance that shot her breathless out the other end a few minutes later.

Ryan was waiting. He hustled her into a dark corner of the dining room and backed her against the wall. He leaned in near her ear. "Is it alright if I kiss you?" he asked and laid his mouth on her jaw. She felt herself flush, suddenly warm all over. He let his lips rove across her cheek and then fasten on her mouth while his hands ran up her back and down again to rest on her hips, tugging her snugly against him.

As his mouth worked on hers, she felt some inner steel within that she had long held firm begin to soften at the impact. She hadn't been open to any man, for any kind of relationship since before Andrew was born. Her mouth opened hesitantly against his and she sank into a kiss that seemed to swallow her whole.

He lifted his head to catch his breath. "Whoa," he said, "that was more than I bargained for." He looked at her swollen mouth and kissed her again. She felt his erection pressed firmly against her stomach.

Someone flicked the light up for a second and they jumped apart, Emily tugging her shirt down as he removed his hand. She eyed him uncertainly but he planted another quick kiss on her mouth before he backed up. "I'll get you a drink," he said.

The crowd eventually began to thin and Emily was saying goodbye to the last of her guests when Ryan came up behind her and wrapped an arm around her waist. He tugged her out onto the porch into the shadow of one of the pillars. "Listen, Emily. I've really enjoyed myself tonight and I..."

Emily burst out laughing and he laughed along with her, his eyes amused.

"Really enjoyed yourself, have you?" She giggled again.

He stopped her with another kiss. "I love your kisses," he said when he came up for air. "I can't seem to leave you alone. I know you're moving out of town, but I want to see you again. Is that possible?"

She looked uncertain.

"Maybe we could even get to know something about each other, besides that we like to kiss."

Emily looked rueful. "I don't really date. I have a child. It keeps me tied down."

He nodded. "I know, Tami told me all that before we got here. It's okay with me. I like kids. Listen, I don't want to pressure you, I'll give Tami my phone numbers and let her pass them on. Is that okay?"

She nodded, then smiled up at him. "Okay."

He leaned in and kissed her again. Emily could hear Tami yelling for him from the car at the curb, *was he coming?* But her heart was hammering wildly under her breastbone and it was still a long time before he lifted his head.

## CHAPTER FIVE

It had been a long day. The actual move had been accomplished the day before, but they arrived at the new house this morning to the sight of boxes everywhere, stacked against the walls and on top of furniture. It looked like a daunting task ahead and they decided to start on the bedrooms.

Late in the afternoon there was a heavy pounding on the door and the stamping of many feet. Emily heard loud voices as she skipped down the stairs. She'd just finished unpacking in Andrew's room and getting the crib set up. The thumping became louder and she heard Tami's raucous laugh as she came into the hall.

Suzanne stood at the door that Mrs. Morrison held open. Verna had Andrew slung under one arm and was waving in a crowd of people with the other, all dripping water off their coats and struggling to divest themselves of shoes.

Emily raced forward and hugged the big fellow at the front of the group. "Walt, you wonderful man! Look at you guys!" She swung around in pleasure, hugging Suzanne, accepting Andrew into her arms as he latched onto her neck. She nuzzled him and drew her friends into the room.

"Tami, what a surprise. Julia, come in. Don, what are you doing in town again so soon?" She grabbed the wet jackets and hauled them off to the laundry room to drip. In the kitchen, paper bags were opened and wine bottles produced. Tami pulled out a selection of containers and snapped the lids off to release the wonderful aroma of hot honey and garlic ribs, wor wonton soup, shrimp and mushroom chow mien, chicken balls in black bean sauce.

"Oh, it smells wonderful. Isn't this great? Gee, I don't even know where the dishes were stowed." Emily opened a cupboard and blessed Mrs. Morrison, not for the first time.

"Well, here we go. I've been working upstairs so I wasn't sure how far Verna got down here. But as usual, she did it right." Triumphantly she produced a stack of plates. Someone found utensils in a drawer and scrounged some glasses. Emily settled Andrew in his high chair and began to clear the table of crumpled newspapers and packing material. She shoved it into a pile on the floor in the corner of the kitchen as everyone crowded around and attacked the food.

"Don, what a nice surprise to see you again so soon after the Mid-Winter Bash. How's the career going? Any big silver screen contracts?"

"Speaking of the Mid-Winter Bash," Julia interrupted, "What did I hear about Emily and some strange guy that Tami dragged in off the street? Strictly high school, I was told, heavy necking on the porch in the dark."

Emily's mouth opened, then closed and she felt a blush creep up her cheeks.

Tami hooted. "It wasn't some strange guy, Julia. It was a client of mine who plays hockey with Bill, so I invited him along."

Emily gaped. "He was a client? You invited a client to the party?"

"Yes," she drawled, "And he said he really enjoyed himself." There was a roar of laughter.

Emily felt her face burn as she lunged from her chair to catch Tami by the throat. "Excuse me, everyone. I'm just going to put Tami out of my misery here." More laughter followed as Tami stretched her neck out and urged her to get a good grip.

She finally subsided back on her seat. "So, moving right along," she spoke over the laughter. "Don, how's the career?"

Don leaned back in his chair and pushed his thumbs under his belt. "Not too bad. I have a few offers coming up," he said casually.

"What?" Every head swivelled as they responded in unison. Andrew, now seated on Walt's lap and sagging against his chest, pulled his thumb from his mouth at the noise to gaze around.

Don looked pleased at the bomb shell.

"What contracts, Don? Really? You've got a big deal lined up?" Suzanne squealed. She and Don had been friends almost as long as she and Emily. They'd all attended high school together, and gone off in different directions upon graduation, Suzanne to social work, Emily to law school and Don to study acting.

Don smiled slyly and raised his chin to present his profile to the group. "This face may soon be as well-known as Robert DeNiro's."

"Or Jackie Gleason's," Tami interjected. He laughed good-naturedly.

"Come on, tell us."

Don casually sipped his wine. "Well, I'm back in community theatre for the spring, we're doing a Neil Simon play. *The Sunshine Boys* opens mid-March in Vancouver. We hope for a good run, not like last time." He smiled at the scatter of laughter in memory of the disaster of his last foray into plays, and murmurs of approval at his current success. "But even more importantly, I've nailed down the lead in a new TV series to be filmed in Vancouver, starting next fall."

"A lead?" Tami shrieked. "My God! We know a movie star. Where's my autograph book? Never mind, just sign my boob." She whipped up her tee shirt. "I'll never wash again." She grinned at the roars of laughter.

Don leered at her. "Tami, you're all talk and no action. I've known you too long to fall for that one."

"Oh, I don't know," someone muttered. "Doesn't she have two kids and no husband?"

Tami guffawed. "Who needs a husband, or weren't you listening in sex education class? Besides, if I'd had to marry them all, I'd be too busy doing my own divorces to do anyone else's."

Emily turned back to Don as the laughter died down. "That's good news, Don. I'm really pleased for you. What's the series about, what's it called?"

"It's about a doctor who's more like a private eye. He solves medical mysteries. I landed the leading role. I've only seen a few scripts so far, one's about amnesia. That's pretty predictable. But some of them seem to be a little more imaginative. For instance, one's about proving the paternity of a child. The mother refuses to name the father, and two men are claiming the child as theirs."

"It's usually the other way around, they're both claiming the other one is the father," Tami murmured.

Don grinned at her and plunged on. "And the child is heir to a fortune from the mother's family, which possibly explains the potential paternal interest. It's pretty intriguing. I don't know what the series will be called when it's released, but the working title for now is Medicine PI."

The conversation leaped on into work and careers. Tami reported her law practice in Victoria was extremely busy. She'd taken on a new associate the year before and was just now hiring another. "Soon I'll be just what I always swore I would never be, a big firm lawyer." Laughing hoarsely, she pulled out a cigarette. She glanced at Don and they both headed for the door onto the patio with lighters in hand.

Verna leaned across, took Andrew who was now sleeping in Suzanne's arms, and headed up the stairs. "I think everything's ready for him up there, Verna," Emily called. "The crib's put together and I made it up with some sheets I found. Even his bear is there." Verna nodded and waved to the group's cheerful calls of goodnight.

"How many lawyers do you have working for you, Tami?"

Julia asked as she returned to the room.

"There are ten of us, counting the one I've just hired. And I take an articling student, although most of them aren't very useful for the first six months." There were groans around the table at that comment.

"Come on, Tami," Emily jumped in. "How useful were we when we first started articling? I was lucky because I'd done the Community Law term in school, so at least I'd been to court to set dates, enter guilty pleas and do simple trials But in general, what did any of us know about the practice of law? We all had to start somewhere."

"So, what's the tally here?" Walt interrupted. "Out of the lawyers here present, I work for a law firm, Emily used to work for a firm and has now gone in-house counsel, Tami has her own company, and Julia, you're still with the government, right?" At Julia's nod, he continued, "Those are probably the profession's averages, half as private practitioners, some with government, some with business."

"Then there's always Steve," Tami interjected. They all laughed. "Steve was in our year at law school, Suzanne, and I know Emily must have talked about him. He was the most outrageous person I think I've ever met, and that's going some."

"Steve was as smart as they come," Emily supplied, "but he could have cared less about studying or marks. We always joked that if we couldn't find jobs when we graduated, we'd just open an office next to his and live off all the malpractice suits from his former clients. He was like a loose cannon."

Tami hooted. "Remember the time at the Community Law Centre when we were all sitting around and he offered to expose himself to you, Em? Well, guess what he's doing now?"

There was an expectant silence.

"He bought a clothing factory in Vancouver, he's manufacturing raingear."

"What's this guy's last name?" Don called above the din. "I think I might have met him."

"You'd remember if you did," Emily muttered. "His last name is Alexander, Steve Alexander. He's tall, athletic…"

"Yeah, yeah, I do know him. He was trying to get a contract to supply the raingear on this west coast trek I took last year. I thought he was a maniac, he talked a mile a minute and reduced his price every second breath. By the time he finished I would have been surprised if he made money on the deal but he just walked away with a satisfied grin on his face and made a pass at one of the women on his way out the door. He really stuck in my mind, he was so… outrageous, I guess that's the word."

The others were convulsed in laughter. "That's Steve," Julia supplied, "but I just can't imagine him as a business man. He'll go broke or get charged with something like fraud, blackmail or more likely sexual harassment. The potential list is endless."

Walt and Suzanne set up the speaker system for Emily and got some music playing while the others cleared up and stacked the dishwasher. The friends inspected the premises, walked through the rooms making comments and suggestions, and gave their stamp of approval to Emily's new home. Suzanne was staying the night but the others finally started packing up.

As they were putting their damp coats on to leave, Tami pulled Emily aside. "Ryan's asking after you, he wants a date. I think he's quite taken with you. Shall I give him your number?"

Emily looked uncertain. "Umm. I'm not sure. I mean, I liked him…"

Tami laughed. "That was obvious. You didn't seem to object when he had his tongue halfway down your throat."

Emily batted her on the shoulder.

"Well, why not give him a try? Have you even gone out with anyone since Russ? I didn't think so, and Andrew's almost two! I don't know how you can stand it. I'd go crazy. It's probably doing something very damaging to your hormones."

Emily sighed. "I know. I know. I was very attracted to him. I just feel vulnerable and I'm not sure what I should do."

"Well, think about it." Tami gave her a quick hug. "He's pretty damned interested. I'll be in touch."

After they left Emily came into the living room with a pile of bedding in her arms, a pillow under one elbow. "You'll have to make do on the pull-out couch, Suzanne. This place has four bedrooms, can you believe it? So even with Verna here, I'll still have a spare for a guest room. I just don't have a bed for it yet, but that will be next. So it'll be your last time on this old couch. I know you'll be heartbroken."

Suzanne grabbed her in a hug from behind, then reached to help hook the sheet over the sofa cushion. "This is some nice pad, you even have an office. That's a first. I use my second bedroom in the condo for an office. It's so nice to be able to shut the door on that stuff and not have it spread all over the place."

"And there's a dishwasher." Emily sighed in exaggerated bliss. "I never thought I'd say this but I would have given my eyeteeth for one. I don't even have any dishwasher detergent yet but that didn't stop me from putting all the dirty dishes in it."

"We can go shopping tomorrow, get a first load of groceries and find out where the shops are. I actually spent quite a bit of time up here in Bonnie as a kid, you know, although it's grown a lot since then. My grandparents had a little place on the lake north of town."

Emily sat down on the made-up bed and hugged one of the pillows to her chest. "That's right, I remember. I used to really miss you when you left for the summer. Sometimes you'd invite me to go with you but Mum always said it was too far or too long, or some reason I wasn't to go."

Emily fell silent and Suzanne reached out to grab her hand and hold it. "Those were some tough years, eh, Em? But that's all behind you now. This is a new opportunity for a good life for you and little Andrew. And Victoria's not far, you can come down on weekends. Some of us will come up to visit. It'll be great. So tell me about this guy, Ryan."

Emily laughed.

"No, seriously. That night at the party, is that the first time you met him? Because you looked like you'd known each other, if you get my meaning."

Emily looked stricken. "Really? Did everyone notice?"

Suzanne laughed. "No, just your nosy friends. Did you like him?"

"Well, that's the thing. We didn't even talk. It was so damn loud in there you couldn't hear anything. He poured me some wine and then he danced with me. And he could really dance. He held me close enough that I couldn't help but notice what a great body he had."

Suzanne hooted. "Yeah, I thought he looked pretty hot, actually. Good looking, but lots of muscle. And he kissed you."

"Yeah, for an hour." They broke down in giggles. When the laughter slowed, Emily flopped back on the cushions. "And it really turned me on. He kisses very well, if you know what I mean."

"Does he, now?"

Emily lifted her head to stare at her friend. "On the other hand, I may just have forgotten what it feels like to be thoroughly kissed." Their laughter subsided.

"That's too sad, Em. Why wait so long? Why do that to yourself? Maybe give him a chance. Do it on your own terms. If you come to Victoria, see him while you're there. Might be really nice, you never know."

Emily rolled her head to the side and gazed at Suzanne fondly. "Maybe," she said. Would it be a good idea to see him? She hadn't thought much about sex since before Andrew was born, but suddenly her body had woken up. If it continued to clamor at her the way it had been doing since the party, she might very well need to visit Ryan soon.

"So, tell me about this new deal. What's the owner like? What kind of job is it?"

Emily told her what she knew about her new situation. "So, I'm the Vice President of *Tanner Enterprises*. The wage is more than decent, the work's interesting. And the great thing is, not much night work and very few weekends. I got the employment contracts all signed last month before I started packing, so that's taken care of."

"Just like a lawyer," her friend murmured, "Does this guy know what he's up against when he takes you on?"

Emily laughed. "He's no pushover, believe me. Pretty tough nut to crack, I think. But basically fair-minded and very business-like. So at least I'll know where I stand. And he has a very nice brother, Geoff, but he's engaged apparently so that lets him out."

They giggled together. Friends since grade three, they'd spent many a teenage night talking about boys and who they would marry. Life was far different now as adults for both of them than either had ever imagined in those innocent days.

"You know, Suzanne, that television series that Don is starting sounds very exciting doesn't it?" At her friend's pleased nod, she continued. "And the scripts are interesting. That one about wanting to prove paternity of the child is a good concept."

"I wondered if that one would catch your attention."

"Well, it did. I mean, I've been thinking about it. Russ called me the other day."

Suzanne's mouth fell open. "You're joking. I thought that sleaze had fled the province, if not the entire country. I hope you didn't talk to him."

"He caught me at work and I answered the phone. The secretary was gone for lunch so no one was screening the calls."

"And of course you were working through lunch so you could get home to young Andrew. Does he know about the baby?"

"I'm sure not. I don't think he was even in town when he called. It sounded like he was scoping out the territory. He said he'd missed me. And that he thought he'd give me a call to see how I was." Emily ignored the inelegant snort of disbelief from her friend. "Then he said he had some business to do in Victoria and might be by to see me."

"I hope you told him to take a hike!"

"No, no. Just listen. I didn't tell him anything. I said I had another call and rang off. Then I talked to André. He said he'd fix it so that after I left Victoria, they'd only take messages at the office and forward them to me. They won`t tell callers where I am or how to reach me. I don't see how he can come back to town anyway. The cops must still be looking for him, wouldn't they be? Although that whole mess just died down. No one was ever charged, there was never a trial."

Emily spread her hands dramatically. "They didn't have enough evidence to lay charges. Those land deals happened within days of each other and there were so many names that it passed through with all the options and liens, I don't think they could pin the fraud on any one person. Each one would just claim innocence and cast the blame on the others."

"Even if he's not charged, Emily, he's still bad news. You know he never cared enough about you to look after you. And what does he mean, he missed you? It's been years and he hasn't even called to see if you're alive or dead. Don't make another mistake with him, Em. Please don't."

"Don't worry." She took Suzanne's face between the palms of her hands and looked sternly into her worried eyes. "Suzanne, it's okay. I knew shortly after I met him that he wasn't for me. But he was exciting, and I needed the attention. He's a handsome guy. And I wanted that baby. It may sound crazy, maybe I was kind of crazy at the time, but I needed that baby. And I'm not sorry. I've never been sorry, not for a minute. I have no family and Andrew's my family now."

"I know, Em. I know. It was so hard to see you go through all that. And your mum, the way she was after your brother died. She was like the walking dead. Honestly, my heart broke for you." Suzanne hugged her tight.

"Anyway," Emily shook herself and pulled back. "This is a new beginning for us and I'm very pleased. Did I tell you that I get some shares in the company as part of my compensation package? That`s if I last a full year, which I fully intend to do, no matter how hard it is."

Suzanne grinned at her smug expression. "No, you didn't. Is the company worth much?"

"Quite a bit and it's going to be worth a lot more with me working there!"

Suzanne laughed aloud at that. "No doubt."

Emily retrieved a half bottle of wine and two glasses from the dining room table and returned to the couch. "Now tell me what's going on in your life. Do you have a new man? Or are you still seeing Jake? I liked Jake. How's the training program going at the Hospice Centre?"

## CHAPTER SIX

Walking into the office of *Tanner Enterprises* the first morning, Emily smiled warmly at the receptionist. "Nice to see you again, Shirley. I know Joe`s away, but I just want to spend a little time getting settled in and becoming familiar with the files. I often have documents that need to be done, and I assume you're fluent in all the software, but I have precedents to follow for format. We can go over that later. What are your hours?"

Emily had known what Shirley was like the moment she walked into the office. She'd dealt with people like her before and feared she knew what to expect. Sizing her up carefully, she listened as the woman talked about office procedures and the work that composed the bulk of her job. "So I just look after Joe," she finished, giving Emily a guarded look. "I don't know what you'll need, but Joe will have to be my first priority."

Emily saw an older woman, very set in her ways, possessive, defensive, possibly even a little paranoid. But she'd had to work with worse. And she could be tough. She'd never met a secretary that could run her out of the office. If need be, she'd circumvent her completely. She'd done that before, too. The lack of computer skills would be an issue right off the bat.

Just down the hall from Joe's, her office had a lot of space which would serve her well. She tended to spread out when she was working. Big windows took up a corner of the room, one looking out to the bay across a sweep of fields and the other showing the curve of driveway with lots of light. A good-sized desk and comfortable chair completed the picture along with a decent floor to ceiling bookshelf. There was a table in the corner with four chairs for small meetings, giving her further space to work when she needed it.

Joe was away in Vancouver which gave Emily time to settle in. She made a preliminary list of supplies she'd need. Computer terminal, window screens, a few pictures. Did they have an integrated computer system or were they all stand alone units? She'd find out. She could bring some of her own things from the house but an area carpet would be nice on the shiny hardwood floor. As she worked, she heard voices out in the reception area, then her office door opened abruptly.

"There you are," a voice boomed. Emily turned around to see an older man striding across the floor to greet her, his hand outstretched. "I'm Joe Tanner, Joe Senior some call me. And you must be Emily Drury, our new legal counsel. It's great to meet you. Welcome to the business." He was as tall as Joe, hair grey instead of deep black like his son's. There the resemblance ended. Joe was muscular, the father was whip thin. A smoker, she guessed, his face deeply lined.

He was still holding her hand and Emily gently disengaged it. "Thank you. I'm looking forward to getting organized." She smiled.

"We had quite a family meeting about you, deciding if we needed someone and what we were able to offer them. Geoff and Joe wanted my guidance on the issue and I'm always happy to help out when I can. I like to include the boys in the big decisions, you know? It makes a family business work best when there's respect on all sides.

"We have a pretty busy office here, a lot of work gets done, so I'm sure you'll find Shirley a big help. How are you settling in with Joe away?" He glanced around the office then sat down, motioning her to one of the matching upholstered chairs in front of the desk.

"This was my office at one time. I did a lot of good deals here, met a lot of great people. I have an office in town now, it gives me better access. I can take care of the big picture items. But it makes sense to have you here with Joe, so the two of you can take care of the day-to-day. I know you'll fit right in."

He rambled on for a while, giving her the once over with his eyes as he talked. Finally he stood to shake her hand again, pressing his lips to the backs of her fingers and giving a slightly rakish grin.

"Call me if you need anything, any time. I'm always happy to help a beautiful woman."

She heard him stop again on his way out to chat with Shirley. Their voices went on for a while before the outer door slammed. Emily mulled his visit over as she dragged boxes of books and files in from the back of her car and tried to create some kind of order.

What role did Joe Sr play in the business? Having been interviewed by Joe and Geoff, and then a second time by Joe alone, she'd had the distinct impression that he ran the show. She did know that Geoff and the father were minority shareholders but didn't think either of them had an active role in the operations of the company.

But the elder Joe had taken great pains to give her the impression that he ran it in terms of contacts and 'big picture stuff'. She and Joe could handle the day-to-day for him, he didn't have an interest in it anymore.

Thoughtfully she took her initial list of supplies through to Shirley and laid it on her desk. "This is what I'll need to begin with, Shirley, although there're bound to be other things that I think of later. And if you could show me where the office supply room is, I can set myself up with pens and file folders."

Shirley looked at her in surprise. "I keep the supplies in

my desk. How many folders do you need?" She opened her lower drawer a fraction, guarding it with her body.

Emily nearly laughed out loud. "A box of fifty to start."

Shirley frowned and looked down. "That would clean me out. What do you need so many for?"

Emily dragged a chair closer to the desk and seated herself. "Shirley, I've been hired to do a job for *Tanner Enterprises* and I'll need not only the supplies and resources to do that job, but the support of the other staff. That means I need your support. Now I require a lot of office supplies, especially to establish my office. If you would just dial up the supply house you use, I'll get started. Who do you usually order from?"

Shirley stared at her, then slowly pulled her telephone reel forward. Apparently she kept no electronic file of contacts. Thumbing carefully through the cards, she selected one and dialed a number. When she got an answer she began to go down Emily's list. "What kind of file folders?"

"Top tab, manila, legal size," Emily answered briskly, "black ink pens, retractable, good quality." She was through using cheap pens and finding ink leaks in the bottom of her purse and the lining of her pockets. "A box of yellow highlighters, document corners in blue."

Her list went on. "And I need it this afternoon. That's great. Thank you, Shirley. I'm sure Joe just didn't take the time to go over with you what changes would take place once I started." She noticed Shirley's face relax at her words and then immediately clam up again.

Okay. Apparently reassuring her by saying Joe hadn't done his job was not going to work either. Joe could do no wrong in this office, she was quite sure.

"So when he gets back we could sit down and hash out the details. In the meantime, if you'd show me around your files, please. I need to know what filing system you use. I also need a list of employees, a list of suppliers, a list of buyers. You know, all the stuff to bring me up to date on how the company works."

She smiled warmly at the secretary's slightly belligerent, very flushed face and moved purposely toward the bank of filing cabinets lined up against the far wall with Shirley hard on her heels.

~~~

When Joe returned to the office the following Monday afternoon he found everything peaceful and serene. Shirley looked up to see him enter and smiled. She handed him a pile of messages and told him Emily was in her office.

He'd had quite a weekend in Toronto. Margaret was cool toward him when he first arrived but seemed prepared to forgive him for standing her up in Vancouver, given that he'd flown out to see her. But she wasn't going to forgive him right away. He could pay first. When he arrived Saturday she wasn't in. By the time she called him back she said she was too tired to see him that night. But she'd be able to free up time on Sunday.

He stayed in his favourite hotel right downtown, arriving at her apartment the next day to a hosted lunch for ten or twelve people. One of them, a handsome well-muscled man of about thirty seemed permanently attached to Margaret's side. He sported heavily moussed hair and a shirt unbuttoned to the waist. Joe put in the time; he knew he was being punished.

When the crowd finally thinned, it was nearly eight o'clock. Margaret still showed no signs of wanting to be alone with him. He finally put on his coat. She came across the room toward him then, swinging her hips and dragged him into the minuscule kitchen of her apartment. "Now, Joe," she said. "Don't get on your high horse. I don't want you to go away mad."

He grinned. "You just want me to go away, right?"

She made a moue with her mouth and tugged at the front of his shirt. "No, darling. I was hoping you'd stay the night. It's been a long time, you know. It's been weeks."

"Well, I know how long it's been for me." His mouth was suddenly grim. "I'm not so sure how long it's been for you."

She laughed and flipped her dark hair aside. "Don't get jealous, now, Joe. You're a bigger man than that. I'm asking you to stay the night with me, I'm not asking Jerome."

"Are you saying it's my turn tonight, not Jerome's?"

Her face flushed and she batted at his chest. "Stop it, or I'll get mad at you again."

Joe nodded and bowed his head, willing himself to have patience. "Listen, Margaret. I came out here to talk to you but you don't seem to want to give me a chance to do that. I think I've made a decision and ..."

Just then Jerome ambled into the kitchen. "Hey, Mags, what's going on? Having trouble with lover boy, here?"

Joe grabbed his shoulder and spun him around. "Just wait outside, Jerome. We'll be finished in a minute."

Jerome bounced off the doorframe and whipped back around at him. "Come here, lover boy. I can take you right now."

Joe put up his hands. "Listen, I'm not interested. Just stay out of it. Give us a few minutes and she's all yours".

Margaret had been glancing back and forth between them and now looked up at him with her mouth open. "What are you talking about?" Then she whirled with her arm out and her finger imperiously pointed. "Jerome, out." Jerome walked stiff-legged into the living room.

"Margaret, just listen." Joe started talking before she could. He put his hands on her shoulders to hold her away from him as she tried to wrap herself around his chest. "I've been thinking about us," he managed to grit out, "and I don't think we're going anywhere together. We live in two different cities, we have different interests, completely different sets of friends. And I'm not into that any more. So I'm calling it quits. You're a lovely woman and you deserve more than a part-time guy who isn't very interested in the Toronto scene. I'm leaving now and I wish you all the best."

Margaret's mouth snapped shut. "Don't give me that old line – you deserve better," she said bitterly. "You've got another woman and you think I'll fall for that?" Her voice rose sharply. Joe put his hands up to defend himself as she took a swing at his jaw. Her ring caught his lip and he tasted blood.

"It's not over till I say it's over!"

"Leave it, Margaret, just leave it. We've had a good time but it's finished. It's time to declare it done. You can't be too surprised since you've got your backup plan waiting in the other room. Don't pretend otherwise." He stalked out, rummaging in his pocket for a handkerchief to staunch the flow of blood.

On the flight home, he slept like a baby. Nothing like a clean slate, he thought. Nothing like starting fresh. He didn't take the thought any further, he wasn't ready yet.

## CHAPTER SEVEN

The first few days in the office Shirley was on tenterhooks, trying to ensure Joe had everything he needed. He alternately assured her he was fine and seemed to attempt to fight off her insistent efforts to look after him.

Emily managed to work around the small tornado in the middle of their headquarters as if it weren't even happening. She had experience at this and instead concentrated on listing all the suppliers *Tanner Enterprises* worked with and digging up whatever written agreements existed between them. The files were darned skimpy. It was dirty work, literally. *Tanner Enterprises* had been working with some of these companies for years and she had Shirley digging through old dusty boxes in the back junk room trying to come up with signed documents to verify the relationship.

"Why do you need them?" she kept muttering. "Just phone them and ask."

"Well," said Emily patiently, forcing her temper back. "It's not usually quite that simple, Shirley. If the contract isn't as favourable to them as they'd like, they can just deny there is one once they discover we can't find our copy. We should be aware of our own commitments, that's why we need all the contracts filed in one spot and easily accessible."

She wandered into Joe's office for the fourth time that day, a stack of folders in her arms. "Excuse me, Joe. Do you have any idea what kind of agreement we might have with Jim Grant of Western Timber Products? I can't even find a file on them, frankly. But I imagine there's something. How long have we been doing business with them?"

*We?* He seemed to like the sound of that and smiled at her. She smiled back. "Why don't you sit down, Emily. We can go through the whole list and I'll tell you what I know. Will that help?"

She dropped into the nearest chair, tired from the search. "That would be perfect. I didn't know if you had the time to do that right now. Okay, here's what I have." She began to go through the names, noting any comments he made beside each one. Then he started scrolling through his computer files listing other companies that she hadn't yet heard about and detailing what type of business they did.

"Okay, hold on. So we're talking about Canadian suppliers, companies that supply product for us to market to the US and overseas. Good. Then we have companies from out of country who supply us with product to market in Canada and also in the US in some cases. But then there's a third group of what we might call logistics or expediters. They help us get product through borders and across the country. Right?"

Joe nodded. "There's also another area. Companies that are one time buy/sell. They usually haven't committed yet and are dabbling in the business, putting a toe in the water, or just have an oversupply of product."

"Do you deal with all of these yourself?"

"I do initially, at least until they're signed up and have shipped their first product. Then Ray Gaines in the warehouse in Burnaby deals with them after that, invoicing for shipping, receiving, ordering, etc."

"What information do they have in the warehouse? Maybe there are documents there that we can't find here."

Joe looked doubtful. "Good point. I'll call Ray and see what he can dig up. I'm sorry things are in such a mess.

We've done business with some of these companies for a long time and we have a working relationship but maybe not a contractual one. Dad wasn't big on paperwork. But it's time to move into the modern age, I guess." He gave her a rueful look.

Emily laughed at his expression. "Yes, the modern age. And what role does your father play? Does he find new product locally, or source product from overseas? What's his area?"

Joe frowned. "Dad? Uh, none really. He hasn't been active in the company since about a year after I took over. He's definitely retired, he just maintains a minority shareholder position."

He looked at her searchingly. "Have you met my father? You have, haven't you! Did he come calling while I was away?" He huffed out a breath at her nod, then stood up to pace around his desk.

"Okay, I should have known." He glanced out the window and rubbed the back of his neck. "Well." He seemed to come to some decision and sat back in his chair. "It's this way. Joe Tanner Sr started this company about twenty years ago. He bought local product and sold it off-island. Then he expanded to selling down the US coast, Washington, Oregon and California. At any rate, it supported them very well but in the last years he kind of lost interest. He asked me if I wanted to take over."

He grinned. "Believe me, it was not a smooth road. He thought he'd retain control both in ownership and position. We fought it out and then I bought him out save for a fifteen percent shareholding. So that's what it looks like. Geoff also holds shares, five percent. He had a hardware store and I needed financing so he bought in. That's how it stands. I'm President, I work here, and no one else in the family does."

"He said I had his office, that he has one in town now to conduct business."

Joe snorted. "Yes, you do have his old office. It's the best one in the place." He laughed. "And Dad may have an office in his townhouse, but he certainly doesn't do any business there for *Tanner Enterprises*. He's fully retired. The golf course gets most of his attention these days."

"I see." So Joe Sr had been playing her, maybe because she was new, and maybe because he liked the attention. She swiftly changed the subject. "Oh, by the way, I wanted to make sure you were aware, I'll be returning to Victoria. I have that court case with André, the one that was still pending when I left. I think I already mentioned it, but I'll be gone about a week. I can send you an email for confirmation if you like, so you have the exact dates. You can take a week from my pay for the time away."

He put up his hand. "We don't have to work that way. I'm sure you'll be putting in the time when it's needed, Emily."

She nodded, wondering how this was going to work.

Just then the secretary stuck her head around the door. "Is that it? I found some more of them."

"Sorry, no. I have another list from Joe." Shirley pulled her head back, and muttered something about coffee break.

Soon Emily began to feel like she was settling in. Joe was a fount of information, if not signed documents. She began building a set of files for the company with Shirley's very reluctant help.

The receptionist wasn't going to be able to handle the type of workload Emily was used to producing, not just the volume but the technical work on documents. She called an employment agency in Bonnie and started the process of outlining what kind of person she needed and what kind of skills were crucial.

An email to Joe let him know her thoughts on that. He replied quite promptly to most issues, but there was no reply to that one.

~~~

Joe rounded the corner in the neatly shoveled path with snow piled both sides. His farm foreman Victor was invaluable. What would he do without him? He seldom had to ask for anything to be done around the place in terms of care and maintenance because Viktor was already attending to it.

The snow was fresh, a cold front had moved in and it looked like it wasn't leaving any time soon.

He approached the patio at the side of Emily's house. He thought of it as 'Emily's house' already, even though she'd only been there a little while. She occupied his every thought. Even when he considered the business, his next thought had become *what would Emily think, what would Emily say?*

Geoff was already giving him the gears, threatening to bypass him entirely and just talk to her when he wanted information. It was Emily's opinion he was getting anyway, he teased, just passed through Joe. So why not go right to the source?

He shrugged his shoulders in irritation. Geoff talked so much he had their sister Natalie curious. "When do I get to meet this paragon?" she'd asked last time he was in Vancouver. "Geoff tells me she runs the business. Can I meet her if I come over?" He was alerted by the merry twinkle in her eye but ready to string Geoff up by the thumbs just the same.

And of course, that was sure to trigger Dad's interest which was never a good thing. Maybe his interest had already been triggered. He'd been out twice to poke around and cause trouble. He made a mental note to talk to Geoff about it.

Her patio was drenched in sun, catching the late afternoon heat and melting off any vestige of the latest snowfall. The old cement planters set around the sheltered space were still full of dead foliage from last fall, with a pile of ice in the centre of each. He stopped for a moment at the door, uncertain of his welcome. He hadn't been invited but thought he'd drop by anyway. How else was he to see her on the weekend? It seemed a long way till Monday morning.

He heard soft chatter coming through the sliding glass door that stood slightly ajar to the fresh air. Looking in, he saw her standing with her back to him, working at the counter in the kitchen. The baby played on the floor near her feet, a set of measuring cups, spoons and plastic bowls scattered around him. His pale blond hair gleamed almost white in the dim light.

What a pretty baby. Like a child in a magazine ad or on television. His hair was much lighter than Emily's own honey-blonde colour. Almost white-gold, it sat in tight curls on his head and down around his tiny ears. His eyes, Joe remembered from when he first saw the child, were a dark blue and large with pale lashes sweeping his cheeks. They were definitely Emily's, those same dark blue eyes with the long lashes that were quite devastating in her perfect heart shaped face.

But the baby's face had its own shape, round-cheeked, square-chinned, already looking more masculine, yet still babyish. He must look like his father, Joe thought and felt a pang. He could have been a father watching his own child grow by now. But it hadn't worked out that way.

It looked like Geoff would beat him to that, to getting married and starting a family. He and Vanessa had already set a date for their wedding, sometime early fall. They'd been saving to buy their own home and set themselves up in housekeeping before they actually tied the knot.

Watching the child play, he wondered about Andrew's father. Where was he? Was he still alive or was she a widow? Other cultures made such things much easier. If she were a recent widow, she'd be dressed in black and everyone in the community would know she was in mourning.

As it was, he hadn't a clue. He'd tried to bring the subject up a couple of times but she always managed to sidestep the issue. Maybe she was still married and her husband would show up at some point looking for another chance at married life. After his latest oblique reference to Andrew's father, Emily had commented that she was sure it had no bearing on the job at hand and he'd been embarrassed enough to shut up.

The thought of a husband on the scene had the hackles

rising on the back of his neck. That idea didn't fit well with the way he thought things should work out. What if she decided to leave *Tanner Enterprises*? This no-account husband could woo her away to another city. Strictly on a professional level, the unexpected return of Emily's husband would be a real negative. Of course, the professional basis wasn't the only basis on which he had an interest in any husband of hers. Uncomfortably warm, he made a mental note to investigate further into the marital status of his most recent employee.

Her cat sat on its haunches near the child, watching every move Andrew made. Now and then he put out his paw and played with the spoons or stood on the baby's leg. Andrew patted the animal or shoved the cat's paw out of the way.

Suddenly, he looked up and saw Joe. His expression underwent a swift series of changes from complacent through uncertainty to fearful before he burst into tears. The cat jumped away and Emily turned around. "What's the matter, Andrew? Did Kitty get you?" She bent down to lift him into her arms.

Joe knocked at the entrance then shoved his head through the sliding glass door. "I think I frightened him." Andrew screamed louder and cowered against her shoulder. He looked big in her arms, his head burrowed into the crook of her neck, chubby legs dangling.

Joe held out his hands, palms up. "I just came by to say 'hi' and I guess I scared him when I came around the corner. I'm sorry." He was embarrassed, a little off balance, as he often was around her.

She turned around to greet him. "Hi, yourself." She motioned him in and moved over to slide the door closed behind him. "You should know better than to frighten little children." She smiled to take the sting from her words and turned to the child. "It's okay, Andrew. This is Joe, Mr. Tanner. He lives just down the hill in the big house. You remember him."

Andrew's sobs slowed down, then the noise stopped as

suddenly as it had begun. He peered at Joe around his mother's arm, his face bright red and tears standing in his dark eyes. Emily laughed and motioned Joe further into the kitchen.

"Grab a chair, Joe. Would you like a drink? It must be late enough for a drink." She pulled out a chair from the dining table in invitation and hoisted Andrew higher against her hip with her other arm. "What can I get you? Let's see." She moved away to open a cupboard door. "I have vodka, rum, and scotch. And I have soda and cola. What will it be?"

Her smile totally disarmed him. "Anything at all," he said. "Maybe a scotch and soda, or scotch and water. Here, I'll get it. Point me in the right direction." He rose and walked around the counter, as she pulled down a couple of glasses from another shelf with her free hand.

He took them and set them on the counter. "Doesn't he get heavy? He's a big boy for almost two." He and Andrew eyed each other warily across Emily's shoulder.

"Oh, he's already two. He had his birthday last week. We had a big party to celebrate and now that the official date has come and gone, he's suddenly being a terrible two half the time. The rest of the time he's still his cheerful sunny self."

So that would explain the cars that had all descended on the house last weekend. A couple of them had stayed the night and he'd been desperate to get a look at the guests to see who had stayed, and especially what gender. He already knew she'd gone back to spend at least one weekend in Victoria.

She laughed and set Andrew down on the floor. He clung to her leg, clutching at the hem of her skirt with his chubby hands. "The ice is here." She reached to open the freezer door from where she stood, and lifted out a tray of ice cubes. "I'll have a rum and cola, if you don't mind. Light on the rum."

Joe poured two drinks and brought them back to the table. Emily walked to a chair and sat down, Andrew shuffling along beside her still attached to her leg. She didn't seem to notice. One hand automatically pushed his hair back from his smooth little forehead, the other reached for the glass to raise to her lips. She took a sip and set it back on the table.

"Well, this is nice. What brings you up here?" He watched the way her eyes warmed when she smiled at him. Andrew smiled at the same time in exact mimicry of his mother, his little teeth all showing at once. He couldn't resist the double impact and had to chuckle.

"I thought I'd walk up and see how you've settled in and if you need anything. I guess you found enough room to fit everything in?" His eyes took in the big living room with the comfortable chairs and sofa, a speaker system set up on a bookcase against the far wall. The fireplace had logs piled next to it, ready to use. He'd asked Victor to get some fire wood up to the house before Emily had arrived. There was at least a cord of wood stacked against the back wall of her garage.

"Yes, lots of room thanks. It's a little bit larger than what I left so we had no trouble fitting in. And the office is a big help. I like being able to go to work in there and close the door on the rest of the house. I didn't have that in my old place."

He watched her as she talked, moving her hands expressively. The baby followed her every move and waved his hands when she waved hers. He smiled at the baby and Andrew smiled back. When he held out his hand, Andrew took a few steps towards him and grabbed, hanging onto his thumb with miniature pliable fingers.

"I see the snow is gone from the patio already." He addressed his remarks to the mother while bouncing the baby's hand on his knee. "It probably won't last, we're bound to get more of the white stuff before spring arrives."

Joe watched her as she watched the baby. Her face was so expressive here in her own home, so open and soft, unlike the sober business mask she wore at work just down the hill at his office. Down there she was all efficiency, decisive and task-oriented. He hadn't been able to crack through that guard, couldn't get her to relax, break out of the lawyer mould she disappeared behind when they were at work. Yet here she was different person, her care of the baby showing in tender body language as she reached automatically to steady him.

At the office the receptionist kept an eye on her like a hawk on guard with its young, so there was reason for Emily's caution. Shirley hounded Joe's door whenever he was meeting with her, protecting him from the Lord knew what evil she might have in mind for him. When Joe asked his secretary what she wanted, she would mumble something and move away but when he looked again she'd be back, hovering just outside his door like a bird of prey.

Once he had physically dragged her from her post at his office entrance and taken her back to her desk with the question, "Don't you have anything to do, Shirley? Isn't there something that requires your attention?" She'd flushed.

Emily seemed unaware of it, apparently totally oblivious to the whole thing. She continued to smile at Shirley, address her politely and request the work she needed done. He was glad, otherwise he'd have been even more embarrassed than he already was over the situation.

For the moment he tried to remember to close his door when the two of them were in his office, or more recently he found himself walking down the hall to meet in Emily's office. Shirley couldn't follow without taking the risk of being caught standing out in the hall. So she contented herself with calling him periodically on Emily's phone to give him messages. He got his revenge. He told her to hold all calls. That's what she used to like to do.

Emily's face softened as she spoke to her son then leaned back to sip her drink and watch Andrew as he leaned on Joe's leg. "This trip to Portugal, Emily. When do you think we should go?"

She glanced up at his words, Andrew's head moving in the same direction. "I don't see leaving sooner than six weeks from now. We're not that far along in negotiations. If things go reasonably well, we should have a final draft of the

Portugal contract in a couple of weeks. With that timing we could plan a trip in spring, tour the plant facility, inspect the products and sign the contract. End of March at the earliest."

She paused for a minute, her eyes on his face. "Plus you're away next month, aren't you? A trip to the States? That'll give me some free time to move it along. Yes, end of March should be okay. I'll be ready to go by then."

"Six days," he corrected. "I'm away for six days. I don't want to drag our feet on this. Let's put some pressure on Peralta, tell him we've made plans to be there for the first of March. That might hurry him up. And I'm sure I'll have orders by then for his stuff. What do you have to do to get ready? Do you need a lot of lead time to organize care for the baby?"

Her eyes flashed sharply to his face. "No, not at all. Mrs. Morrison is quite capable of looking after Andrew given a moment's notice. He doesn't hold me back from doing my job." She seemed to realize she'd snapped at him and her cheeks went pink. She rested the cool glass against her temple and looked out the window.

When she turned back she spoke in a calmer voice. "No, what I meant when I suggested end of March was that the drafting of the contract and the settling of all the details is complex when another language is involved. It takes time. And it seems to take an inordinate amount of time to get a response from Portugal. When I send an email with questions and ask for information, it takes a week or more for each reply. I don't know if it's the language issue or what. But if you want to go the first of March, I'll send Peralta a message in the morning and let him know. I'll suggest we finalize the terms of the contract by the end of this month." Her face was flushed.

Joe studied the high colour along her cheekbones, realizing there was something else here that he'd triggered by his comment but not sure what it was. "I didn't mean anything by that question, Emily. I was just curious what you do when you have to go away without the baby, that's all.

Having a nanny must be the ideal answer, I guess."

Her cheeks went darker and she averted her face to study the last slanting rays of the sun across the patio as it lowered toward the horizon. "I'm sorry if I sounded abrupt. Some people are uncomfortable hiring a woman with family responsibilities in case those responsibilities get in the way of the job."

Joe just nodded and patted at Andrew's hands as they lay on his knee. The baby laughed and patted back. Then he reached up with both fists and grabbed Joe's thumbs. "Up," he said, drooling on his jeans-clad leg. "Up."

"Oh, no, Andrew. Come here sweetheart." Emily made a grab for the baby but he batted her hands away.

"Up," he said again. Joe reached down and with great satisfaction set him firmly on his knee.

## CHAPTER EIGHT

Emily left her office to check on Shirley's progress with the final edits on the contract. Joe had been hustling around all morning, getting ready for his trip to the States. He was courting a new manufacturer that was interested in having *Tanner Enterprises* market his product, a small efficient solar light panel that he'd developed. The contract had to be ready to go with Joe when he left but she had to proof read it first and it seemed to be taking a long time to produce.

The secretary frowned when she saw Emily coming down the hall and threw up her hands. "It's not done yet! Goodness sakes. I'm going as fast as I can." She took a sip of her coffee. "It's been a busy morning. I actually think I need some help in here. You can't expect me to do all the work for both of you, for heaven's sake. It's not logical."

"How far along are you?" Emily looked impatiently over her shoulder to see the computer screen. "I see." She thought quickly. "Actually, just take what you have and send it to me. I'll be able to get it done before Joe leaves. I'm more familiar with the wording."

Shirley smiled. "Yes, that makes perfect sense. It's just as fast for you to type this up as it is for you to give it to me. Now, how would I email it to you?"

Emily motioned her out of the chair. "I'll do it." She clenched her teeth together as she attached the file to a message and sent it to her own terminal. "There. All done. Thanks, Shirley."

She finished up the file, did her proof reading and printed out two copies. Joe was just closing his briefcase when she took the documents into his office. "Here they are, two contracts. You both sign with a witness and add the witness's name and address below his signature. He keeps one, you keep one."

He grinned. "I think I've done this before."

She flushed darkly and closed the office door. "Of course, sorry. It's just that I'm having trouble getting my work done. I've contacted an employment agency and I'll be interviewing a couple of people this week. Just so you know. I can't get anything done with Shirley and perhaps she just wants to do your work. I'm fine with that. I'd only need someone part time to begin with."

He gave her a level gaze. "I see. I wondered how it would work out. Let's sit down and discuss it when I get back. We'll make a plan. Okay?"

Emily nodded. "Oh, and one other thing. I'd like to get over to Vancouver and visit the warehouse, meet the staff. They must have information in their files."

Joe nodded. "Good idea. I've been wanting to take you over there. We'll arrange it when I get back."

~~~

Five days later Joe drove into the yard and parked in front of the garage. One day he'd take the time to clean all the stuff out of there that his folks had abandoned and he'd actually be able to use it to park his vehicle. He dragged his case out of the truck and headed toward the front door. It was late and the night was pitch black.

The trip to Oregon had been worthwhile but the solar panel manufacturer hadn't signed. Joe told him he didn't handle merchandise that was already listed with another distributor. It wasn't worth the work and he didn't want to use up space in his warehouse. He knew the man would find that everyone took that approach. But the inventor was not persuaded and decided he'd wait to make his decision.

The trip had still been fruitful. He'd made time to call on two other companies that he handled and had been rewarded with more product. His plans for expansion were beginning to show fruit and it was exciting, if exhausting to get it rolling.

He heard a burst of sound and lifted his head. There was company up at Emily's house. He saw two cars pulling out of her drive and heading toward the main road. But there was still a truck parked in front that looked unfamiliar. He frowned. The woman sure had a lot of company. Did one of her girlfriends drive a truck? Not likely. He snorted to himself and admitted that he was just a little disgruntled.

Later that night he could still see the truck parked in front of her door. The upstairs rooms were dark and there were a few low lights in the living room. Didn't she have to get some sleep? It was going to be damned busy in the office tomorrow. What was she thinking, with her son and a nanny in there with them?

~~~

Joe raised his head as Geoff walked into the office. His black hair was disheveled from running his hands through it all morning.

Geoff, on the other hand, looked composed, his dark brown hair neatly brushed, his casual jacket and open necked dress shirt pressed. He whistled as he pulled up a chair. "So, big bro, how goes it? I've got the whole afternoon set aside to work on this presentation night. Let's do it."

Joe rose from his desk. "I'll get Emily and we can meet around a table somewhere." He walked to the door. "Shirley, can you put on a fresh pot of coffee? And tell Mia we need something to eat for the three of us in about an hour." Joe's housekeeper was a whiz at getting things done for him. He led the way down the hall to Emily's office and pushed on the partly open door.

She sat at her desk, her ear pressed to the phone. She

looked stressed, her colour high. "I know, André, I know. I'll be careful. I just..." Her voice was tense, her fingers white where they wrapped around the phone. She looked up as they poked their heads through the door.

"Trouble?" asked Joe, frowning. "Problems with André?"

Emily shook her head and swung around to speak into the receiver. "I have to go, I'll talk to you later. Yep, right. Bye." She hung up and swung her chair around. "No, no problem. Hi Geoff, how are you? Are we working on the presentation night?"

Joe eyed her for a moment before stepping back to let her precede him down the hallway. What was wrong? She'd looked tense and her voice had sounded strained. Something was going on.

They settled outside in the sun for an hour in a sheltered corner of the huge patio at a round table and laid their papers out. His dog sat at his knee, his hand dropping down periodically to rub the furry head. The air was still and almost spring like, the snow gone.

Shirley brought coffee. She set it in front of him with an ingratiating smile, then frowned at Emily before she stalked back into the building.

~~~

Geoff watched Emily organize her files and wondered how she dealt with the secretary and her negative body language. Her face was as serene as if she hadn't even noticed. He glanced at Joe, who was watching Emily too, but obviously for a different reason. Joe was so dense sometimes. He couldn't see what was right in front of him. Or maybe he just didn't want to deal with it. Couldn't blame him in some ways, there was a ton of stuff on his plate right now and it only seemed to get busier. But this was clearly not working.

When Joe went back to his office to get some material he'd forgotten, Geoff turned to her. "How are you getting along with Shirley? Is she helping you get your work done?"

Emily glanced up from her folder and regarded him for a moment. "Shirley does her best. Why?"

Geoff shrugged. "Just wondering. Sometimes I've thought it might be time for her to retire and let Joe bring some new blood into the office. He doesn't pay much attention to stuff like that, but he doesn't have the same need for staff support that you probably do with the different roles that you fill."

"Well, I have thought that someone with more skills would be an asset, now that we're moving into international connections. The drafting of documents is going to be a challenge. We'll see how it goes." She fell silent as Joe came back through the doorway.

Geoff immediately launched into his offensive. "Joe, have you thought about getting some office help in for Shirley? This place is busy. It's more than she can handle." Joe shook his head as Emily smiled and leaned back in her chair.

"That's one of the things on my list I'd like to talk about," she chimed in. "The presentation night is the first item, but yes, I've been thinking Shirley needs help. I'd be happy to give you a profile of what we need in the way of additional staff."

Joe's mouth was open. He paused and then nodded his agreement and buried his head in his papers. Geoff shot her a smile.

"Okay," Joe said from behind his papers. "Let me know what you find. By the way, did you get any sleep last night? Your company stayed fairly late." He shot a keen look her way.

Emily looked surprised. "No, my company left early. Oh, the truck. Yeah, my friend Don had been to see his folks up island and stayed the night on his way back to Victoria. We had a good visit." Geoff watched Joe's jaw clench as she glanced down at her notes.

"Now," she continued, "the presentation starts with an informal gathering from four thirty to six o'clock."

"Yeah," said Joe. "That'll give everyone time to get a little oiled up before you do your presentation at six."

"Not too 'oiled up' though," she said. "I really want their attention. This format is pretty successful and it'll make a good impact if they're sober enough to grasp it."

"Yes, okay. Not too oiled up. Geoff, you're in charge of that. Keep the group sober enough to hear Emily and understand the concepts she's presenting. They can drink all they want after that."

"Sounds good," said Geoff. "Maybe we should keep the pre-presentation time to an hour. Something like five o'clock to six. Some of these guys can move pretty fast when they're thirsty."

"Will Joe Sr be there? What role will he play?"

The brothers looked at each other. Geoff said, "Why, have you seen him up here?"

Joe nodded. "He's been in at least twice to see Emily and offer his help wherever needed. Of course, he waits until I'm not in the office before he comes visiting."

"Three times," said Emily.

Geoff pulled a face. "I see. Well, he won't be here for the dinner. He doesn't really have any part in the running of the company. He doesn't make decisions, he doesn't give instructions. If he tries to pull that with you, just tell him you'll check with Joe. That's usually enough said."

Emily looked between the two of them and seemed to take the comments at face value. "Okay, I'm filled in on that topic."

Joe just grinned and shook his head.

"So," she continued, "I know the Presentation Dinner is the more immediate thing, but I wanted to sound Geoff out on a few things regarding the Portugal venture." At the word 'venture' Joe raised his eyebrows a fraction. "Okay, maybe venture is not the right word. Gambit?" she teased.

Geoff burst out laughing at the expression on his brother's face.

"No, no, just joking. Our plan for expanding into Portugal, how's that? Anyway, here's what I have so far. The target is the south of Europe and maybe Turkey. We're beginning with Portugal. It's a different dynamic than Asia, which is easy to reach from the west coast and it makes sense to have our warehouse in Vancouver near the western seaports for that market.

"However, Europe will be more effectively served by the east or at least central Canada. We'll look at warehousing near Toronto or Montreal. A lot of companies settle in Mississauga."

She smiled and Geoff wondered if she knew Joe had had a girlfriend in Toronto. He guessed not.

"Our first priority is to find product with a reasonable price and a reliable source. I've identified two areas of interest. One is the spirits market, i.e. port and wine from the Douro valley in the north. And the other is ceramics both for the table and the garden. They're really quite lovely and should have a good reception here and in the US. Meanwhile we start looking for markets."

Joe looked bemused, Geoff was smiling. "When you've finished that, would you come and manage my stores while I go on my honeymoon?"

Joe laughed. "Forget it, little brother. So, what have you left out? I can't think of anything. Our agent will be travelling with us in Portugal, right?"

She nodded.

"Have we narrowed down the ceramics product? "

Emily consulted her notes. "Hard to know until we see it firsthand. But really the kitchen stuff, like soup tureens, ceramic hot pads, cappuccino cups and saucers are absolutely gorgeous. The garden ornaments and pots are really lovely but heavy to ship and more expensive compared to Mexican. But they're ever so much nicer. I imagine it will decide itself when we pin down prices and your sales people start marketing.

"But Geoff, I thought you might canvass the hardware and building materials business, you sell a lot of garden stuff. You must have a good idea of what will go and what won't."

They were interrupted when Mia came to tell them lunch was ready. Over lunch Emily reminded them that she was in Victoria the following week on the Supreme Court trial with

André. Joe seemed gloomy after that reminder.

Then Geoff stepped in. He talked about when they were small and Joe had untied their father's launch by accident. It drifted out into the bay before they noticed. Joe had to swim out and catch the rope before his father dove in to help him pull it back to the wharf.

"So, you two lived here your whole childhood? "

Joe looked at her quizzically. "Not just two, there are four of us."

"Oh, sorry. I don't think I've heard anyone refer to other children in the family."

"Sorry, Emily," said Geoff teasingly. "There are more of us to deal with. There're three boys and a girl. Joe's the eldest, then me, then our sister Natalie and our youngest brother Jonny. Natalie lives in Vancouver. She went over there to do a degree in urban planning and stayed to marry and have children, thereby requiring further urban planning."

He grinned as Emily laughed at his comment. "And Jonathan lives in Bonnie. He has a bookstore."

"Oh, a bookstore. I love bookstores. I'll have to call in and see what it's like."

"It's great. He carries used books, buys and sells. Mum went into business with him a couple of years ago and he bought her out recently. Sole proprietor now, although Mum still works there a little bit to help out and keep her hand in."

"What street is it on?"

"It's on Maple Bay Avenue, just off the highway."

"I've been in it! Verna and I found it the first time we went to town to do some shopping. Someone told us about it and we went over to have a browse. It's a lovely shop. I don't know if I saw Jonathan. Does he look like you two?"

Geoff couldn't resist, even as his brother raised a hand in vain to stop him. "I'm sure he'd like to think he doesn't but we all look quite a bit alike. Tall, dark hair, a strange squint…"

"You're being silly, now. Well, good for him." Emily smiled warmly and Joe smiled as he watched her. Geoff watched Joe watching her and thought, *yep, I was right. He's in deep. This should be interesting.* Joe was usually so guarded, he didn't get involved. His girlfriend Margaret hardly counted. She was a barracuda and he didn't seem to care that much if she was there or not.

And that relationship was over anyway, if Joe had stuck to his stand on it after his last trip east. Now, here he was lusting after the corporate legal counsel and Emily wasn't even aware of it. Was she in the market for a guy right now? And what would Margaret have to say about all this? She wasn't the kind of woman to give up without a fight.

## CHAPTER NINE

Emily threw her jacket onto the back of the sofa and picked Andrew up to give him a cuddle. The meeting with the Tanner brothers had lasted all afternoon and she was tired, but it had gone well. She liked Geoff. She felt more relaxed when he was around. He made things easier, unlike Joe who seemed to question most of what she said and frown on the rest. With the younger brother acting as a buffer, things smoothed out.

Part of the problem seemed to be her trip to Victoria for a week. Joe always frowned and changed the subject when it came up. Yet he'd known about it weeks ago, before she even started here. She sighed. Well, it was what it was.

She stood Andrew down and he went back to his play, piling blocks on top of each other, then knocking them down. Kitty watched, occasionally knocking some down herself which irritated him. He was getting cranky when Verna suggested a quick snack before she took him off to bed. They all sat down and had a bite to eat, and the nanny packed Andrew up the stairs for his bath.

Emily rooted through her briefcase to find the pad of paper with the phone number André had given her. She stared at it for a brief moment. There was no name, just the number but in her mind's eye she could see the name spelled out clearly in large letters. RUSSELL. Taking it into her office, she softly closed the door. When she made this call she needed to be calm and unruffled, no distractions.

She sat in her chair, took a deep breath and dialed the number on her cell phone. He picked up on the second ring. "Russ here."

Emily closed her eyes. His voice hadn't changed at all, she'd recognize it anywhere. She was astounded that it could still affect her, cause a small rustling in her mid-section, a little leap of the heart. "Hi, Russ," she said. "How are you doing?"

"Emily?"

"Yes. I was talking with André earlier today and he mentioned that you'd called the office looking for me. He gave me your number so I thought I'd phone. Are you back in town?"

"Emily, it's about time. I didn't just call the firm once, I called five times and dropped in there but I never seem to catch you in. Where are you?" He sounded rattled.

This was exactly the question she didn't want to answer. "I've taken some time off, so I haven't been into the office for a bit. What's all the fuss? Save for that call a few weeks ago, I haven't spoken to you in years." Emily gripped the phone with both hands, trying to keep her voice steady. Her breathing was shallow.

"I just wanted to talk to you, Emily. We were pretty close at one time." His voice dropped seductively. "I miss you. I wanted to see you, spend a little time. We're old friends, surely you can spare time for an old friend."

She remembered that voice. He was so persuasive, he used to be able to talk her into just about anything. Even now she felt her nerve endings stir in response. But she was older now and, she hoped, wiser. She certainly had a lot more to protect.

"You must be joking, Russ. You left town and didn't even say goodbye. And that was at least three years ago. Why in the world would I want to see you?" She paused and let the question hang, hoping he hadn't been able to hear her voice shake.

For a minute he seemed to be lost for words. "Emily. Emily, that's not how it was. I *had* to leave town, you know that. The cops were hot on my trail. I couldn't contact you. They were probably watching you, waiting for me to get in touch. I don't have to explain all that. And it wasn't three years ago, maybe two. Doesn't mean I didn't care about you. I did. You know how it was between us. We were good together, really good. I know you haven't forgotten."

She didn't let him get any further. "Don't be delusional, Russell. You surprise me. I've long since moved on. And no, I don't have any interest in seeing you. Good bye."

She pressed the off button. Her hands shook as she put them up to her cheeks. They were ice cold. *Oh, God.* Don't let him find out where she was. Don't let him even start looking. She just didn't want to deal with him. And if he found out about Andrew and guessed that he had a son, there would be no way to be rid of him. He would demand paternity tests and be in her face and in her life forever. He wouldn't do it because he wanted to take responsibility for the baby. No, he'd do it because it would give him a hold over her, and he'd try to use that as leverage for his own benefit. All she had to do was lie low and make sure he never found out about Andrew. Surely he had no real interest in her after all this time.

He could find another woman easily enough. A handsome man, he was also charming and engaging when he wanted to be. She didn't doubt for a minute he'd had other women since he left town. Hopefully the cops were still interested in him and their interest would make him decide to move on again. Maybe she could help that happen. She laughed hysterically and put her head down on the desk in despair.

~~~

Emily packed her briefcase, throwing in all the documents and trial notes, snapped it shut and lugged it out of the courtroom. André had left right after the trial was finished but Emily waited at the courthouse to make the final appearance when the judge returned to deliver his verdict. A partial win. They'd won on the technical issue at trial but the damages had been far less than their client had hoped. Well, it had still been worth going to trial, the issue was an important one.

She switched on her phone and listened to the messages. Tami had called about the evening's agenda. André left instructions on the trial wrap-up. There was one from Verna who was bringing Andrew down to meet her tomorrow, and a few from Ryan about his plans for the two of them. It had been four weeks since she'd met him at her house party and she was nervous and excited to see him again.

Then there were two terse messages from Joe, asking her to call.

She stood on the courthouse steps, wondering if she should phone now or just wait until she got back to Bonnie. There was nothing she could do for him down here late on a Friday evening. He'd seemed really testy about her coming down in the first place and she was having trouble figuring out why. Yes, there was work waiting for her in Bonnie. But he'd known this trial was pending from early days. She'd been up front about it when she first started with *Tanner Enterprises*. She sighed resignedly and called the office number but had to leave a message. Obviously everyone had left the Tanner office already.

She held the phone in her hand for a minute, debating with herself, then called his cell phone. He answered on the second ring. "Tanner."

"Hi, Joe. It's Emily calling."

"Hi." His voice seemed to relax. "How did the trial go? Is it finished or carrying on to next week?"

"Finished. We just wrapped up, got the verdict a half hour ago."

"Okay. Good. Did you win?" He chuckled.

"Well, yes and no."

"Uh, oh." She could hear the wince in his voice. "What does that mean?"

Emily laughed. "We won. But the damages weren't what the client was hoping for. We tried to tell him before we went to trial that the losses he suffered didn't all flow from the breach of contract, but, well…. There you go. Sometimes the argument isn't worth it. Sometimes it's okay to just walk away. But he has the comfort of knowing he was proved right."

Joe was silent for a minute. "Yes. I guess I know the feeling." There was a pause. *He did? What did that mean?* She waited.

"Well, I wanted to know if you were back in our offices Monday. Your new girl is starting, and I wasn't sure what I'd do with her if you weren't going to be here. I thought maybe we should postpone. But if you think you'll be back…"

"Oh, yes. I see. It could have been awkward with Shirley."

"No kidding. Okay, I'll leave it as is. Have a good celebration and I'll see you Monday."

"Thanks, Joe. I will." She pressed the button to disconnect and looked thoughtfully down the steps to the sidewalk. Her final day in the office last week, Joe had been abrupt with her and short with his comments. She wasn't sure if there was something else going on or if he was upset that she wasn't going to be available for a week.

They had been meeting in her office, going over last minute details for the days coming up when Shirley came to her door one more time and asked for Joe. Apparently someone was there to see him and the secretary had put them in his office to wait. He'd shot a dark look in the secretary's direction and stalked out.

A few minutes later, Emily saw the visitor briefly as he escorted her out of the office and down the hall to the main house. It was a woman, tall, slim, very well dressed and extremely good looking, not pretty but striking. Shirley had lost no time in coming in to see if Emily needed anything and offhandedly filling her in on the story while she was at it. This was Margaret, Joe's girlfriend, a decorator from Toronto. She'd been mad at Joe but had come to Vancouver Island to make up with him because he'd begged her to come.

Joe didn't return to the office that afternoon. Emily spent the last hour sending him a dozen emails with details wrapping up their conversation and putting a stack of files on his desk for immediate attention. She was amazed that he'd leave in the middle of finalizing a half dozen issues when he seemed so put out that she wasn't going to be around the next week to work on them. Maybe she had it wrong and it was about something else entirely.

Suddenly her gaze cleared as she saw someone waving to her from the bottom of the stairs. Ryan, Tami's client from the Mid-Winter Bash, stood smiling up at her and she went swiftly down to meet him.

~~~

Emily had come home Saturday night with a very tired Andrew. It snowed again the next day. She'd been surprised by the wet blanket of white but according to the old-timers who hung around the upscale mall in downtown Bonnie, it wasn't unheard of this time of year. It stood in dirty piles along the edges of the road with tree limbs and twigs garnishing the untidy heaps. Branches were down everywhere.

The arbutus trees kept their leaves all winter and were prime targets for damage. Great gnarled limbs and whole trees had fallen, the broad leaves acting as baffles as they caught the wet snow and were pulled apart. Exposed roots and broken trunks littered the gravel drive and the edges of the road where they had been dragged out of the way by passing motorists.

*My God, what kind of weather is this for late February?* Emily had just gone to the gym in Bonnie and done a bit of shopping. Verna would be returning tonight. Andrew had stayed at the gym nursery while she did her workout. When she left home it had been raining but the snow had started before they even got to town. She should have just turned around and gone back, but it was hard to find time to get to the gym and she needed the workout and the relaxation it provided. But really, snow now?

Joe had warned her against driving in this kind of weather. He'd even offered his four-wheel drive truck but she'd been too proud to accept the help. She couldn't believe she'd been so determined to do everything on her own and not be beholden to anyone, especially her employer. Especially Joe.

She had a good time with Ryan in Victoria but for now she'd decided not to take it any further. He was attentive, good looking and a turn on with his kissing. But Ryan wasn't who she was interested in.

Her body had woken up, however, and had stayed awake. Her hormones must be working overtime because they didn't give her any rest. And Joe was the man who seemed to keep them humming. Why was that, when he charmed everyone else and glared at her? Maybe that's why she'd turned down his help with the truck. His face had gone all hard when she told him 'no thanks'.

Her son was still thrilled by the sight of the white stuff, though. "Snow," he crowed, pointing with his chubby fingers.

"Don't worry," she said, "they have lots of it up here. It's not like Victoria weather, they get a real winter in Bonnie."

She wasn't far from home but hadn't realized it was so late by the time she left the grocery store. The receptionist at the gym, someone she was surprised she knew from high school, had invited her for coffee and it had delayed them further.

It was colder now that dusk had fallen and the snow was coming harder as she bundled Andrew into his car seat. She wheeled their way out of the parking lot. The highway was in good condition, mostly clear, but as she turned off onto the country road leading to Arbutus Bay, the snow fell faster. The wipers struggled to keep the windshield clear. It was so heavy she could see the tree branches sagging with the weight of the water held in the frozen white stuff.

Andrew fussed in the back seat, hungry and tired. Finally he started to cry.

"It's okay, baby." She reached between the seats to pat his leg. He continued to howl. Nervously she came around the corner on the two lane road a little too fast and as her lights swept the trees she caught the gleam of eyes in the darkness. Gingerly she touched the brake with her foot and the car skidded wildly. She frantically turned into the skid as she'd been taught years ago in driving school but simultaneously hit the brake too hard in a sudden panic as a deer leaped in front of the headlights.

There was a crunch and a sickening series of bumps as they were dragged sideways and finally ground to a halt. The car stopped at an angle across the road, the lights shining into the forest as the snow fell in a steady sodden silent blanket around them.

Shaking, her hands trembled on the steering wheel. Was the deer alive under the wheels of her car? She pulled at the door handle and shoved weakly against it with her shoulder. Placing one running shoe into the snow she snapped her seatbelt off and stepped out onto the road.

Her headlight was damaged, shining down at an awkward angle toward the ground. And beneath the fender lay the deer, legs crumpled, dark eyes staring. When it caught sight of her, it lunged to try to free itself from the weight of the car, then lay trembling as blood trickled from its flaring nostrils.

Emily staggered down the side of the car, leaned against it heavily and was sick into the snow by the back wheel. She wiped her mouth with one gloved hand, trying to control the involuntary heaving. Andrew screamed in the back of the car, lunging against the straps of his car seat. Dry heaves claimed her attention and then she sagged weakly against the vehicle until her legs steadied.

She tried to block out the sound of Andrew's crying. Bending down she grabbed a handful of snow and rinsed her mouth out. What should she do? She needed to get the car off the road and out of the way of traffic. She was a sitting duck for any on-coming motorists. They'd have a hard time not hitting her, parked as she was at an angle in the middle of the right of way. Wrenching the driver's door open, she fell back into the car.

"Hush, Andrew, hush." Her voice was hoarse, her throat

sore. She put the car into reverse. The wheels spun. She tried rocking it, first in forward, then reverse. The car moved and she heard the deer's shriek of pain. She slammed the car back into park.

Bolting from the door, she ran around to Andrew and pulled him from his seat. He fought her, arms flailing wildly. "Come on, Andrew. For God's sake, don't do this. Not right now, please." She felt her nail break to the quick as she grappled with the snap on his seatbelt.

At least she could get him out of danger, away from the stranded vehicle. If she left the lights on, surely anyone coming would see them and perhaps could stop in time or get by to avoid a collision.

How much traffic was there on this road in such dreadful weather? Maybe no one would be coming for a long time. That was a scary thought, too. They might be stranded. There was no cell phone reception on this stretch of highway. She'd lost a call on her mobile more than once while travelling through here. She could walk, but would have to carry Andrew and it was a long way home. Well, if she had to, that's what she'd do.

Andrew shrieked in her arms, pushing at her shoulder and arching his back, making it hard to keep her grip on him. "Andrew, shush now. It's okay." As she staggered toward the verge of the road, the sweep of lights behind the trees came from the direction of town. What if the driver didn't see her car in time, what if they couldn't stop? She and Andrew could be caught in the backlash of a collision.

Panicking, she ran in the heavy snow at the side of the road, slipping and sliding as she headed down the bank toward the ditch. She fell and landed on her knees in the water and dirty slush. Andrew gave a renewed howl and thrashed in a full blown tantrum. "Andrew, stop it!" She slapped his bottom through his padded coat.

Later she realized she'd never smacked him before. Shocked, he simply froze in her arms, clamped his mouth shut and lay his head down against her collar. Emily wrapped her arms tighter around him and rubbed his back, rocking him gently as the wet seeped into her shoes.

The louder hum of a truck engine approached. She raised her head as the headlights swept around the curve, slowed and then stopped right behind her car, holding the scene in their powerful glare. Instinctively she ducked. Anyone could be in that truck. The door opened and a set of overhead floodlights on the top of the truck cab flashed on before a boot descend into the snow. A hulking black figure emerged and walked around to the side of the car, peering in through the windows, then moved to the front to inspect the deer still struggling against the car's undercarriage.

Then, "Emily? Emily!" She saw the figure head toward the ditch, easily following her trail in the snow to where she knelt, her knees dirty and shoes soaked.

"Joe?" She staggered to her feet. "Over here." Shifting Andrew in her arms, she ran at the side of the ditch, slipping and falling back down the embankment. Andrew whimpered. Joe was suddenly beside her, taking the baby from her with one hand and grasping her under the arm with the other.

Hauling her up the bank, he dragged them both across the road and into the headlights of his truck. "Are you all right? What were you doing down there? I thought ..."

He encircled her with his free arm and crushed her against his jacket. She thought he pressed a kiss to her temple. She gave a sob against the snowy fabric, then covered her mouth with her gloved hand.

"Are you hurt?" He stood her away from him to examine her and reached down to brush the mud and snow from the knees of her jeans, Andrew slumped in his other arm.

"You're soaking wet. Get in the truck, the heater's on."

"Oh, Joe," she protested. "Did you see? What am I going to do? I think the deer is still alive."

He wiped the hair back from her damp cheeks. "It's okay, Emily. I'll look after it. Just get in the truck and get warm."

He wrenched the passenger door open with a gloved hand and handed her up. Scrambling to reach the high seat, she pulled the truck blanket over her knees. "Joe, the deer," she said as he handed a limp child up into her arms. She peered at him out of staring pupils. "What are we going to do?"

"It's okay. I'll look after it." He slammed the door shut. She huddled down in the blast from the heater, leaned her head against the back of the seat and closed her eyes. Her arms were shaking but she tightened them around the baby dozing on her knee.

She heard him rummaging in the back of the truck and the clank of tools as they rattled against each other. Then he went by the window and disappeared on the other side of her car. Some minutes later he backed her car to the side of the road but she didn't see the deer again. Joe climbed into the truck, flipped off the floodlights and put it in gear.

"Where's the deer?" Craning her neck, she tried to see out the back window as they moved past the spot toward home.

"It's okay. Don't think about it, sweetheart." His big arm came around her shoulders and pulled her in to the warm hard wall of his chest. "We're almost home."

Joe got them into the house, pried off his boots and carried Andrew into the living room. Emily wrestled the little boy out of his jacket and boots and he carried him up the stairs as she led the way. "Are you going to be all right? Where's Verna?" He looked around as if he expected her to appear out of thin air.

"She's off this weekend, visiting her daughter. We're fine, Joe. Thank you so much. I'm not sure what to do about the car." She sniffed and wiped her nose on the back of her hand. Joe passed her a cold wad of Kleenex from his pocket, his mouth a firm line.

"I'll look after it, Emily. I'll get Victor to go back with me and help tow it home. I don't want to leave it out there for fear someone will hit it. But it isn't a good vehicle for up here anyway. It's probably time to find something that's more reliable for our weather." He pulled her into a long hard hug, rubbing his hand comfortingly on her back.

"Are you okay?" He peered into her face, his gaze sharp.

He seemed to hesitate, then reluctantly let her go. "I have to go and get the car off the road."

She nodded. When he was gone she felt bereft. He carried the feeling of assurance with him, an air of control and comfort. She missed him already.

## CHAPTER TEN

The next weekend Emily drove her new vehicle down to Victoria and out to the ferry terminal. The car was new to her, and very nice. She still couldn't believe it. Joe had mentioned a few days after the accident that a vehicle was part of her remuneration package and he'd found something that might work with her little family.

*What part of the remuneration package?* She'd mentally gone through all the documents she'd written and had him sign, and finally pulled them out to read them again. There was no mention of a vehicle. Joe drove a truck, *Tanner Enterprises Ltd* stencilled on the cab doors. But that was different, he was the owner of the company.

The next day he poked his head around her office door and quirked an eyebrow. "Don't you want to see what kind of vehicle I've found? I thought you'd at least be curious." He gave her a slow grin.

"Joseph Tanner," she said. "What are you playing at? And what vehicle in the remuneration package? There isn't mention of one in there."

He laughed. "Did you actually look?"

She flushed to the roots of her hair.

He added, "I just got the call back about your car. It's a write off. You can pick up your cheque Thursday."

She made a face. "I'll have to find something else, I can't be without a car."

"That's what I've been saying. I've found the perfect car. We won't be gone long, back before you need to get home. Come on. I have to go into town now anyway." So she put on her coat and went out the door, Shirley frowning in her wake.

Joe stopped at a car rental place on the highway and pulled his truck into the lot. He climbed out and held the door for her, then pointed to the line of cars. "There it is, what do you think?"

It was a light grey car in the next row of vehicles. "An SUV," Joe said, "one year old, just coming off lease. It has all wheel drive so it's safe in the snow. It's good and heavy, won't slide around, and has great traction. Four doors so you can get Andrew in and out easily. It's got limited trunk space. That was the part I wondered about, whether that would work for you. But otherwise it's a very functional vehicle. Do you want to try it out?"

He waved away the approaching salesman and walked her over to inspect it. The snow was gone as if it had never been and the day was clouded but warmer.

"Uh, I'm not sure. I don't think I can afford it." She pondered the price on the ticket tucked under the windshield wiper. "No, I'm sure I can't. I need something a little cheaper." She smiled up at him. "Thanks, anyway."

"No, you don't understand. This is a very practical vehicle and it's safe. And you can afford this. I've already negotiated a better deal. Don't worry about the sticker price."

"Joe." She laughed. "Even if you negotiated a great deal, I couldn't afford it." She made the calculations quickly in her head.

He eyed her with a gimlet expression. "Yes, you can," he insisted. "*Tanner Enterprises* has a new Vice President and she needs to be driving a car that goes with her status. So think of it as a perk, or a bonus. Or something. If you like it, let's take it for a drive and see how it handles. It's safe, that's the main thing."

Seeing she had started to waver, he smiled and beckoned the sales guy over with the keys. "Thanks, Mack. We just want to do a test drive. See if we like how it handles. We won't be too long."

"Take your time." The salesman gave them a thumbs up and returned to his office.

So Emily climbed into the driver's seat and took a test drive. The car handled like a dream. She couldn't believe how it rode. Joe talked her into pulling over and examining it inside and out. They checked the seat heaters, the air circulation. He showed her the phone and GPS programs. The back seat was very functional, certainly enough room for Andrew's car seat plus extra passengers. Airbags everywhere made her feel safe. They inspected the trunk for space.

When they pulled back into the lot, he turned to her with an eager quirk to his mouth. "What do you think? Do you like it?"

She contemplated him, wondering what this was really going to cost her. But she couldn't resist. "Yes, I like it."

"Good." He grinned with satisfaction. "Let's go in and sign the papers. You drive it home and I'll follow in my truck when I'm finished my business."

~~~

Now she parked her new-to-her car in the long term lot for the ferry, grabbed her overnight bag and climbed out. She walked across the barricade and spied Walt's car in the ferry lineup.

Suzanne was with him. "This is going to be so much fun, I can't wait. Does Don know we're coming?"

The line began to move and Walt pulled his car down the ferry ramp. "I talked to him again yesterday. He knows and he's got a party for us to go to afterward."

They had a late lunch on the ferry and got into downtown Vancouver early enough to check into their hotel and relax in the bar before the show. *The Sunshine Boys* was having a very popular opening at the historic Orpheum Theatre. Their seats were front and centre balcony, Don had upgraded them before they arrived and Walt picked up the tickets at the front box office.

When they were finally seated, Emily gazed around appreciatively. "What a fabulous building," she whispered to Walt. "I just love coming here, and the sound will be great in the centre of the balcony like this."

"I know," he grinned back. "Can't get better seats. Look at the detail in the architecture. You could never afford to build something like this today. Good thing they didn't let it fall down, but finally put some money into refurbishing it."

The lights dimmed and a hush fell over the crowd. Emily leaned forward to look down on the main floor. There wasn't an empty seat. The production manager stepped through the gap in the curtains and made his introductory comments then it became truly dark and the curtain lifted.

At intermission, Walt took them downstairs to get a drink at the bar. The lobby was thick with guests milling around and when someone tapped Emily on the shoulder she turned in surprise. Steve Alexander stood there grinning down at her before he hauled her against him in a tight hug. "Emily," he drawled. "I haven't seen you for ages. I couldn't believe it was you." He looked her up and down, before hugging her again. "You're looking pretty damned good."

Emily laughed and managed to extricate herself from his grasp. "Steve, long time, no see. You haven't lost your grip."

He laughed appreciatively at the double meaning. She looked over her shoulder and waved to Walt and Suzanne. "Did you see Walt? And this is Suzanne, a friend of mine from Victoria."

Steve greeted Suzanne, shook Walt's hand and they chatted about old times. "Is it true you're into clothing manufacturing now? I think I heard something about that only a couple of months ago." Walt grinned and winked at Emily.

Steve chuckled. "Well, I am and I'm not. I have a company that produces rain gear but I'm in the process of selling it to Westcoast Gear out of Kamloops. And now I've started work in the movie industry. I'm going to supply equipment to the grips and production crews. It's great. I've got some stuff in this *Sunshine Boys* production, that's why I'm here tonight. Big party later, after the play. Want to come?" He quirked a brow at Emily and threw his arm around her shoulders again. "It'll be fun, say you'll come."

Emily smiled but looked a question at Walt. "We're already going to a party with Don. It might be the same one. But we'll see you after the play and take it from there." Steve nodded and signaled a woman standing across the room to join him on his way back to his seat. Emily looked over at her. She was beautiful, tall and slender with a swath of red hair pinned back on one side. She gave Emily a pointed look, then turned on her heel and met Steve at the aisle.

"Whoosh," Suzanne breathed. "She really gave you a once over. Not sure you're her favourite person. The way that guy kept hugging you probably ticked her off."

Emily laughed. "That's just Steve, that's what he does. Right, Walt?"

They fought their way back to their seats. The second half of the play was even better than the first. Don played the character of Willy Clark, and the makeup they had used was fantastic. That, along with his clever body language made the audience see that this late twenties man was much older and severely disappointed in life. Willy wanted to make a comeback in the entertainment industry but was past the time where that was possible. So he was settling for a reunion with his old comedy partner, whom he hated with all his heart.

The machinations of the two old men were hilarious and yet hit Emily as being sad. She thought it might be her state of mind, with everything that was going on in her life. Ryan had been such a magnet down in Victoria, yet she hadn't been so tempted that she'd slept with him. He was getting impatient, pressuring her to come down by herself for a weekend with him. She hadn't said 'yes'.

But her body was yelling at her with a vengeance and

urging her on full force to satisfy it. She had a battle on her hands that tugged her first one way and then the other.

When the curtain came down for the last time they all sighed and relaxed back in their theatre seats. "That was great," enthused Suzanne. "I loved it. Don was amazing. I'm not surprised he's getting offers for a television series."

They found their way backstage, having to wait outside the stage door until Don could be located to let them in. They hung around chatting while he removed all the paint, false hair and extra padding tied around his middle. After he showered and changed, they caught a cab across town to the party.

Suddenly Emily leaned forward to tap Walt on the shoulder in the front seat of the taxi. "Steve! We forgot Steve! I told him we'd check with him afterward before we headed out."

Don took her arm. "Don't worry about it. Steve will probably be there. He turns up all over now that he's plugged into the entertainment industry. I've seen him a few times since we were up at your place in Bonnie."

The party house was packed. Don was on a real high after the performance and slugged back a few stiff drinks the minute they arrived. He introduced his friends and began to move through the crowd, chatting and gathering congratulations. The others followed casually behind. Suddenly Suzanne grabbed Emily's arm. "There he is."

"Who?" Emily's head twisted around to see Steve plowing through the crowd with his red-headed date in tow.

"Guys, here you are. I figured we were heading to the same place." He grinned boyishly and tugged the redhead forward. "Everyone, this is Rachel, a friend from the industry." Rachel gave them all a cool look and Emily couldn't help smiling.

Steve turned his back on the girl and leaned in close. "Emily, I need to talk to you for a minute. Come with me, okay?" He took her arm and eased her away from the group. Down a hall and through an archway in the back of the house, he opened the last door on the left. He looked around and led her inside someone's office.

"Goodness, this is very cloak and dagger. What's so important?" She looked up, puzzled, into his handsome face as he closed the door. "You really are a good looking guy, Steve," she commented. "Why hasn't some woman made an honest man of you?"

Steve stilled, just looking down at her.

"So, what's the big secret, that you had to bring me back here to tell me?"

Steve studied her a moment longer. "Emily, I've missed you so much." He moved suddenly, took her into his arms in a firm embrace and placed his mouth over hers. The kiss immediately became possessive. Emily was taken off guard for a minute, and he took the opportunity to tighten his hold. She waited a second to gauge her own reaction.

Ryan kissed her like this, and she'd grown to crave the fire it sparked in her, the physical need. But she didn't know if she was attracted to him or the excitement and sexual urgency he ignited when she was with him. Experimentally she kissed Steve back. It lit an intense heat that left him panting against her cheek.

"Emily," he whispered, "I want you." His breath was coming fast, his chest rising and falling rapidly as he lowered his head to kiss her again. He backed her up against the door, his body grinding into hers and she realized he wasn't joking. He did want her, at least physically. She grabbed his shoulders and held on as his mouth started to roam across her cheek and down her throat.

One hand slid under her sweater and gripped her breast, his thumb rubbing across the lace of her bra to bring her nipple to fierce attention. For a minute she almost lost her head. She was so lonely for someone who knew her and wanted her.

That thought brought her back to herself. Steve didn't know her, he probably didn't even know she had a child. This had to be pure physical reaction. She tried to push him away, but he captured her hands and held them above her head in one of his while he pulled her snug against him again. He ground his hips lightly against her. "Emily, come on, let me. There's a couch right here. I'll lock the door."

She pushed harder. "No, Steve. Stop it, stop now." He didn't seem to hear, his hands roving all over her. "Steve, stop." She grabbed a handful of his hair and tugged his head up. The eyes that looked into hers were glazed with passion. He leaned in to kiss her but she turned her head away.

"Listen to me." She gave a shove and he staggered backward. "Listen to me. The answer is 'no'."

He blinked in confusion for a minute, then a ferocious frown appeared. "What do you mean, the answer's 'no'? You were kissing me just as hard as I was kissing you. You didn't object when I had your sweater pulled up around your neck and I didn't imagine your nipples standing at attention!"

Emily shook her head. "Don't be silly. Just because I kissed you doesn't mean I'm going to have sex with you. Steve, you have to have grown up more than that by now."

He gave a low growl and turned sharply away to stalk across the room. "Get out, Emily. If you're just going to play games with me, then get out."

Emily studied his rigid back. "Do you really do this kind of thing? You come to a party with one date, grab a different woman and drag her into the back room for sex?"

He rounded on her, his face flushed an angry red. Emily couldn't stop herself from retreating a step from his almost threatening stance. "I don't just do this kind of thing. I'm not that wild, even if my reputation says different."

His mouth thinned to a flat line. "Emily, I haven't seen you in nearly three years, since we both finished articles in Victoria. And I've missed you. I think about you all the time. Still. You're stuck in my head, okay? I can't get you out, every woman I date gets compared to you even if she doesn't know it."

His face washed pale. "I want you. I always wanted you. But you were a settle down type of girl and I wasn't that guy.

But I want you even now."

Emily turned her head slightly, it was so hard to look him in the eye. He advanced on her again and hesitantly gathered her into his arms. His voice softened. "I still think about you, wonder about you. I want you." He buried his face in her hair and groaned, and she let herself be hugged.

When she found her small group again in the front rooms of the house amongst the pushing crowd of actors and theatre goers, Suzanne was ready to leave. Rachel had apparently wandered off to greener pastures and Don had gone with a woman friend from the production crew. They eventually tumbled into a cab and ended up back at their hotel. Walt steered them into the bar for a nightcap before they headed to their rooms.

As they settled around a low table, he turned to Emily. "So what did Steve want, if I can't already guess. You came back with your hair all messed and no lipstick left." Suzanne giggled, and Emily felt a blush climbing her cheeks.

"Oh stop it, you two. Is this the inquisition?"

Walt yawned. "Well, yeah. Steve is always the subject of an inquisition. He's one strange wild character." He gave her a searching glance before lifting his highball glass for a sip. "You just have to be careful around him, that's all. Really careful." He winked to take the sting out of his words but his face showed concern.

Crawling into one of the beds in their hotel room, Emily could hear Suzanne's deep breathing and knew she was already asleep. She felt foolish for what had happened tonight and realized it wasn't all right to keep Ryan dangling. She would have to end it with him.

If nothing came of her interest in Joe, then she'd live with that. Life was too busy anyway. Russ had called again and he was serious about talking to her. He'd said he'd be by to see her. He thought she was going to be a big part of his new plan, whatever that involved. And she was equally determined she would not.

## CHAPTER ELEVEN

The sky was a dull overcast grey with dark clouds thick across the low horizon. And the sea was calm, tiny, tiny waves lapping against the rocks, almost no movement at all. Joe had seldom seen it so still. Across the bay, giant log booms floated in irregular flotillas, big logs tied so close together he knew he could walk across them. The sea lions huddled in a group on the small island on the long stone-filled beach.

They'd arrived a few weeks ago, such funny furry animals. They had a mile or two of exposed rock to sit on but they had chosen a couple of boulders and huddled together, writhing and climbing on top of each other. They barked non-stop. That was the noise he'd been hearing.

Emily had just gotten home from Vancouver he noticed. Verna was still in Victoria, apparently she'd bring Andrew back tonight. They did a lot of travelling down island. Was she settling in or just putting in the time?

When he'd found her car askew in the middle of the road that night, lights glaring into the woods and an injured deer caught under the fender, he'd nearly had a heart attack. They were gone and the car was damaged. Then he'd followed the tracks through the deep snow and found them in the ditch by the side of the road, her jeans and runners soaked and dirty. His whole body reacted, arms tight, chest constricted and gut in a knot.

He'd hauled them out of there and got her into his truck. All he wanted to do was take them home with him, settle them into his house, and keep them safe. Instead he'd done what he had to, dealt with the deer and towed her car.

Then he'd had to go back to acting as if nothing had changed – he hadn't hugged her against him, he hadn't kissed her temple, he hadn't longed for her.

As he walked down to the water, he wondered how the lions got any sleep. The barking continued day and night. It was much louder down here. They were protected from a lot of the sound up at the house by the stands of trees.

The lighthouse on the island flashed a green and white light and the sedge grass grew brown through the snow among the pebbles in a ragged uneven line. The rocks were grey-green, the colour of lichen, with patches of brown-gold set off by the dark smudged red of the winter branches on the low willow bushes. A Navy ship was coming through the pass, probably part of the ocean exploration team he'd heard about, here to have a look at the sea lions. This was new for the area, the lions had never come this far north before. Nobody knew why they were here this year.

Fifteen men stood on the deck of the boat and another ten up on the prow, all looking at the sea lions, binoculars flashing in the dull light, gesticulating and talking amongst themselves. And the sea lions barked.

He saw her ahead of him in the snow. She must have heard them approach because she whirled around to find the sheepdog sitting at her feet and Joe standing just behind. "So, it's you down here," he said inanely, then winced at the awkward remark.

Emily smiled and slanted him a look. "Yes, I was out for a walk. I heard the noise and wanted to see the sea lions."

"I thought I saw someone down here by the boats. I just wanted to check." He gestured toward the far off beach. "They're quite a sight, aren't they?" She turned back to look out at the scene.

A mist rose from the remains of the melting snow around

them and the ocean gleamed in the near dusk. Through the hazy light, all he could really see was her white woolly toque and great dark eyes, the slant of her brows. He'd missed her this weekend. When he didn't see her every day in the office, he had a powerful urge to end up at her house to find out what she was doing and if she was home.

He put his hand on her shoulder and took a step closer to stand beside her. "I've just been thinking …" He gazed down into her eyes as she lifted her head to look at him questioningly and she was so close it was more than he could resist. So he leaned closer to see the clear dark blue of her irises. "I was just thinking …" he said again and lowered his mouth to hers.

She was still for a moment and then imperceptibly her face turned toward his. That was all the encouragement he needed. He deepened the kiss and felt the sudden emotional impact in his chest, wondered if it was shock. He raised his head. Her eyes were wide, the pupils dilated. She placed her gloved hand over her mouth.

"Emily", he breathed, "that's what I thought." He didn't know if he'd spoken aloud. He took her wrist to move her hand away and kissed her again. She leaned into him as he opened wider, slanting his mouth over hers. Her taste was like magic, like music, like a potent drug.

When he lifted, she stepped back. "Joe," she said, "I have to go," and she turned and walked swiftly away.

He watched her leave through the rising mist until it swallowed her whole as she climbed the hill and he realized that, in fact, he hadn't been thinking at all. But the kiss had told him that she was open to him, for at least that moment. She'd let him in, pressed against him before she lost her nerve and ran.

Turning, he looked out to sea, past the island and the lighthouse. The Navy ship was still out there, drifting near the beach. His boat was gently rocking at the dock down below on the calm water, but his mind was still firmly on the look in her dark blue eyes.

When he first saw her those few months ago as she stepped out of André Dubuy's car, it was like having a veil removed from his eyes or maybe a sledgehammer to the side of the head. He didn't know which.

He must have been living in a fog before and he'd been clear-eyed ever since, his gaze resting squarely on her. He glanced up the hill again but she was long gone from view.

*My God, what now?* She'd run like a scared rabbit. If she was still here beside him, he'd probably blow it anyway. He wouldn't be able to stop himself and she wasn't ready for that, obviously not ready. He released a pent-up breath. Suddenly it seemed like the most important thing in his life to make this go right, whatever it was. He couldn't screw it up. No matter what, he had to do it right.

~~~

Joe eased his arms into his suit jacket and shot his cuffs. He adjusted his tie and gave his hair one more swipe with the brush. He heard Geoff whistling and the sound of his heels striking the marble in the entrance hall. Good old Geoff. He was one reliable guy and very good at these functions. With a dozen suppliers and manufacturers coming in for a pep-talk, wine and dine, flag-waving, it took all of *Tanner Enterprises'* thin resources to pull it together.

He had to admit his housekeeper, Mia, had been more useful than Shirley in getting everything organized. She arranged for the food, the liquor, mix and appetizers and even hired extra staff to serve. Shirley had bogged down after drawing up the guest list and sending out the invitations. She flustered and balked until Joe simply left her out of the procedure altogether, telling her to hold down the office while the rest of them worked on organizing the event.

Emily's secretary Anna, new as she was, had been much more resourceful. There was something to what Geoff had said about looking for new office help, but now wasn't the time to worry about it.

Emily was very organized. She was presenting an overview of the corporation, its recent growth and future potential.

She'd drawn up quite a body of information and this morning showed him a folio to be presented to each of the attendees. It was very professionally done. He shouldn't have been surprised, everything she'd undertaken since starting with Tanner had been first class.

Since the day down at the water though, when he'd kissed her, she hadn't been alone with him in the same room. She managed to keep Shirley present, be on the phone, call on Geoff to lend his presence. Whatever he tried, they were never alone. The last few days had been busy, ramping up this presentation while putting the pressure on the Portugal deal but he'd not had a chance to talk to her about that kiss. Maybe it was best, maybe he'd stepped so far out of line she'd never let him near her again. The thought struck terror in his heart.

He watched her. Today she'd seemed really jittery. She'd been on the phone as he approached her office earlier in the day. The tone of her voice rather than any words he could make out made him pause outside her open door. She'd sounded stressed. When he stuck his head in, she'd just rung off and gone on with business. But her pale face and the tightness around her mouth gave her away.

Now he was anxious to see how she held her own in the midst of a group of twelve businessmen, some of whom even he found intimidating at times. Most of them were pretty good people but a few were sometimes tough to handle, especially around women.

He took the stairs two at a time, arriving in the living room in time to see Geoff greet Emily with a kiss on the cheek. She looked stunning. Her dress was black, mid-calf length with a short jacket. As she leaned forward for Geoff's kiss, he realized it was probably strapless. The cleavage was modest but enticing. Her hair was swept up in a sleek roll on the back of her head, glittering earrings dangling almost to her shoulders. Geoff took her hand and turned her around, whistling in appreciation.

Joe shook his head silently, meeting his brother's amused

gaze. This was going to be a very interesting evening.

~~~

Emily greeted another guest, shook another hand, smiled and chatted. She was doing her best to get to know these people, make them feel welcome and comfortable. She'd been more than ready for the evening, everything was so organized it made her look like a machine. But that phone call this afternoon had thrown her right off stride. How did Russ get her work number, for heaven's sake? It was a total disaster, that he could just pick up the phone and call her at the office. He'd said he called to chat.

The whole idea was so upsetting she didn't know how she carried on with her day. She was thankful Joe hadn't heard the conversation. All she needed to do was contain the situation, get it under control. Somehow she had to neutralize Russell.

But he'd been asking her questions about working up in Bonnie and what had triggered the move. He needed her help, he said, and surely she was willing to help an old and very close friend. She winced inwardly, recalling the low tone of his voice, the sexual innuendo contained in the statement.

She smiled and shook another hand. She knew all of the names of their suppliers now and had been able to put faces to them without too much trouble. It had helped having Geoff standing beside her as they mingled before dinner. He made a point of using names whenever she joined a conversation or when another manufacturer was referred to until she had them all in her mind. And he'd been faultless in treating her with courtesy and respect. She couldn't say the same for some of the other men in the room.

Her presentation had gone well. She'd considered using overheads but in this relaxed setting it seemed too formal and overdone. So she'd settled for a flip chart and professional printed posters that she'd used for illustration. The folio of information had gone over well. She led them through the data, quickly pointed out the meaning of the charts and graphs that showed how businesses associated with *Tanner*

*Enterprises* could profit. Joe looked satisfied, she thought, although his expression was often difficult to read and was almost inscrutable tonight.

Since he'd kissed her in the snow down by the bay, he'd been more guarded around her. Although she wasn't entirely sure if it was him or her. She hadn't known what to do about that kiss, so decided to ignore it. That seemed to be her best strategy lately, maybe her only strategy. She wasn't in a position to let it jeopardize her position. It was funny really, in an odd sort of way. After a two year hiatus she was suddenly being pursued by three different men.

But until it felt right, nothing was going to happen. No matter that her friends gave her such a rough time about not being with anyone for so long, since before Andrew was born. She'd decide if and when it was right. So far, she hadn't made that decision.

Having Steve drag her off to a secluded room and try to seduce her that night in Vancouver after the theatre had shaken her to the core. What kind of signals was she suddenly giving off? None, her friends had assured her. That was just Steve. Yet if he really did feel that strongly about her while they were at law school, she'd been unaware of it. He liked to flirt but that could mean anything. He was just Steve, zany, crazy, a bit mad.

The kiss with Joe had been totally different. It had felt right. The way he'd taken her in his arms and fit his mouth over hers. It felt wonderful. It felt welcome and it scared her to death. There were so many reasons why she shouldn't go any further, too many to count. It would have been so much safer for her to choose someone else.

And yet she was powerfully attracted to him, drawn to his dark grey eyes and big shoulders, his intense gaze that focused on her mouth. It drove her crazy, scared her to death and lit her up.

Tonight when she'd finished her talk, Geoff had given her a big thumbs up that made her smile. Most of the businessmen had seemed impressed. The wine and hard liquor had certainly helped to relax things after that.

Geoff put on some background music and then Joe rescued her neatly when one big fellow, Harold Bull, had tried to sweep her into a too-tight grip to attempt a tango. This man was aggressive, put his hand on her knee under the table during dinner, and ogled down the front of her dress. He made sure she knew he was the owner of Bull's Custom Lumber, a specialty lumber supplier. She assumed she should have been impressed and tried to appear so but stopped smiling altogether just as dinner began when she grabbed his wrist in a death grip and told him in a hissed comment to keep his hands to himself.

Joe must have been aware of what was going on because when she excused herself for a moment from the table, she returned to discover he'd changed places with her. "Just have to discuss a few things with Harold here, Emily. Hope you don't mind."

With relief she took Joe's place across the table between Debendra Singh, the owner of a small quilt factory and Steve Gaines, manager of the Tanner warehouses in Vancouver. They were both interesting men and Emily learned a lot about the fabrics industry and the difficulties of running a hand-craft factory.

The evening eventually wound down. The living room was empty save for a halo of smoke from Harold's cigar. Joe had done his best to keep the smoking outside, but Harold Bull was a stubborn man.

Geoff grabbed Emily's hand and twirled her around. "That went well," he said as he drew her into a dance around the rug. "I was mighty impressed, Ma'am. Mind if I feel your knee while we have dinner?" He leered and she burst into laughter.

"Did you know that's what he was doing?"

"Well, I hoped he restricted himself to your knee. I could see he was up to something Joe got there before I could."

"Oh, God." She covered her flushed cheeks with her palms.

## CHAPTER TWELVE

Joe watched them, leaning against the kitchen doorway. "All right, you two. You can't make fun of my business colleagues like that."

He crossed the floor in a couple of strides. "Harold Bull is one of my major suppliers. And if he ever puts his hand on your knee again, I'll break his arm."

After Geoff drove off, Joe poured Emily a drink and one for himself. "Whoa, that's over." He sat on the sofa beside her and took a deep gulp from his glass. It was his first drink of the evening, and he knew she'd been drinking soda water. He had a policy, never be at a disadvantage with his business associates. And a night like tonight meant too much to risk that.

He blew out a breath and leaned his head against the back of the couch. "Man, that was excruciating. Most of those men are really good guys, like Lou Walker, the customs agent. He's honest and competent, easy to work with. But there are a couple..." He peered at her. "Harold being one of them. What an ass. Good for Geoff for tipping me off. I didn't notice at first."

Emily laughed and sipped her drink. She seemed relaxed and even a bit giggly. She was probably feeling a huge sense of relief after the tension of the evening.

He reached to take her hand. "Your information package went over well. Enough information to get them interested but not enough to overwhelm. I heard a fair amount of talk around the table about it."

She smiled at him, her eyes twinkling. "I've used that format before. It always goes over well. People think they're really perceptive to pick up on the crucial points so quickly but it's because you spoon feed them with that kind of information. It's like baby food, goes down easy."

He grinned. "Yes, Mum. You know all about baby food."

She laughed softly. "That's true. I do. It did go well, didn't it? I think a couple of those people have already decided to join forces with us. And there was definite interest from Active Enterprises to market our products from Asia. I think we'll see a lot of business from this."

When he tugged on her hand, she fell gently against his shoulder. "Thank you, Emily. You were great, you really pulled it off."

She hummed for a minute under her breath, then leaned forward to set her drink down and turned to him. "Joe," she said. But he moved to carefully touch her lips with his. She didn't pull away. His lips clung and she opened her mouth, letting him in. His arm tightened around her back, pulling her against him as his heart started a wild tattoo in his chest. He deepened the kiss. As she reached to touch his cheek, he placed his hand at her waist.

He leaned back to see her face. "I want to apologize for the other day down by the sea lions. You seemed taken by surprise with that kiss. But it just kind of happened. I thought I scared you." He watched her face for clues as to what she was thinking.

"Not really scared. But you did take me by surprise. I wasn't sure…."

He nodded, his stomach clenching. "I'm sorry, I didn't mean to embarrass you. You just looked so enticing there, with your fuzzy white hat. You looked serious and beautiful." His fingers closed convulsively on her waist.

"You're very beautiful, Emily. I want to ..." He paused. "Well, I want to kiss you. May I?"

She nodded, her eyes huge in her face. He leaned forward again and placed his mouth over hers. So lovely, so soft. She smelled like heaven, tasted like wine and woman. His hand moved up her side and around her shoulder. His fingers slid beneath the little bolero jacket.

"Oh my God." He dropped his head, his forehead touching hers. "I've been looking at this dress all night and wondering. It really is strapless. That thought kept most of these men from concentrating very hard on what you had to say. Myself included." His thumb brushed along her fragile collarbone, back and forth.

She snuggled closer and he kissed her again, angling his mouth over hers. He dropped his hand to the front of her dress and pressed his palm against her nipple standing proud under the silk fabric. Then he slid his fingers up and around her bare shoulder under the little bolero top, rubbing her soft skin before he reached under the bodice of her dress to touch her. He groaned as he ground his mouth against her soft lips. Her breath quickened and she wrenched her mouth free.

"Joe." She pushed his chest to get his attention.

"Sorry. Going a little too fast, eh? I can slow down." She fit so nicely into the curve of his arm. "It's hard to go slow with you, Emily. You're like a magnet. I should try to resist, right?"

She laughed breathlessly.

Maybe he was going too fast but he didn't want to stop. He kissed her again.

"Joe. I have to go."

He blinked and squeezed her breast softly. "God. Sorry." Reluctantly he withdrew his hand. This was worse than high school. Somehow, he didn't seem to have the stamina he used to have. Then he'd work all night just to get a feel of the girl. Now it was different altogether. Was it possible he was more desperate than he'd been in grade twelve? That was a discouraging thought.

He watched Emily rise to her feet, tugging her bodice into place. Her breasts giggled as she adjusted her dress, and he felt an uncomfortable tightening in his groin. He rose awkwardly to his feet and reached for his suit jacket.

"I'll walk you up," he said, his voice a little hoarse.

"Thank you."

He placed her wrap around her and squeezed her shoulders lightly before opening the door. The air was balmy, a true spring evening, not a hint of snow remaining. His sheepdog bounded to his feet and stood at attention waiting to see which way they'd head. The night was starry and the air smelled clean and slightly salty from Arbutus Bay down across the field.

Closing the door behind them, he tucked her hand into the crook of his arm and covered her fingers with his. The walkway was clean. He could thank Victor for that. They meandered up the path, the dog trailing.

Joe told her about the property and how Victor was near retirement age but still carried the main load of caring for it all. "I just tell him to hire the local boys when he needs help. He never oversteps with me."

She patted his arm. "You're a nice man, Joe Tanner." He gazed obliquely at her profile but didn't reply. He knew he wasn't always nice.

She reached into her purse for the key as they approached the door.

"Good night." He regarded her solemnly before he leaned down to kiss her and her tender mouth just drew him in. Before he knew it, his hands were lost in her hair and he was breathing heavily against her throat. Then his hand slipped back into her dress, inside that enticing bodice and his mouth followed down the smooth slope of her breast.

The feel of her turgid nipple against his tongue, the taste of her skin, the scent of her lit him on fire. Her arms were clamped around his head, as much for support as in passion, he thought. He inhaled and felt dizzy from the headiness of her perfume.

"Oh, baby. Oh, baby, let me come inside with you. Please." He heard himself beg, a low growl of sound, but didn't care. His heart was doing triple time in his chest, clamouring to get out.

"No, Joe. I can't. Verna would hear and I just don't."

"You don't?" he croaked, confused.

"I don't. She'd hear. You're a big man and you make a lot of noise. It'd sound like an army troop coming up the stairs. She'd probably call the cops before she opened her bedroom door to find out what was going on." She sounded petulant that he was so large and noisy.

He laughed softly. "I see. Okay." He kissed her again, trailing his mouth down her throat and across her smooth shoulder, licked at her collar bone. She had a death grip on his neck and panted in his ear. He finally paused, just holding her against him to regain some sanity.

"Shall we go back to my house? We can make all the noise we want there. We can just walk back down the path."

She shook her head stubbornly.

He considered her for a minute, then leaned in to kiss her again. She raised her face to him and he was soon lost. When he finally came up for air, his hand was under her skirt and she was draped across the front of his jacket, her fingers threaded together at his nape. His lungs were labouring in his chest but his brain was crystal clear.

"Which room is yours?" He leaned his head back to glance up at the house.

Emily craned her neck. "I'm at the back, the big one overlooking the patio. It's got a balcony."

"Perfect," he said. "You go in and I'll meet you up there." He leaned to give her a parting kiss but lingered and embellished until she was propped against him again, her head on his shoulder as he plundered her mouth. His hands were trying their best to get under her clothes. He pulled back. "Emily," he whispered, "you go inside. I'll meet you up on the balcony."

"What?" She tried to get a grip on the lapels of his jacket

with her fists. "What are you talking about?"

He placed his hands gently over her wrists. "I'll climb the trellis. Just go inside and I'll meet you up on the balcony. Go on." He gave her a hard kiss and tried to pry her hands off the front of his jacket, but she hung on.

"So, you're Romeo now? You're going to climb my balcony?" She laughed breathlessly. "This I have to see."

"Yes, Juliet. That isn't all I'm going to climb." She reached up to place a soft kiss on his mouth, finally turning to fumble with the lock. Joe watched her disappear inside and close the door behind her. He heard the lock click. Taking a deep breath he stared at the flat surface of the door, the knocker hanging just below eye level.

He couldn't believe it, she was so soft and receptive, so open to him. He had to do this right, but more than that, he had to do it. He'd been driving toward this moment almost from the day he first laid eyes on her, and he'd finally arrived. She'd been very guarded and right now her guard was down.

He turned and stepped carefully down the path and around the side of the house.

~~~

When Joe heaved himself over the railing of the balcony to the sound of the wood of the trellis cracking beneath his foot, Emily tugged on his arm to help him up, convulsed in laughter.

"Shhh," he hissed as she clapped a hand over her mouth. Taking his arm she led him toward the open sliding glass doors. The interior looked so inviting he stalled as he stepped inside. His mouth went dry. A small lamp on the dresser cast a low glow around the walls. The bed was covered in a rose coloured throw. Pillows were piled at the head of the bed and a soft cushioned chair sat to the side.

He paused to take off his shoes and placed them on the little mat inside the door, then slowly slid the glass closed behind him. Emily had stopped laughing, her face solemn as she gazed up at him. He took her in his arms, gently pulling her against his body and just held her. When he lowered his face into the soft cloud of her honey-coloured hair which was freed now on her shoulders, her perfume rose to engulf him.

Oh, how he wanted her. The feelings had been growing so strong he had trouble controlling himself when he was around her at the office, and he was restless and agitated when he wasn't. If he met up with Geoff for lunch in town, his brother would ask what his problem was. Could he please just concentrate for a minute so they could discuss some issue, and Joe would try to pull himself together.

All his concentration had gone out the window, it was centred on his new vice president. Emily and her small son. Emily and her ideas about promotion, negotiation, legal issues. Emily and her caution around him. It was as if his mind wasn't his own, he'd lost control.

Yet, here she was, right here in his arms. He walked her backward toward the bed. She began to peel his jacket off his shoulders and he helped. Then he searched for the zipper on her dress and found it under her arm. The garment slid to the floor in a whoosh of silk and she was naked in front of him, or nearly so. When she bent to peel off her pantyhose, he caught his breath at the sight of her leaning forward, her naked breasts moving with her motions.

Fumbling urgently with the buttons on his shirt, he peeled it down his arms to discover himself caught with cuff links anchored at the wrists. Emily giggled and gently dislodged each one, setting them quietly on her dresser.

He took her in his arms. The feel of her bare skin under his hands, her breasts pressed against his chest made him catch his breath. He fell with her onto the bed. "Don't change your mind," he whispered.

She shook her head against his throat and he touched her, one hand smoothing down the silky skin of her back. She eased away from him with a grimace and he hastily unbuckled his belt and slid his slacks off, dumping them with a jingle onto the floor. Her panties followed, lovely black lacy things. But what was underneath was even more exciting. His palms tingled to touch her.

"Oh, you are so lovely. Sweetheart, I don't have a condom. I never thought … I mean it was a business meeting, and I didn't consider… I'll go back to the house and get one." He felt suddenly bleak at the thought, but determined as he sat up and reached for his shirt.

"It's okay," she said. "We're okay.

"I promise you, I'm clean. I'm healthy, I always use protection. Except for tonight." His face felt hot.

She pulled his head down for a drugging kiss that made him forget what he'd been saying. He lost all sense of time, seduced by the slow mesmerizing flow of movement, the feel of her skin, the wetness of her, the heat, the small sounds. The rubbing and slipperiness.

When he raised himself above her and used his hand to guide his entrance he had lost all thought.

She hesitated.

He pressed and she tensed. "What? What's wrong?"

"It's been a long time," she whispered. "Just go slow."

"I will," he gasped. "I'll go slow." And he pressed again and was finally inside. He waited, his heart thumping like a jackhammer, feeling her relax around him. Then he began a slow movement that would, he hoped, keep him from finishing too quickly.

But she wasn't going to wait, with sudden haste she rose to meet him. He tried to hold a measured pace, but she was anxious, seeking and faster, urging him on. He delayed, attempted to hold off but she didn't let him and culminated in a tumultuous climax. Hastily he covered her mouth with his palm to try to contain her groans and came right after, slamming into her hot slick flesh. He lay there gasping, his face ground into the pillow trying desperately to catch his breath. His heart pounded, his lungs bellowed.

Eventually he rolled over, taking her with him in his arms, chest still heaving. "That was a stellar performance," he murmured into her hair when his heart finally began to slow down. "I'll try to do better next time."

She laughed weakly. "It was me. It kind of caught me by

surprise."

"By surprise all right." It had caught him by the throat. The feel of her had his heart pounding harder before he'd even pressed inside. It was like being wedged in a tornado.

He turned his head and kissed her temple, ran his hand down her back and around the globes of her bottom. Her skin was like satin. His hands had a plan of their own and as they encompassed her flesh, she began to make small breathy sounds, pressing her face into his shoulder. He moved her head slightly to find her mouth and began a slow seduction.

*This time, I'll have some control. No rush to the finish line.* He'd woo her properly with careful lovemaking, so she'd want him again and again.

But something about her seemed to take the reins right out of his hands. She writhed under him, tugging his head down for a ravenous kiss that sent his thoughts into a jumble, then flying right out of his head. She rubbed his chest, nuzzling him. Her hands gripped his buttocks and dragged him against her and into her.

It was the fight of his life. He battled bravely and ended with a mindless climax that left him in shattered pieces. He tucked her against his shoulder and slept.

Deep in the night he stirred and pulled her back against him, familiarizing his hands again with all her warm and secret places. "Emily," he murmured. "I won't stay." He pushed the hair back from her face and kissed her cheek, her forehead before resting at her mouth. "I just want to kiss you, sweetheart. I just want to hold you."

She stirred in his arms. "Joe, maybe we should..."

"Shhh," he murmured. "I won't make any fuss." He touched her breast, stroking the velvet skin and heard her breath catch in her throat. The pebbled nipple rose to meet his searching fingers. He lowered his mouth there and suckled her gently, then more insistently. Bodies shifted, skin against skin. She gave a little gasp as his hand slipped across her belly then down between her legs. He used his thumb to rub that secret place, massaged her until she was breathing unevenly against his neck.

Covering her mouth with his, he felt her give and yield and demand more. "Come on top of me," he whispered, guiding her with his hands. He fell onto his back, pulling her over him. As she straddled him and then lowered herself, he stifled a groan and felt the sweat pop out on his chest.

"I don't think this helps," she panted.

"Does it hurt?" He stopped her motion, gripping her thighs in his big hands.

"No, no. It feels…. Oh, God. It feels…. It's just been too long and I can't…"

"Can't what?" he murmured, trying to control her sudden plunging, holding her off then slowly lowering her. "Can't what?"

She collapsed forward till her mouth was on his. His hands came up to cup her breasts. She moaned. "I can't go slow. I just need this."

And she began a steady rubbing that had him rigid in her grip. He held on and gritted his teeth, his fingers digging into her hips as she rocked on him, on and on, and finally came in a smothered gasp. He continued moving until she was limp in his arms and then took his own release.

## CHAPTER THIRTEEN

As Joe climbed down the trellis he felt his pant leg catch and rip on a broken piece of wood and he grinned to himself. Why did life work out like that? Here he was sneaking out of a house on his own property, *his* house, in his best suit and dress shoes. Who would believe it? He dropped the last few feet to the ground, took a deep breath of the night air and looked up at the sky.

When he was a kid, the Domingo family used to live in this house. Davey Domingo was eleven and Joe was ten, they clicked immediately. Mr. Domingo, Davey's father, had been the farm manager for quite a few years. Some of the land had since been sold off, but back then it was a big farm in the Stocking Valley and Joe's father had always had a manager on site to look after the whole operation. The boys ran wild all summer long. After Davey and his little sister had been put to bed by his Mama, he would climb down the trellis and run out to get into mischief with him.

Joe had never really been sent to bed when he was a kid. He looked back now and wondered what his parents had thought he was up to when he was out at night. They never asked. He and his brothers and sister would wander off to their rooms when they were tired and after his mother came to tuck them all in and say goodnight, no one came back to check or looked in to see how they were doing.

One night he remembered he was in the process of pulling on his shoes by the back door around eleven o'clock in the evening. He and Davey had decided to go down to the wharf onto the Tanner launch that was docked there. They'd turn on the light, play cards, share a beer from the fridge. Pretty innocent stuff really. But his parents didn't know that. This night, his father came down the hall, drink in hand just as he tied the last shoelace. Joe froze where he sat on the floor.

"What's up, Joey?" his father asked.

"Not much," he'd mumbled.

"Okay." And his father ambled back down the hall to join his mother in the living room by the fire. Joe had let out his breath and eased out the door. He ran up the hill, climbed the trellis and knocked gently on the sliding glass doors. Davey's head appeared between the heavy drapes and they were off on another adventure.

Now he couldn't believe how this evening had evolved. Emily had been so open and then so passionate he was still shaking from the reality of it. His heart hurt. There was a pain under his breastbone, this must be what heartache felt like. He took a deep breath and shook his shoulders, trying to ease the pressure.

It was just starting to lighten in the east, dawn wasn't far off. His hound sniffed at his feet and he leaned down to ruffle his ears. Good old Dog, always there when he needed him. He walked around the side of the house and down the hill, hoping for a few hours' sleep.

~~~

Emily closed and locked the glass doors and crawled back into bed. She pulled the covers high and lay staring at the invisible ceiling in the dark above her head. What did she think she was doing? She couldn't believe it. It had been fantastic.

It had been such a long time, the total lovemaking thing. Something had shifted that night with Ryan at her party when he'd managed to get past her armour and inside her fortifications. She'd thawed. Yet he wasn't who she wanted.

This was so different that she didn't even know how to characterize it in her mind. She felt totally replete. She had no energy left, wrung out in the best possible way. And enormously excited. Excited at the pleasure Joe gave her and the heat, the slide and loving, the possibility of more. That was her heart talking, her body.

But her mind said she knew better. And she could say it was the drink she'd had, but she'd only had one, after everyone left. Maybe if she was single without commitments or responsibilities she could do this but that wasn't her situation. She hoped André Dubuy never heard about it. He'd be mortified to find out how she'd handled herself after he'd recommended her for the position. She writhed in mental discomfort.

The thing was, she hadn't handled herself. She'd been swept away. She'd been aware of Joe at a deep inner level when she was in his presence right from the very beginning. She liked to pretend that he was critical of her but she had to admit it was more that she'd been afraid of the chemistry between them.

And she'd known he was as aware of her as she was of him. She'd been focused on him. Her time with Ryan had warmed her up, softened her up for Joe.

Sleeping with him was something that had been waiting to happen and she felt shattered. The fire, the passion scared and exhilarated her at the same time. This had the makings of a dream or a disaster. With everything going on right now, it was more likely to be disaster. How could she work for someone and have a casual relationship with them? With Russ poking around trying to find her, how would she keep things on an even keel with Joe? What a mess she was in. What an utter mess.

The tears leaked slowly into her hair, finally the sobs overtook her and she buried the noise in her pillow. She wanted him again already.

~~~

Joe eased the throttle on his boat to idle and set out his fishing gear on the deck. The motions were automatic, he'd fished for years in this bay and just outside into the channel beyond. He knew the best spots by the time of day and the time of year. There weren't as many fish as there'd been when he was a kid but he always came back with something in his bag.

He hauled out the toolbox full of lures and opened it on the deck beside his gear. Setting his downriggers, he attached the lines and lowered the weights as the line reeled out. When he was alone like this, he only put out two downriggers and two lines. It was always a mad scramble when he got a hit to pull in the spare rod while keeping the fish dancing on the hook. He'd spent more than one afternoon untangling lines all over the back deck.

He put the boat in gear, trolling slowly down the bay and out into the channel. The sea lions were gone from the island and the smell had abated somewhat. They left as suddenly as they'd arrived. Joe passed close enough to see the sand all churned up from the winter's activity. The marine authorities were still confused about the sudden appearance of the animals this far up the inside of the island, yet he knew from personal experience that the sea and its inhabitants were always unpredictable.

He kept one eye on the tips of the rods, watching for any sudden movements to indicate a fish on the line as the boat chugged slowly through the water leaving a small wake. The sky was grey and overcast, the water a bit rough. It looked like it might rain.

After a time, he turned the boat in a wide arc and headed back the way he'd come in the same pattern he'd used dozens of times trolling for salmon. The chinooks were running and he was hoping to catch a few. His wharf was a small speck in the distance up the coastline. Dog would be laying there or sniffing around the rocks on the shore waiting for his return.

The downrigger gave a strong jerk. His pulse skipped a beat before he realized he'd gotten too close to shore and was dragging his weights on the bottom. He put the boat in idle and walked back to wind up the downrigger and coax the gear off the rocks.

That was a damn fool thing to do. He knew better, but had to admit he was a bit distracted. That's why he'd come out on the water in the first place. It always calmed him down. Everything was slow motion and measured progress, he had time to think.

Sometimes that was a good thing, sometimes it wasn't. He jerked the line off the clip with more force than was necessary and wound up the downrigger with impatient strokes.

Emily. It was always about Emily. What was the woman doing to him? He'd been walking on clouds when he left her bedroom that early morning. He felt complete, like a man who had his whole life in order. At one and the same time, he thought he'd never need sex again it had been so fulfilling and he needed her again right now, because it had been the most exciting night of his life.

He'd gone home and slept like the dead for a few hours, then rose and faced the day with incredible anticipation. He couldn't wait to see her walking into the office on Monday, all prim and proper. Her hair was always confined, pinned up or held back with combs. She wore little jackets with her dresses or slacks. It turned him on no end to think of her sitting with her laptop at the desk while she talked on the phone and made notes or argued some point of law with the person at the other end of the line. It was like the buttoned up librarian who threw off her glasses and jumped his bones.

And yet he hadn't been able to get near her since Sunday night. It was incredible. She turned hot and cold so fast it made his head spin.

He'd seen her the following morning in the office for all of about ten minutes. He had to take a phone call and by the time he was free, she had gone. Shirley told him she had a meeting in Bonnie. With who, he'd like to know. He certainly hadn't asked the secretary, he didn't need problems on more fronts than he already had.

By the time she got back that afternoon, she picked up her messages and went home. So he'd called by her house that evening to see if she wanted to go for coffee or a walk and Verna answered the door. No, Emily was out, but she'd give her the message. Would he like to come in for a cup of tea? *No, thanks, just give her the fucking message.* He'd steamed back to the big house.

The next day she wasn't in the office at all. She phoned to tell Shirley she had business in Victoria and would be back late the following day. She was working on contracts for the Portugal trip they had coming up in a few weeks, so he couldn't fault her for that. But when she returned she had booked Geoff in for the day to go over other issues that had arisen and get his feedback.

It was galling. He caught her alone in the corridor coming back from the washroom while Geoff was there and tried to ask her if she'd like to go for dinner but she acted like she didn't even know his last name.

Logic told him she was running scared. Emotions spoke a different story and he seemed to be ruled by emotions these days. They swung him around like a cat by the tail.

Geoff was no help. He and Vanessa were into the thick of planning their fall wedding and he wasn't paying attention to his own stores, let alone *Tanner Enterprises*. They were in the throes of trying to buy a house. He spent all his spare time with a realtor in tow or on the line giving him updates on what appeared to be an hourly basis.

Joe tore the fishing line from the clip with irritated fingers and began to reel it in. This wasn't working and he might as well call it a day. Just then the other line jerked and popped off the downrigger. He quickly finished hauling in the first line and grabbed the second rod, yanking the tip up and starting to slowly reel it in.

He suddenly had a fight on his hands and forty minutes later the muscles in his arms were burning, he was breathing hard and a thirty pound fish lay flapping on the deck of his boat.

The elation was always the same. He grinned, he couldn't help it. He used the fish bonker to put it out of its misery and pulled up the downriggers. Now he'd call it a day. Maybe he could offer some of his catch to Emily, a peace offering, for what offense he wasn't sure.

When he appeared at her patio door, he peered in to see Verna knitting in the easy chair with the cat at her feet. He tapped on the glass. She moved to lay down her knitting and come to the door. "Afternoon, Joe." She greeted him with a smile. "What have you got there?"

"I just caught a nice Chinook, so thought I'd bring some up for your dinner. Where is everyone?"

"Come in," she said. "Come in. What a lovely idea. No one home but me. The others are out for the afternoon. Emily's gone to the gym, I think. But that looks like a nice piece of fish. I'll just get it into the refrigerator, best to keep it cold."

"You know, there's a decent gym up at the house. She could use that any time she wants. I should have thought to offer."

"Well, she might be interested but I think she likes getting into Bonnie and having her own time. She can meet up with her friends and socialize a bit. But that's a generous offer, Joe. Would you like a cup of tea?"

"Uh, no thanks. Just say 'hi' for me."

"Okay. Why don't you come back for dinner? They'll be home by then and we can all sit down to a nice meal. How do you like your fish cooked?"

Joe marched back down the path toward the big house. *Out for the afternoon, huh?* She must have known he was going to come by. She hadn't been in the same place twice since the night of the presentation to the buyers. He swiped savagely at the deadheads of grass as he stalked past.

## CHAPTER FOURTEEN

Emily pulled the baby stroller up beside a table in the food court and paused. She looked around at all the tables but didn't see Steve. Sitting on the nearest chair, she pulled out the little container of Cheerios and pried the lid off for Andrew. He held it carefully, picking them up one at a time with his chubby fingers and popping them into his mouth.

"There you are!" Emily turned her head to see Steve bearing down on them with a grin. He dipped his head and she moved quickly so that he pressed a kiss to her cheek. "You look marvelous. How's my girl?"

Emily squinted at him with a small smile. He looked good, his dark brown hair a bit long and shaggy, but it suited him. He always dressed well and his athlete's body carried itself with confidence. Ever the same Steve. She frowned. "I'm not your girl, Steve. But I'm fine. How are you and what are you doing in Bonnie?"

"I come here occasionally. It's a nice little city. But right now I've got an order for raingear so I'm just looking after my customers."

"Oh, I thought you sold the business. Not yet?"

He frowned. "It didn't go through, although it looks like it might now, especially with the big orders I've had coming along in the last few months. That just might light a fire under them to get moving on it." At that, his face cleared. "Who's this?" He turned to examine the little boy.

Emily placed her hand possessively on the stroller. "This is my son. Say hello, Andrew." The baby grinned but remained content to continue shoveling in the Cheerios while he eyed Steve.

Steve contemplated him for a minute. "I'd heard you had a baby but I didn't know for sure," he said slowly. "How old is he?"

"Why? Are you trying to figure out who the father is?" Emily clamped her lips shut, wishing she hadn't let that sharp comment pop out. "He's two," she added abruptly.

Steve gave her a baffled look. "Who the father is?" he paused. "I haven't a clue. I was just wondering if you were pregnant when we were still articling. He's a good-looking little guy. His hair is a true blond, even lighter than yours."

He contemplated her hair for a minute as if he were distracted, then clapped his hands and shifted in his seat. "What do you want to do? We don't need to eat here, there are nicer places in town."

"I know," she said. "But it's easier with Andrew. His mess isn't as noticeable along with everyone else's mess, if you see what I mean. We like Vietnamese. Andrew has the spring rolls, he likes to dip them in peanut sauce."

Steve laughed and stood. "Stay here, I'll get us some stuff."

Just as Steve arrived back at their table with a loaded tray of food, Emily felt a hand on her shoulder. "Hi, Emily. You're in town today, are you? Good to see you." She looked up into the smiling face of Geoff Tanner.

"Geoff! Are you working today?" One of Geoff's large hardware stores was at the other end of the mall.

"Yes, the odd Saturday." He shot a quizzical look at her table partner. Emily turned to Steve. "This is Geoff Tanner, he's one of the owners of *Tanner Enterprises*, where I am now. Geoff, this is Steve Alexander, a friend from law school"

The men eyed each other and Steve set the tray of food down to straighten and shake hands. He was a few inches taller than Geoff and broader in the chest. Geoff seemed to take him in with one swift glance. He chatted for a few minutes then wished them a good lunch and moved off to catch up with a couple of other men who were standing to the side waiting for him.

Lunch was interesting. Andrew wanted to sit on Steve's knee which gave him pause. But he eventually lifted him up and let him spread his spring roll all over the table and down one pant leg. Emily laughed and didn't interfere, thinking this might be the closest Steve had been to a small child in his entire adult life. It might even be good for him.

He was full of stories and had her in gales of laughter over his antics, real and imagined. Andrew laughed whenever his mother did, even when his mouth was full and Steve was kept busy trying to good-naturedly keep the mess off his shirt. When most of the food was gone and their coffee cold, Emily cleaned Andrew up and tucked him back into the stroller.

"Thank you, Steve. That was a fun lunch. I don't know how you stay in business if things like that happen all the time."

Steve grinned, his eyes bold and teeth white. "Well, they don't happen all the time, do they? Just most of the time."

She chuckled.

"It was nice to see you, Em. Maybe we can do it again sometime."

Emily eyed him a bit warily but smiled. "That would be nice."

He leaned forward and kissed her, lingering for a moment before pulling away. "I'll hold you to that," he said, his gaze steady.

~~~

When Emily walked into the house, Verna was peeling carrots and Joe sat in the big overstuffed chair chatting with her. A giant filet of fish marinated in a serving dish on the counter.

"Joe!" Andrew cried and released Emily's hand. She made a grab for him and wrestled his boots and coat off before he tore across the room.

Joe stood. "Hi, Emily. Hi Andrew."

"Hi, Joe. See my book?" Andrew darted over to pull his book out from under a pile of blocks. "Read me."

Emily looked from Verna to Joe and back again.

"I've been invited for dinner," he said, then hooked his hands under Andrew's arms to pick him up. "Let's sit here." He sat back down in the overstuffed chair. "How was the gym?" He eyed Emily's snug pants and tight sweater.

Emily smiled tentatively at him, knowing she didn't look like she'd been to the gym. She turned to Verna, "How are you doing with dinner?"

Verna spoke from the counter. "Joe brought us our meal, so I invited him to stay. It's as fresh as can be, he just caught it this morning. He says it's really good barbequed." Her eyes twinkled.

Emily paused, then forced a smile. "Lovely," she said. "Thank you Joe, it looks like a really nice piece. That must have been a big one, to have a filet that size." She looked around helplessly and then down at herself. "Well, I'll just get changed and come down to help." She headed for the stairs to escape.

~~~

Joe found himself staring at the empty staircase. Andrew tugged at his shirt and pointed to the page, drumming his heels against his shin. "Then what?"

Looking back at the little boy, he began to read the storybook about the naughty kitten. Andrew was riveted, as always. He'd only heard it about two hundred times. The idea of a naughty kitten really caught his imagination.

Dinner was a little stiff at first. He talked about catching the fish, which Andrew found fascinating, then started on the presentation night as Verna asked questions. He was proud of

Emily's role in the event and wanted her to know.

She had begun to talk to him instead of around him by the time Verna left to give Andrew his bath. He rose to clear the table. She hovered uncertainly for a minute, then reached for the serving dishes. "You don't have to. We can manage."

Joe turned to look at her, a platter in his hand. "I don't mind. I had a great dinner, I'll help with the dishes." He headed for the kitchen, Emily hurriedly following.

"There aren't many. I can handle it."

He paused, then placed the dishes on the counter. "Emily, we have to talk. Come outside, just for a minute."

"I don't want to talk," she said. That mulish expression had appeared.

He almost smiled, she looked so childish, but knew it would be a huge mistake to let her see his grin and he was getting a little desperate in his attempts to spend time with her. "Then we can chat right here. What happened the night of the presentation was…"

Instantly she held up her hand. "I can't, Joe. I can't talk about it." There was the sheen of tears in her eyes.

"Okay, all right then." He took a deep breath and let it out slowly. "Don't talk, just listen." His voice became softer. "It was wonderful that night, you were wonderful. It was magical." She lowered her head and he could only see the side of her face and one pearl earring glinting in the low light.

He took her hand and rubbed the back of it. "Emily, if you don't want me, I have to respect that. But I'm begging you, if you do, if you have any interest at all, please tell me. I miss you so much. I don't know what to do, how to handle it. You're hot and then you're cold. You like me and then you won't even speak to me."

She let out a sob.

"Sweetheart," he said desperately, "Don't cry. I don't want to make you cry. I just… I don't know how to handle this. Did I hurt you?"

She shook her head mutely.

"Did I do something that offended you?"

Another shake.

"Can you tell me what I did wrong, what made you unhappy?"

She shook her head again. "It's not that, Joe." Her voice was a whisper. "It's not that. It's just too much... I'm so confused and I'm caught in a bind. I don't want to jeopardize my position and I made a mistake letting things go that far between us. I know I can't turn the clock back but...." Her eyes were wide and luminous with tears.

"Do you not care for me at all? Do I turn you off?" He peered down into her face.

She gave a wet laugh and sniffed. "You know better than that. You had me on fire."

"That's what I thought too," he whispered as the tremendous pressure in his chest eased a little. "On fire. That's what I can't forget."

"But I can't do this right now, Joe. Please believe me. I'm in a precarious position. I have other concerns and I'm not sure how to handle them, so you have to let me make the choice of what happens now. Please, let me decide."

He nodded. "Okay, I can do that. Does that mean we can't spend any time together? I mean, I'd like to take you out to dinner, maybe visit some people. My family always comes to the big house for Easter. I thought you, Andrew and Verna might like to join us for the meal. Is that out of the question? There wouldn't be any pressure, just a visit and some food. You already know Geoff and you've met his fiancée Vanessa and Dad. What do you say? Can we do something like that?"

"Yes, that would be nice. I'd like that. Thanks, Joe."

"Don't thank me," he said, "I'd like to do a lot more but I can be patient. I can wait." He wondered how long he'd have to wait.

~~~

The next day Emily left the office early, taking a briefcase full of files with her. With Joe in Vancouver, Shirley had been incredulous that she was leaving. Luckily Anna was there to look after calls and emails. When she got up to the house, Verna already had her coat on, car keys in hand. "Oh, there you are, Emily. I knew you'd be on time. I'll just head out. If I'm not back tonight I'll call and it will be about mid-morning tomorrow. Is that okay?"

"It's fine, Verna. No problem. And don't worry. I can work from here just as easily as at the office. If I have to, I'll take Andrew down with me to get anything I've forgotten. Drive carefully. Just let me know when to expect you. And give your daughter my best."

Verna flew out the door.

Emily closed it behind her and walked over to the fridge. She'd worked through lunch to try to get as much done as possible and she was starving. There were a few containers that looked interesting, she pulled them out onto the counter. The front doorbell rang. Verna must have forgotten something. She ran back down the hall and pulled the door open.

Russell Barrie leaned nonchalantly against the doorframe, hands in his pockets. His hair was the same curly white blond, cut short at the sides and back. He was leaner than she remembered and had a deeper tan. He wore expensive chinos and a button down shirt, with a windbreaker over it.

He gave her a slow grin. "Hi, Emily. Long time, no see." His gaze travelled casually over her before fastening back on her face. "You're looking good. Can I come in?"

Blocking the door with her body, she flashed a panicked look down the drive.

"Don't worry, I waited till your friend left. We're all alone. Except for the child."

The blood left her head. How did he find her? She glanced reflexively down to the big house. Was there anyone there who could help her? Only Shirley, and she didn't like to help.

"Well?" One eyebrow was cocked. "Can I come in, or are we going to have this conversation out here?"

"Russell, I don't want you here. Leave me alone."

His eyes became hard and cold. "I came about the child."

Emily backed up and he walked in. Andrew was playing on the floor with his train set. Russ paused and examined the baby, then looked quizzically at Emily.

"Is he mine?"

Emily tried not to panic. She was totally unprepared for a confrontation with him, had never allowed herself to imagine that he'd find her. It had been too frightening to contemplate. Yet, here he was in her living room.

"Russ, how did you know where to find me?"

"It was easy. I found an old directory and got your last address in Victoria. When I called around there, your tenants were happy to let me know how to reach their landlady, my old friend Emily Drury from law school." He didn't mention how long he had to hang around the house before he caught the guy at home alone, because the wife wouldn't talk to him.

"I see. So what do you want? I was serious when I told you we were finished. It was over a long time ago, and you know it. You simply left town. Don't try to tell me now that your heart was broken. I'm quite sure I'm the first thing you forgot as you shook the dust of Victoria off your feet."

Russell grinned. "No baby, that's not true. You're a mind-sticker. I didn't forget you. It just wasn't safe to maintain contact. You know what it was like. It would have been suicide to keep in touch. The police would have been on me like a shot."

"What possible interest could I have in you now?" Her hands were shaking in her lap, but she hoped he didn't notice as she clenched them tightly together.

"Just this." He gestured at Andrew. "Is he mine?" He sent her a rueful grin. "After all, a man should know if he has a son."

Emily slowly shook her head. "You're incredible. Such ego." She stood, hoping her legs would hold her. "No, he's not yours. He's not even two years old. I would have had to be pregnant for a year. The world's first twelve month pregnancy."

She motioned toward the door. "Now, I want you to

leave. I have someone coming and they'll be here shortly. I'm sure you don't want to hang around and be introduced. Please go. And don't come back. I'd hate to have to call the police and lay a harassment charge, because the cops are still probably interested in you for other things."

Face set, Russ rose to his feet and stepped closer, making her perform an involuntary retreat till the backs of her legs bumped up against her chair. "Don't threaten me, Em. If that little guy is mine, then I want to know about it. A man deserves to be in his son's life. And in the life of the son's mother as well. I wouldn't mind being back in you, so to speak."

He pushed his head forward aggressively.

She jerked her face to the side.

"In you, Em. That was exciting, so exciting." He was waiting when her head swung back and he smiled into her stricken face. "I need some help and you're going to give it to me.

He walked to the door, then paused and looked back. "His hair is just like mine when I was a kid." He opened the door and left.

Emily collapsed in her chair, covering her face with her hands and trying not to cry. Andrew grabbed her skirt and tried to climb into her lap. "Mummy, Mummy."

Dropping her arms, she pulled him up into a hug, then rose hurriedly to lock the front door. She trembled all over. Locking the patio door, she carried Andrew upstairs. They would both have a nap. And she'd come up with a plan. Because now she had no choice.

## CHAPTER FIFTEEN

The smell of roasting turkey permeated the house. Joe scanned the room. Audrey, his mother was in full cooking mode. Mia had prepared the potatoes and baked some apple pies ahead of time and Audrey had arrived to baste the bird and put the vegetables on the stove. His sister Natalie was in charge of the salads. The men supervised the children, set the table and served the drinks.

Joe Sr was well into his cups by this time and had Jonny cornered, grilling him on the performance of his bookstore in Bonnie.

Natalie stepped in and sidetracked him with talk about the children and how well little Kenny was doing in kindergarten. She had always been able to wrap their father around her finger, and Joe was just as happy to leave her to it.

Everyone in the family was aware Jonny hadn't been doing well in the last few months. He said he was taking his medication but was having trouble getting out of bed. His store stayed closed when he didn't get there to open it for business.

Joe suggested he have his part-time employee open for him. That way there was more incentive to get into the shop later in the day to relieve her. Geoff had offered to fill in if he was really stuck. Even Mum had said she would schedule a few mornings to open the store to take the pressure off.

Dad had his own views. He always maintained there was nothing wrong with Jon, he should just decide to get on with his life. *Measure up, son.* But things had never been that easy for the youngest son. His depression began when he was a teenager and had never gone away.

At least now with medication he was able to function quite well most of the time, but the last thing he needed was Dad hounding him about non-performance. Today he seemed in pretty good shape and was holding his own with their father. For once he'd shown up for the family dinner.

When the doorbell rang, Geoff was the closest and beat Joe to the door. Emily, with Andrew and Verna in tow stood on the verandah. She'd never looked lovelier. Her honey-coloured hair lay around her shoulders in a soft curl and the colour of her large dark blue eyes was picked up by the silk sweater she wore. Andrew looked cute as a button in a little suit with vest and tie. His pale blond curls had been brushed till they shone and his face glowed pink from washing. He grinned at Joe but stayed with his mum, holding her hand.

Geoff invited them in and Natalie rushed over to meet their new in-house legal counsel, Joe Sr right on her heels. He couldn't get near them for the crowd so just stood back and watched as his father hustled over to schmooze the most beautiful woman he'd ever seen.

Dad was practiced in the art of charming women. In Joe's opinion, his mother Audrey had been way too patient with him but they seemed to have some kind of agreement that worked.

Now he was standing too close to Emily, smiling too widely and making too many low voiced remarks for Joe's liking. The fact that he'd already had more than his share to drink was starting to show. There was no telling what he was saying, but if she started to blush Joe was going to deck him no matter what his mother might have to say about it.

Natalie deftly cut Emily away, taking her with Andrew to meet the other children, so Joe seated Verna on the couch and got her a drink. Jonathan struck up a conversation with her that soon had them both engrossed.

Andrew slowly inched away from his mother's leg to approach Natalie's two children. Kenny at five was tall for his age but gentle and his little sister Olivia was a big-eyed three. She stared at Andrew, who looked totally intimidated by her direct look but Kenny took his hand and led him over to the toys. Andrew peeked back at his mother and grinned.

"Emily, come and meet our brother Jonathan and this is Ken, Natalie's husband." Geoff was doing the honours. "And our mother, Audrey...."

"Is right here. Pleased to meet you Emily. We've been hearing all about you from Geoff and Joe so it's nice to finally meet you."

~~~

Emily looked around the room. She was fascinated by this family. Neither of Joe's parents struck her as parent types, but she knew from personal experience that appearances could be deceiving. In her own family, her mother had appeared to be the perfect homemaker, apron and all, yet her father had been the approachable and caring one, the one she could tell her sorrows to or confide her deepest secrets. Not that her mother didn't care, she just cared in a different way.

She turned to Jon, "I think I've been in your bookstore. It's on Maple Bay Avenue, near the highway, right?"

Jon nodded, looking pleased.

"Remember, Verna? We stopped there when we first moved up here. It's lovely. We found about ten books we wanted, Andrew found a lot more but we had to put a lid on the number we bought. And we haven't even read them all, it's been so busy."

"Joe's working you too hard. I'm not surprised." Jon shot an admonishing look at his older brother and Joe let out a snort. "No, I'm serious, you work too hard, Joe. And you probably drive your staff too hard as well."

Emily shook her head. "No, it's not that. There's just been a lot to do to finish up at my old office, then the move and getting settled in. I'm looking forward to summer, all of that will be behind me and things will settle down for a bit. But I loved your bookstore."

When dinner was served Emily found herself seated beside Joe Sr who was at the head of the table, with Andrew in a high chair beside her. At first she struggled with it, but his low-voiced comments meant for her ears alone began to embarrass her as it ensured she couldn't join in the general table conversation.

Rising, she moved Andrew's chair to her other side. "I'm right handed, Mr. Tanner. I can feed him better this way. Otherwise my aim is bad." She laughed lightly. Joe stood to help her.

"You should bring Andrew to the play-school, Emily. He'd have a good time and meet some other kids his age." Vanessa nodded at Andrew. "He's two, right? The children start at two and go to age five, you know. Until they enter grade one. We have a lot of fun. It's called the Rumpelstiltskin Playschool."

"Vanessa works there. She's drumming up business," Geoff interjected.

She frowned at him. "I am not. It's just that Andrew probably doesn't have anyone to play with out here, and he'd enjoy it. Lots of the children only come a couple of days a week, that way they can be at home some days."

The conversation moved on to business in general and the men soon entered a somewhat heated discussion on pros and cons of having more than one store in the same large market. Obviously they were talking about Geoff and his big hardware store in the mall plus a lumber yard out on the highway. Natalie had her own very vocal opinion to add and Ken made a face at Emily. "Sorry, this is what it's like to live with a family that's in business. It never ends."

Emily laughed. "That's all right, Ken. I like business."

Joe nodded his approval and gave her a slow grin.

Audrey refused any help with the dishes. There would be staff in tomorrow, she said. Jonathan suggested they have dessert in the living room. He helped Emily from her chair and picked up Andrew. "Come on, little guy."

He seated her in the corner of the sofa and sat beside her. "You'll be more comfortable here. Sorry about dinner, usually one of us is quicker to protect our guests. You'll have to learn how to give Dad a nudge in the balls." He snickered at her shocked expression. "I mean if you don't, Joe will and that would cause a huge family row. Now tell me about working for Joe here. Is he a tyrant? He was when we were kids, you know. An absolute tyrant."

"He was not," said Natalie, laughing. "Don't listen to him, Emily. Jon was the youngest and always complained that everyone picked on him. Joe was a good big brother, wasn't he Geoff?"

"I complained because everyone *did* pick on me," said Jon.

Geoff snorted. "Jon's right, I cannot tell a lie. Joe was a tyrant." Jon joined the laughter and Joe looked offended. "Of course, he was seldom around, so a spare time tyrant," Geoff added.

The ribbing carried on until the pie arrived. Joe Sr walked in, looked at the seating arrangements and took a place on the loveseat by the window. "Come and sit by me Emily and I'll tell you all about what these children were like when they were small."

Joe snickered. "Stay where you are. You won't learn anything new there. Dad's the last one to know what we were like when we were little. He hardly noticed we were around unless there was bloodshed. If there was blood, Dad was right there with his first aid kit."

"Well," said his father. "I trusted you to use your good judgment. Was I wrong?"

Joe sobered. "No, I don't think you were wrong. None of us got into trouble, did we? Not serious trouble anyway." He looked around at his siblings, then said abruptly, "Oh, no you don't. I don't want to hear all those old stories. You'll scare Emily back to Victoria."

"Oh, I don't scare easily. Tell me," she said, fixing him with a teasing look. "I can keep a secret."

~~~

Joe looked at her mischievous expression and thought, she's coming back to me. I'm not sure what happened, when she got scared after we made love. But she's opening up again and coming back to me. He worried about her other fears, not knowing what they were, but that could wait until she trusted him enough to tell him.

So he told the first story about Geoff falling out of the apple tree and getting his scarf caught in the branches. Joe had stood below holding his brother up by the legs to keep him from strangling, and bellowing at the top of his lungs for help. Victor Alberto was the one who heard and came running to the rescue. He was the one who scolded and warned them to take better care of each other.

Vanessa looked alarmed and said, "I've never heard that story before. Thank you, Joe, for keeping him from hanging. Mind you if we don't find a house soon, I might hang him myself".

Geoff guffawed. "As if I'm the one who can't decide what kind of house we should buy."

~~~

Verna held one hand and Emily the other, Andrew between them, as they ran up the path in the rain. Emily pushed the door open. "That was fun."

"It *was* fun." Verna took her coat off and shook it in the hallway. "Aren't they a nice group of people? That Natalie is really sweet and clever. Did she tell you she has a small business in Vancouver, even with the two little children? Her husband Ken talked about it."

"Yes, she runs a temp company, cleaners, caregivers, nannies. I think that's very smart of her. They seem to be an entrepreneurial family, don't they? They all have a business of some kind." Emily peeled Andrew's shoes off and left them at the door. "Jonathan is a very nice man. And his bookstore sounds like the perfect business for him. Let's make time to visit it again soon and see what we can find. You'd like that, Andrew. We could look for some more children's books. And now it's time for your bath." As she lugged him toward the stairs, the phone rang.

"You get that," said Verna. "I'll start the bath."

Emily handed Andrew over and walked into her office to pick up the phone.

"Emily, this is Russ."

Emily's breath caught in her throat and she reached to close the door. "Russ," she said impatiently, knowing her voice sounded weak. "Why are you calling? I don't want to talk to you. I hope you haven't turned into some kind of stalker."

"I enjoyed our little chat last time, Emily. I'm just wondering when I can see you again."

"You can't see me again. What do you want?"

Russ grunted. "I want to talk to you, I have a proposition to make. If you don't want to pick up where we left off, well, I can deal with that. But you'll still be interested in this. Don't forget, you have my son. I can make things easy for you, or I can make things very complicated."

Emily laughed, but it came out strangled. She could hardly breathe, her heart had risen into her throat blocking the air. She stared at the wall and tried to sound calm. "You have to be joking. Anything you're involved in would be suspect from the word 'go'. How did you get my home number? It's unlisted."

"I called *Tanner Enterprises*. The name's on your gate. The secretary, Shirley was very helpful and gave me your home phone number because you were never in when I called you at the office."

Emily groaned and rested the phone against her temple. She could hear his voice but couldn't decipher the words. *Shirley gave him an unlisted phone number?* She knew Russ was pretty persuasive, especially around women, but that was such a lapse in judgment it was astounding. And yet right now it was the least of her worries.

"Come off it, Russ. I'm not interested, I'll never be interested. Don't call me again." She slammed the phone down. Her legs shook and she sat down in the chair before she fell down.

The phone rang again. She stared at it, knowing it was him. What to do? She'd just let it ring and hope Verna didn't pick it up.

Now he had her number. It was unlisted, he shouldn't have been able to get it. But it meant that even at home, he could reach her. His reach was long and she was starting to realize she might not be able to evade it.

*Should she disconnect the house phone?* But that wouldn't work. Verna needed a phone in the house.

She needed to talk to someone, get some advice. *Should she call the police?* It would look bad if she did that and it came out later she was using the police to help hide her child from its biological father. She could be disbarred by the Law Society. This was her worst nightmare.

# CHAPTER SIXTEEN

Shirley buzzed her office line. "There's a call for you, Emily. Line three." Her voice was distinctly disapproving. Something was obviously annoying her again. Emily's heart speeded up. If it was Russell, she didn't know what she'd do. She pressed the button. "Emily Drury speaking."

The female voice on the other end said, "Hi Emily, this is Natalie Tanner. We met on the weekend."

"Oh hi, Natalie. That was a lovely dinner and it was nice to be invited to join you."

"Well, we mothers have to stick together, don't we?"

Emily laughed. "That's so. How are you?"

"I'm fine. I was calling Joe, but he's out so I thought I'd chat with you for a minute. Your little boy Andrew is very sweet, how old is he?"

"He just turned two in February. He's a bit big for his age. Wow, the time flies. You must notice that with your two. They were very open to having a new youngster play with them and share the toys. Your little Kenny is so gentle."

"Yes, he is. He's a good little guy. Now, the reason I phoned, I was wondering if you can advise me on something, and I was calling Joe to tell him I was going to talk business with you, but he isn't there, so I'll go ahead and talk with you first and tell him later. Poor Joe, he's always the last to know these things." She laughed. "Anyway, in my business I hire temporary workers to fill contracts with my customers. The contract I'm currently using with my temp workers isn't very good. I've had a few different ones but none of them were written for me and they always leave something out. What do you think? You can just bill me directly. It's a Tanner job, kind of. Just a different Tanner business than the one you usually work for."

Emily smiled. "Sure, Natalie. Why don't you send me what you're using now and a list of the types of work your people do. I'd imagine you need two contracts, one between you and your workers, one between you and your customers."

"You see," said Natalie. "That's exactly why I needed to talk to you."

"You arrange most of your business by phone?"

"Well, actually by internet. And it means we all have a record of the contact, we can access the information any time of the day. If I'm busy with the kids I can still take phone calls and check the email when I get home. I'm actually getting so busy I'm thinking of hiring a temp worker to help me out!"

Emily chuckled. "A temp service hiring a temp worker. Well, lawyers have their own legal representatives, don't they? You know how the old saying goes, a lawyer who acts on his own behalf has a fool for a client. So maybe you'd be better to hire some help and not get bogged down."

When she rang off with Natalie, she jumped up from her desk to head for the washroom, nearly knocking Shirley over in the hallway just outside her office door. Emily stopped abruptly, grabbing the older woman by the arm to steady her. "What's going on, Shirley? What are you doing outside my door?"

She frowned, looking around the hall. There was absolutely nothing there to occupy the woman. "Shirley, answer me. Were you listening to my phone call?"

Shirley's face was bright red. "Well, I was just trying to see if you needed anything."

"You would have knocked if you thought I needed something. You knew that was Natalie on the phone, right?"

"Of course. She called to talk to Joe and then she goes and talks to you for so long. I couldn't figure what it could be about. I didn't know if it was an emergency, so I thought I better… I mean Joe needs to know. She called to talk to him, not you." She clamped her mouth shut.

"This is clearly a serious breach of protocol." Emily took a deep breath and held it. "I've overlooked all manner of things because I know you're very loyal to Joe and you've been here a long time."

Shirley nodded, her face now mottled with colour.

"But this is the limit. I won't work under conditions like this. I won't have staff be rude to me, listen at my doors, drag their feet on tasks I give them. This is serious. I'll deal with Joe on this."

Shirley was now pale, beads of sweat standing out on her forehead.

"In addition, you gave out my unlisted home phone number. What were you thinking? You didn't know this person. You could have simply taken a message so I could get back to them."

Shirley looked down. "He said you weren't calling him back and it was an emergency. If you don't call them back, you aren't doing your job so I gave him your home number."

Emily's jaw tightened. "It isn't for you to decide if I'm doing my job. Go back to your desk, Shirley. We'll speak about this again after I've had a chance to talk to Joe."

~ ~ ~

Emily marched into Joe's office the next morning before he'd even gotten his jacket off. She was clearly ready for an argument but he took the wind out of her sails. "How is Anna working out?" he said. "She looks like she knows what she's doing."

"She's good," she answered cautiously. "So far. This is only her second week. But she knows the software and she's quick, picks things up easily."

"Yeah. I called the office yesterday and she got the call. Very professional, takes instructions. It's a novelty." He lifted his brows in mock alarm.

Emily burst out laughing. "Yes, a novelty. I need to talk to you about Shirley. Do you have a moment?"

He sat down at his desk, folded his hands and winked at her. "All the time in the world."

"I'm serious. This is serious."

"I'm well aware. Tell me."

Emily sat down on the edge of a chair. "She was listening outside my door yesterday."

He frowned.

"I was on the phone," she continued, "and she was listening outside my door to the conversation."

Joe lowered his chin, his face getting warm. "You're joking."

"Your sister Natalie phoned and asked for you. You weren't here, so she asked to speak to me. Shirley wanted to know what she said to me. When I caught her, she told me Natalie was calling for you and you should be told what the conversation was about. She didn't deny listening."

He leaped from his chair and started around the desk, a flash of adrenaline pushing him forward.

Emily raised both hands. "Just listen, Joe. There's more and we have to decide how to handle it. This is tricky."

He hesitated, then leaned against his desk, arms folded. "Okay, go ahead. I'm listening."

"Okay. She gave out my unlisted home phone number to someone who called for me here at the office."

"What?" He felt his heart start to thunder in his chest.

"Her argument was that I wasn't doing my job because they said I hadn't called them back when they left a message. So she gave them my home phone number."

"Jesus!" Joe gripped his head. "Who? Who did she give your number to?"

"It doesn't matter who. It's just that she did. I don't trust her with any of my personal information. I don't think she wishes to harm me but she thinks she's defending you, so if I'm harmed it doesn't matter."

Joe glared, then averted his face in embarrassment. "We have to let her go, Emily. There's no alternative."

"Yes and no. I've looked up the law…"

His head swung back and he felt his lips curve in a smile. "Of course you have. And?"

"And we need to give her a formal warning. I think you've spoken to her before about her work. Now we need to give a written warning. The next infringement she's fired. After the warning, we change her work conditions so she isn't doing anything sensitive for me. We can give that to Anna."

Joe was undecided. "I don't know. I think we should let her go. She's been here a long time, which deserves some consideration. I'll pay her what she's due and she can move on. A warning could just make her more determined to put you in a bad light, because that's what she's been trying to do. A clean cut might be best for everyone."

She pursed her lips and he tried not to smile. He was starting to recognize that look. It usually meant she was digging in her heels. *What tack would she take?* He didn't have to wait long to find out.

"There are a couple of things to consider. Anna's brand new and doesn't know her way around the company yet. We're going away shortly and she would be left here floundering around trying to run the place when she isn't fully prepared for it. It's not the best start for a new employee and Shirley is certainly capable of holding the fort until we're back. And she deserves some notice. When we get back, if Anna is settled in, we can do it then. It'll be a smoother transition. What do you think?"

Joe had to smile.

"What? Is that an agreement?"

He nodded. "It makes sense. Let's talk to her now. We'll write up that letter and give it to her. Maybe it'll be enough to keep her in line until we get back from Portugal and Anna is up to speed."

Joe asked the secretary in to join them in his office. She was red-faced and belligerent by the time they were finished.

"You're a fine worker, Shirley," Emily told her. "But there are rules about privacy that have to be observed. You were out of line and these things can't happen again."

He let her do most of the talking. She was clear and precise, leaving Shirley no wiggle room, yet compassionate. She'd been more lenient than he was inclined to be.

~~~

Joe rounded the path and knocked at the patio door. He waited a few moments before Verna came into view down the hall. She smiled and slid the door open. "Come in. How are you doing? I haven't seen you since that nice Easter dinner. It was lovely and I want to thank you again for inviting me."

He grinned. "You're welcome, it was nice to have you there."

"Emily and Andrew are in Victoria for the weekend because she's leaving next week for Europe. They won't be back until Sunday afternoon. And I decided not to go, but stay here and have a quiet time. Would you like to join me for lunch? I was just about to put something together."

"Thanks, Verna. I'd like that."

"Well, I have some cold chicken and I was going to make a salad. There's cornbread from last night."

"Why don't I go down to the house and get a bottle of white wine to go with that?"

Her face brightened. "That would be lovely. That will just set the meal off nicely."

By the time he got back, she'd put the salad together and was slicing chicken on the cutting board. "Just put it there, Joe. There are glasses in the cabinet to the left. We can eat here in the kitchen, that'll be most relaxed."

The cornbread was on a dish on the table and their places set with fresh napkins.

"Sit down. We can start right away. Do you say grace, or shall I? There, I will." She bowed her head and said a prayer.

Lunch was tasty and relaxed. He found himself talking about Emily under Verna's expert prodding. When he tried to find out who she was visiting in Victoria, she professed to know only that she usually stayed with a girlfriend and there was a young man down there who was interested in her, but she didn't know if she would see him on this trip.

He had a hard time hiding his reaction to that information.

Verna clearly saw his anger. "Emily's very careful who she sees. That's all I know. But I wonder if you know what her life has been like."

When he shook his head, she continued. "She's entirely on her own. Her older brother died in a car accident when he was sixteen and she was eleven. I think they were very close, and after he died she missed him terribly. Her parents went into a decline, that's the only way I can describe it. I don't know firsthand, of course, but I've heard enough from the Dubuys."

"From the Dubuys? I thought they were business acquaintances, Emily and André." He had stopped eating and just listened.

"Well, they are that too. But they were friends of Emily's parents and saw the whole thing unfold. Angeline Dubuy doesn't have too many good things to say about Emily's mother. Mrs. Drury was a very proper lady who doted on her son. When he was gone, she didn't seem to be able to pull herself together, not even for her young daughter. And the father withdrew into his work. He was a lawyer as well and a friend of André Dubuy professionally. So Emily was eleven and more or less abandoned. She gravitated to the Dubuy household. Angeline said she was there every weekend, often overnight. She'd ask her to stay, claiming she needed help with the grandchildren who were always visiting."

Joe looked thoughtful, and took another bite. "Where are they now, the parents?"

"They died, first the dad, heart attack. Then the mum, probably suicide. The coroner ruled she'd taken too many sleeping pills. By then Emily was nineteen and she'd been living in that silent house for almost eight years. She was left to tidy up the estates of her parents and get on with her life. She loves the Dubuys as if they were her parents instead of just good family friends."

Joe nodded, speechless at this tragic story.

She continued. "That's not to say she didn't earn her place at André's law firm. He always said she was the best associate he'd ever hired. She didn't article there, she articled at the Attorney General's office, then went to work for André. He loved her and led her right along. She's one clever girl."

"Well, I know that," he said. "It's been easy to see right from the start. She ran the show in our first interview." He grinned ruefully. "That's a little hard to admit for a businessman, but it's true. But what about Andrew? Where's the father?"

Verna looked amused. "I don't have any information on that. Andrew is who he is. He's one fine little boy, and his mummy loves him dearly. She'd do anything for that child. He's her whole family. So anyone who accepts Andrew," she continued, "is a hero in Emily's eyes. She's very protective of herself and careful about her decisions. You have to work around these things when you're dealing with her."

He grinned again. "I think I'm being coached here, Verna. I have to say I appreciate it." He looked into her kind knowing eyes. "She's hard to read sometimes, and she blows hot and then cold. It's as if she'd really like to be close but then decides it might be dangerous. I'm never sure what triggers the fear. I try to be patient, not ruffle too many feathers, but it's hard." He knew the colour was high on his face, his collar suddenly too tight. "But I'll take my help wherever I can get it. I'm not proud."

Verna leaned back in her seat and said cheerily, "Well, that's just fine then. That's what I thought of you, clever lad. You do need to have patience. But I just want the best for her, for her and the little guy. Only what's best for her, Joe."

He nodded, determined he would be what was best for her.

# CHAPTER SEVENTEEN

The pace was frantic, they had one more day to complete any work that needed to be done before they left for Europe. Emily had packed her briefcase and was finishing up files on her desk, leaving some for Anna to work on, some to be sent to Ray Gaines at the warehouse. The new secretary handled all of Emily's work now, documents, meetings, phone calls.

Just then Anna popped her head into the office and made a face. "Emily, sorry to interrupt when you're so busy. There's a phone call for you, it sounds like it's personal."

Her head whipped around. They were in her office making a list of what had go with them to Portugal.

Joe took in her startled expression and rose, saying, "I'm finished with this. I'll just get back to my office and clear up a few things." He gathered a file and some folders and walked out the door.

Anna looked a question at her.

"Which line?" she said.

"Line three."

She waited till her door was closed and lifted the phone with a heavy feeling of inevitability. "Emily Drury."

"Emily, it's Russ. Don't hang up. I want to meet with you. Don't put me off, it's important."

"Russ, I'm just on my way out of town, leaving first thing tomorrow morning. I can't possibly meet with you." She looked at the calendar on her desk. "We're not back for eight or nine days."

"Is this a vacation?" His voice sounded strained, tight.

"No, not a vacation. It's a business trip to Europe. I can't do anything about it. I don't understand this need to see me. You saw me at my house. What else is there to say?"

"It's not about that. This is business. What day are you back? We can arrange a meeting for the day after you return, okay? Give you time to get your rest. When?"

She sighed. "I don't want to see you, Russell. I don't see the point."

"Emily," he gritted. "Don't give me a hard time. I know that's my son. Now, I can haul you into court for an order to get DNA tests or you can cooperate with me. Got it? Now what day?"

She felt the sweat start to run under her arms. She'd always known it would come down to this very thing, a demand from Russell for her help. She pulled her calendar across the desk toward her.

~~~

They arrived in Oporto, Portugal at dawn local time, after interminable hours of travel. Emily was so tired she was having trouble being civil to the wine agent who met them at the luggage terminal. Joe pointed out their cases to a porter and headed out to the waiting car, fingers pressed to the small of her back. He opened the back door and handed her in, tucking her coat tail beside her before shutting the door. She would have been irritated at being escorted like a child if she hadn't been so wilted.

They'd been travelling since early the previous morning. The plane from Victoria to Calgary left at seven a.m., which meant they left Bonnie at three o'clock in the dead of night. The next flight, Calgary to Toronto was four and a half hours and left after a lengthy delay. The eight hour flight from Toronto to Portugal was one of the hardest exercises in patience she had ever experienced. Even though they were travelling business class, it had been a grueling trip.

The agent took them straight to their hotel and left them there, promising to collect them for dinner that evening. Joe checked them in and took Emily up to her room. "Now, I'm right next door and I'm not going anywhere. So go straight to bed. If you want to talk to me, just dial my number. I'll knock on your door around three and we can put our heads together before we meet the agent for dinner. How does that sound?"

She could do no more than nod her head and close the door.

She felt a little better at dinner. The agent was good company and talked in general terms about the two vintners they were going to visit. He seemed to represent both companies so was impartial as to which they went with.

The tour of the wineries the next day was very exciting and the countryside was magnificent. She enjoyed it immensely. She barely got a look at the city of Oporto other than the picturesque view as they drove in from the airport.

Situated on the river, its colourful image was reflected in the still water wherever she looked. The colours were so European, she wondered why she was surprised. Not so much European perhaps as Mediterranean with the tan and ochre coloured walls and red tiled roofs.

The following day they took the train down to Lisbon. This was her first visit to Europe and she was enchanted. The Portuguese people were so charming and ready to help that she was completely won over and dreamed of coming back for a vacation one day when she was free to spend some time.

The owner of the ceramic factory, Mr. Fredo Peralta met them at the train station and took them to their hotel. He insisted on treating them to dinner at his favourite restaurant, where they were served a delicious and lengthy dinner featuring giant lobster.

She'd been enjoying herself, Mr. Peralta was flattering yet she wondered how it would be to do business with him. Perhaps he'd flatter her and do business with Joe, she wasn't sure of the niceties of the Portuguese culture where business and women were concerned. They were lingering over coffee when she suddenly felt distinctly queasy. Afraid the lobster had been bad and pleading fatigue, she left the two men to their coffee and went back to the hotel by cab.

She let herself into her room. Oh, now she felt positively ill. Must be the food. She loved lobster, but knew fish products were sometimes uncertain choices. She was sick once into the toilet bowl and fell into bed, already asleep when Joe knocked softly on her door. She didn't hear him, and slept through till morning when he called her room. "How did you sleep?"

"Fine." she yawned. "I slept like a log."

"That's good." There was a pause. "I thought you weren't feeling very well when you left so suddenly."

"I know. I thought it must be the lobster. I was quite nauseous. But I'm fine now. Whatever it was, it's passed. What do we have on today?"

~~~

They had some free time. Mr. Peralta had gone home to Sintra, a small town to the west of Lisbon where they would meet him the following morning. They spent the day in Lisbon touring the sites. Emily wanted to see the Castelo de St. Jorge. "The Cashtelo," she whispered, reminding Joe of the Portuguese pronunciation. *Cashtelo.*

The Castelo was on top of a huge hill overlooking the picturesque city and river, the Rio Tejo below. They walked along the castle ramparts, Joe clasping Emily's hand in a death grip, his heart in his throat. "I can't believe this," he muttered. "There aren't even any railings to stop you from falling to your death!"

He pulled her back sharply from a particularly rough area where the steps were cluttered with rubble. "You'll stumble, Emily, and likely keel over the side." He peered doubtfully down at the boulder strewn floor that seemed to be about forty feet below. "You wouldn't walk away from a fall like that. Let's go back the way we came."

They negotiated the narrow steep stairs down from the top of the ramparts, each step with shallow depressions worn into the stone from the impact of countless feet over centuries. The walls were crenulated, interspersed with arrow slits with funnels built into them. "That must be to pour boiling oil down on your enemy," he pointed out.

She grimaced. "Sounds like fun."

He suddenly grinned at her expression. "Well, it was decisive. You didn't have to negotiate everything like we have to now, you could just fry them."

She laughed.

There were chickens in cages inside the courtyard, a half dozen turkeys wandering loose in the moat. Goats grazed freely and climbed the rocks. Joe picked a large slab of stone to sit on, and spread out their lunch. "How are you feeling today?" he asked casually. He tried not to scrutinize her face as he opened the napkin-wrapped loaf of bread. "Any better?"

Emily looked surprised. "No, I'm fine. It was just the lobster, I'm sure." She gazed around at the Portuguese families everywhere, resting on stone benches, drinking wine and smoking. A mother was washing her children down at one of the waterspouts that flowed into the high courtyard. She breathed deeply and relaxed back against the rock behind them. "Isn't this great? I didn't think I'd get to Europe for years. Too many other things on the list. I love it."

She smiled at him, and he gazed at her thoughtfully. "What other things are on the list?"

"I don't know. Andrew, I suppose. Student loans. Debt in general. Life's expensive, no?" She grinned and took a piece of bread from his fingers. "What else do we have to eat?"

"Oh, hungry are we?" he teased. "Aren't you the one who didn't want to bother stopping to pick up a bit of food? Too impatient to get to the top of the Cashtelo."

"Of course you're right, Joe. You're always right." She glinted at him and he laughed.

"That's a first," he muttered good-naturedly. "Well, there's some salami style meat, not sure what it is, but it tasted good in the shop. There's a nice creamy cheese. Big black olives, pickles. Some nuts, I think they're filberts, salted. Sound good?"

"Sounds delicious." She took a bite of her bread, then spread some cheese on it and looked around again. "Look at all this stone, Joe. I mean the benches are made of chunks of stone that are at least four feet long and they're about two feet thick, sitting on more chunks of stone. Fabulous."

Joe looked where she pointed, but spent most of his time watching her. Her face reflected her total delight in the place and in just being there. She was charming him all over again. They finished their lunch and wrapped up the leftovers. He tucked them in his pack and offered his hand to her where she sat. He tugged her up and stepped forward at the same time so that she fell straight into his arms.

"Oops," he grinned. He pressed a kiss to her lips and she stilled against his chest. He deepened it, just for a minute, just because he had to. Her mouth was soft and so sweet beneath his. Plunging his tongue between her lips, he felt her shiver in his arms. When he finally lifted his head, her cheeks were pink. "That was nice," he whispered.

Then before he went too far, he stepped back and turned toward the entrance. "Come on, let's walk back down. Are you okay with that?"

"Sure," she said and he felt her relax as he took her hand. The smells of urine and mold receded as they walked out of the Castelo grounds and started down the hill. The streets were lovely, too narrow for a vehicle to navigate, white stone everywhere, steps set into the lanes every few yards as they descended the slope. The red roofs added gorgeous definition to the scene.

He took her to a little traditional restaurant for dinner, recommended by the hotel concierge. "I don't know if that means it's owned by his brother-in-law," he said. "But it's as good a lead as any. And he says there's some traditional singing, it's called Fado. You might like that."

Her eyes shone with anticipation as the waiter seated them at a tiny table inside the place. Everything was wooden, tables, chairs and side bar. And the building was stone, just like every building they'd seen since they arrived. The menu was limited but Emily decided to have the pork in sauce, wanting to stay away from fish for the night. Joe had cod.

By the time they were on dessert, the singing had started. A large woman in a low cut dress that was gathered at the waist stood at the microphone. She began to sing as her accompanist played a Portuguese guitar. The Fado song was slow and almost dirge-like. There was enthusiastic clapping after each rendition. They listened to a few songs but Emily was clearly flagging. Joe paid the bill and hustled her out onto the sidewalk.

"What did you think of the singing?" He smiled at her and tucked her hand under his arm. "Not quite like at home."

"No, but that's why a person travels, isn't it? To see and hear things that are different from back home. On the other hand, I'm not sure I'd like to hear it all the time. Pretty dismal in mood."

Joe strolled down the sidewalk toward the hotel. "Do you miss Andrew?"

She smiled slightly and nodded. "Yes. We're hardly ever apart, so it's hard. But I'm okay. And so is he, I'm sure. I'll call Verna about mid-week, just to see that everything's alright."

"You can call her every night, if you want. If it sets your mind at rest." He looked inquiringly at her. "I don't mind."

"No, that's fine. I'll call mid-week, first thing in the morning so that I catch Verna still up. She's sent me a couple of emails already, so I know everything's all right."

He pulled her against his side in a loose hug. "That's good. She's a nice woman." He turned his head slightly to catch the scent of her. This was the closest he'd been able to get since that night back in Arbutus Bay and he wanted another kiss.

~~~

They took the train the following morning to Sintra, and

Peralta met them at the station. First he took them on a tour of the small town, up the mountain to see the view from the Penna National Palace, then to his home to get settled and left them to rest. He'd put them in adjoining rooms with a bathroom that was shared.

Joe looked at Emily with a twinkle in his eye. "Just call and I'll come running," he said, pointing to the bathroom door. Emily laughed self-consciously. "I'll use it first, then you can have it," he continued. "You can lock my door when you use it. Just don't forget to unlock it!"

He took his shoes off and lay down on the bed. This trip was going okay. They had some good leads from the Oporto stop, and he might just carry both the port and the wines. Why not? He was glad to finally get to Sintra to spend some time with Peralta. Peralta's warehouses must be stuffed with items he'd want to bring to market back home. It was just a matter of forging the link and making the best choices. He could make an agreement on a personal level but Emily was here to make sure he was protected with contract.

He turned his head to contemplate the bathroom door as he heard the water turn on. It sounded like she was filling the bathtub. Great. Now he could lay here listening to her splash and imagining what he'd see if only he could get in there. That thought warmed him all over.

To his surprise he was wakened by a gentle tap on his door and a call to dinner.

## CHAPTER EIGHTEEN

They were seated around a large table with Mr. and Mrs. Peralta and their children, including a grown son and his wife and little boy. He was about two and very cute. It gave Emily a pang in her heart over being so far away from Andrew. They talked about family. Peralta and his son both spoke excellent English. The younger children were obviously learning and excited to try out their skills on the visitors.

The next day was all business. Peralta took them to his office and they hashed over the last rendition of the contracts. Emily thought it had all been settled and was surprised to be going over it yet again. So they spent two hours discussing why the contracts didn't meet Peralta's needs and what had to be changed to get where they needed to go. By the time the changes were made, Emily insisted they be signed right then. Peralta looked surprised but she said, "If they don't meet your needs, let's work on them till they do. If they already do the job, there's no reason not to sign."

He gave her a considering look, reached for his pen and signed. Before he could change his mind Emily shoved the copies over to Joe to add his signature. "There," she said. "Done. I'll act as witness." She bent over the pages, knowing Peralta was gauging her actions. "Here's your copy. I'll keep this one. Now we're ready to do business."

She saw the look of dawning respect in Fredo Peralta's eyes. He'd been very courteous with her when he met them in Lisbon. Now he was fawning. He took her hand and led her off for coffee, Joe trailing forgotten in their wake.

The afternoon was spent in the warehouse. There was a small showroom to the side and Peralta had runners going back and forth into the giant structure to bring them different items, or different colours of the same item. Primarily he dealt in pottery. Emily was inclined toward the ceramic hot pads, some with cork around them, some with rope, some plain ceramic. They were light, decorative and exotic. Joe agreed with her, and they picked out eight or ten types to put aside. There were lovely soup tureens and ceramic water bottles with matching cups that would work well on a sideboard or office desk.

She was doubtful about carrying full sets of dishware. It could backfire trying to stay in stock with the passing fads but they took lots of pictures and gathered all the brochures Peralta had to offer. Platters, platter and jug sets, vases, she added them to the list as they worked through the product line.

Large ceramic planters were pulled out and examined. Joe was doubtful, Emily was enthusiastic, but deferred to his judgment, cautioning that the high end market would really respond to these fabulous designs. By the end of the day, they had apparently seen all the pottery the manufacturer had to offer.

When they got back to the house, Emily went to have a rest while the men had a sherry and cigars in the garden. After an early dinner they headed back to their rooms. Emily murmured, "I didn't know you smoked cigars."

"I didn't either," said Joe. "I was a bit dizzy. I guess I shouldn't have inhaled."

She laughed and closed her door in his face.

Next morning they were back in the warehouse to look at Peralta's store of copperware. They started with the pots, strainers, paella pans and moved on to decorative ware. The items were so lovely that Emily was totally enthralled.

Finally she sat back. "Joe, I'm not feeling very impartial about this stuff, so I'm not a good judge. I think these things would simply fly off the shelves, but that's just me. Perhaps we should take photos and make decisions later."

Slowly he shook his head. "No, not necessarily. Pick out your ten favourite products and we can start there. I like them too, if that's any reassurance. Take your pick."

"Okay." She pondered for a few minutes then began to pull out the most distinctive items and set them aside. "There. That's my best guess, plus these little containers. Aren't they darling? I just can't resist." They were cast copperware fruit, apples, peaches and pear shapes with the stems soldered to the lid. They opened in half to form a charming container. Like everything else in the warehouse, they were beautiful.

~~~

They wrapped up business and ate lunch at a small local bistro. Peralta took them back to his home and he and Joe headed off to the gym for a workout. Emily decided to walk the hill behind the house and tour the Castelo de Mouros at the top. The Moors had been quite a presence in Portugal's past and the structure on the mountain was renowned for its beauty.

It was a lovely shaded road winding up through trees to the top of the low mountain and dozens of tour buses passed regularly in a line as she climbed. She was almost halfway up the hill when she suddenly felt unwell again, dizzy, her head spinning. She stopped climbing and stood on the side of the road to catch her breath. A huge tour bus whizzed by, buffeting her with wind.

Maybe she hadn't eaten enough at lunch. She swayed for a minute then began to climb again. Again she stopped. A roiling sense of nausea rose in her throat and she forcefully swallowed it down. Not this again. She'd had fish at lunch. Damn.

She looked around and spied a cool grotto up ahead by the side of the road.

Managing to reach it, she tottered in toward the small peaceful pool. The alcove held a lovely porcelain Madonna and Christ Child in its shelter. As she sat down on the moss beside the pool, Emily could still hear the traffic behind her but it was quieter here and cooler. Putting her head back, she just allowed her body to sink to the ground.

Ah, that was better. Or would be if she could just lay here and wait for a bit, let the sickness pass. They were going home tomorrow. She couldn't wait. She'd feel better as soon as she was back home, eating regular food, getting enough sleep. She prayed for the feeling to leave her, for a good trip home without any illness.

After a while the sick feeling began to ease. When she sat up, she stayed there for a few more minutes to ensure the nausea was gone. Then she pushed her hair back with her hands and got to her feet with a renewed feeling of peace from that lovely place and headed out to the road.

The Castle at the top was magnificent. She'd never seen Moorish architecture and was enchanted with what she saw, the coloured tile, high arches and defensive walls meandering across the hilltop.

She felt refreshed but slightly wobbly so sat on the wall and rested for a while before attempting the walk back down. Joe appeared on the road coming up the hill. When he spied her he promptly came across, looking her over critically. "Are you okay? Mrs. Peralta said you went up the hill a long time ago. She expected you back before now and was worried."

"Yes, I'm fine. I was just heading down. Did you want to see it? It's lovely." They wandered back into the Castle and Emily sat and waited while he walked out the top of the great long wall stretched over the crest of the hill. When he came back, he took her hand and turned to the winding road down the hill.

At the grotto, she tugged at his arm and pulled him down the path to show him her discovery. "Isn't it lovely? It's so peaceful. I sat here for a while on the way up when I got dizzy from the climb."

"I wondered." Joe brushed her sweater and removed bits of grass from her hair. "I could see you'd been laying down somewhere. Was it here?"

"Well, I think it was the fish at lunch. I can't seem to eat fish here. But after a while I felt better."

Joe nodded thoughtfully. "We'd better get back. It's our last night, and they have a big dinner planned for us."

"I hope it's not fish," Emily muttered. "I really don't think I want any fish."

Joe grinned at her and held her gently against his side.

~~~

Joe seated her in the airport lounge and went off to chat with the airlines personnel. When he returned he had boarding passes for first class. "I told them you weren't feeling well. They've found space for us up front and we can board now."

His hand was gentle, his grip firm as he took her arm and hefted their carryon luggage in the other hand. "Come on. Just a little ways down the corridor and you can settle in." He found the seat and helped her into it where she relaxed back with a grateful sigh. He left briefly to return with a couple of drinks in his hands. "Here's a soda water. It might settle your stomach. I know you haven't eaten anything today. This is tomato juice. If you can keep it down, it'll give you a little energy." He dragged some pillows and a blanket out of the overhead bins and settled himself beside her.

"Come here, sweetheart. I'll make you comfortable." Emily relaxed with a tired sigh against his chest as he tucked the blanket around her. His arm held her securely as he reclined against the seatback. She couldn't wait to get home. All she needed was enough rest and the right food and she'd feel well again.

The stewards had been through all the pre-flight announcements and the plane was finally airborne before he spoke again.

"Emily," he whispered against her hair, "are you awake?"

She nodded and turned her head to look up at him. His

eyes were so close she could see the flecks of gold in their centre, radiating out in a spiral of colour. "I want to talk to you for a minute. Sweetheart, I'm worried about you. You're ill and you don't seem to think anything should be done about it."

"I'm not ill, Joe." She frowned. "I've just got the flu or something. And I did do something about it. We went to the Pharmacia in Lisbon this morning and got some pills for nausea. We even talked about going to the Hospital Ingles, but I didn't feel sick enough to wait in emergency."

She shrugged. "Besides, we're on our way home now. I'll be getting enough sleep and eating the usual food. I'll be fine. I can see my doctor if I still don't feel well." Her mouth was dry and she reached for the soda on the tray in front of her. His big hand beat her to it and held the plastic cup to her lips.

"You're not well," he muttered. "And I don't think it's the flu. I've never seen the flu cause someone to faint during a walk."

She stirred against him. "I didn't faint, exactly." She paused then added helpfully, "I just felt dizzy and had to lie down."

"Yeah, at the side of the road. And you couldn't get up again."

She refused to honor that with a reply.

"Emily," his voice was strained now, low and dogged. "Have you thought that you might be pregnant?"

She startled against his arm, turning to stare at him. "Joe, that's impossible and you know it."

"Why is it impossible? Anything's possible."

Her face got hot. "I haven't been with anyone else, if that's what you're driving at."

"I know that," he snapped. The colour was strong on his cheekbones. "That is, I assumed that. You're not the kind of woman to be seeing two men at the same time. Do you know if you're *not* pregnant? That is… Have you had your period since that weekend?"

She was confused. "Joe, you can't, so it isn't a question of whether I'm pregnant or not!" she whispered fiercely. Her cheeks felt as if they were on fire and her gaze dropped when she could no longer meet his eyes. "So I can't be pregnant."

"What do you mean, I can't? We both know I can and in fact did. More than once!" His voice had risen slightly and she looked around uncomfortably at the other passengers.

"Keep your voice down! Are you trying to inform the whole plane?" Of course he'd done it more than once. More than twice. That was one of the things she couldn't forget about that night.

He lowered his voice and pushed his face closer to hers. "What do you mean, I can't? Are you trying to say I'm impotent? That's ridiculous!"

"Not impotent, silly, just sterile. Shirley already told me. And it's okay, it doesn't matter. So it isn't a question of my being pregnant, is it?"

"Shirley told you what?" he gritted. "What did that damn woman tell you? She doesn't know anything about me, for God's sake!"

"She told me you were sterile. That you and your wife had tried to have a child but then you found out that you were sterile and that's partly why you divorced. It's okay, Joe. I'm not about to talk about it if that's what worries you. It's no one's business."

He swore under his breath and pressed his head back against the seat. *Was he upset that Shirley had told her?*

But when he leaned down to her ear, he whispered, "I'm not sterile, Emily. What the hell she was talking about, I don't know and I mean to find out the minute we get back. But whatever it was, it's not true. What else did she tell you?" He pulled her chin around to look into her face.

She couldn't meet his gaze. "That's all. Just that Marie wanted a child and you didn't. And then you found out that you couldn't have any and so...."

"And so?"

"Well, then Marie left and married someone else. That's all." In confusion she picked at the blanket with her nail, back and forth, back and forth, his eyes following the motion.

"Emily, look at me."

She raised her head a fraction of an inch. She couldn't look at him.

"Marie and I didn't want to have kids that young. I was in a hurry to build the business and she had other things in mind. The marriage just didn't work. It had nothing to do with whether we had or even wanted children."

She nodded in bewilderment.

"You might be pregnant."

She went still. This couldn't be happening to her.

"Do you use birth control?"

She turned her head toward the window, feeling the weight of his gaze on her face, the weight of the world on her shoulders.

He sighed. "Probably not. After all, you weren't having a relationship with anybody and you thought I couldn't father a child. So what was the point of birth control? Have you had your period since that weekend? This is entirely my fault."

His voice softened. "But you took me by surprise. That night, I just couldn't hold back..." His jaw clamped shut.

She watched him stare at the back of the seat in front of them. "No," she finally said, "you took me by surprise."

He laughed, an unexpected, soft, confused sound. "Well, nobody was more surprised than I was." His expression was bemused as he studied her. "And I should have been prepared. Have you, Emily, have you had your period yet?"

"I don't think so." She rubbed her forehead with her fingertips. "But it hasn't been... I mean, it's only been two or three weeks, so..."

"It's been thirty days." Her head swung around in surprise and she saw him cringe at the comment. Her colour deepened as he continued, "I remember every one of those days. Thirty days since I climbed the trellis to your bedroom door. So if you haven't had your period, that would mean you're late, wouldn't it?"

She stared at him horrified. "No, it hasn't been that long.

It can't have been..."

"It's been thirty days, trust me." His eyes smouldered as he looked down at her and his hand caressed her skin where her arm was bare beneath the sleeve. "Oh, Emily, you're so soft and lovely. Your skin is like silk. I've missed you so much, my arms have been empty. You feel just right against me when I hold you." He watched as she frantically searched for a safe place to look.

"So is that a no, you haven't had your period?" His hand was so tight it crushed hers and she wiggled her fingers until he relaxed his grip. He didn't let go.

"I don't remember. I've been so busy, and sometimes it's a few days late..." Her voice trailed off and she looked away again.

Joe waited but she stared out the window wondering what she was going to do. How many balls did she have to have in the air at one time? How many complications did she have to create for herself? Finally he reached to take her hand and lay it on his thigh, stroking the backs of her fingers.

"Emily" he said finally, his eyes determined. "We need to talk about what we're going to do. You don't have to worry. I'll look after everything."

"What does that mean, you'll take care of everything?" Now he was going to make her decisions for her? Everything irked her, that she had another issue to deal with and that he thought he'd solve it for her. "How do you think you'll look after it?"

There was silence, then he tightened his hand around her fingers. "I think we should get married. Then there'll be no problem."

At least he'd sort of proposed, unlike Russell. But it sounded like a business decision. She winced.

~~~

Joe watched her face as she processed his statement. Not very romantic. But she kept him at such arm's length that he couldn't get close enough to be romantic. The idea of marriage had impinged on his consciousness the day she left dinner early in Lisbon because she didn't feel well.

It came back to him with greater clarity when he found out she'd collapsed on the side of the hill above Sintra. He realized then that she wasn't well, that she may be pregnant. It came to him suddenly, and even the housekeeper at Peralta's had made an aside to him about the Senora maybe having a bebe in her tummy, poor lady to have to travel at such a time.

Joe heard the click in his head. He'd been thinking the same thing without being aware of it. And he'd seized on the idea as a chance to marry her. She'd feel pressured to look after herself and Andrew and this would be the best way to deal with it.

She looked at him with a wide gaze, her eyes dark and shadowed. "Get married? Joe, we hardly know each other, and besides I don't think I'm…"

"We know each other very intimately." His voice was a low growl, a husky hum of masculine intent. "I've never known anyone like I know you and want to know you." He saw the confusion in her eyes, saw that he was rushing her but couldn't stop himself and plunged on. "And I'd be good to you. I like your little guy and I'd be good to both of you. I'd look after you. You wouldn't have to worry about anything, I'd look after both of you," he repeated. "We'll get married."

"Don't you think that's a little high-handed? That isn't how you get married, Joe, by just announcing to a woman that you're going to marry her." Her mouth was set in an obstinate line. He recognized that stubborn expression, had seen it on her mouth before.

He was silent for a long time, studying her face. Then he took both her hands in his and threaded their fingers together. "Look at me. Will you marry me, Emily? Will you?"

She gave him a long measured look. "If I'm pregnant, I'll think about it." His burst of laughter startled her. Heads turned towards them at the deep masculine sound. His hand tugged on hers.

"Good," he said, "that's good. You'll think about it." He continued to grin, flattening her hand against his chest and holding it there. "Look at it this way. You'll get a husband and father for your baby and Andrew would get a dad. I'll be a good dad to him, Emily. He's a sweet little fellow and very easy to love."

Her eyes misted with tears and she wearily laid her head on his shoulder. He gathered her close.

"When I get back, I'll go to the doctor and we'll know right away. We'll see."

He squeezed her more firmly, vowing she'd be his one way or another.

# CHAPTER NINETEEN

It was two in the afternoon before Emily got into the office. Through the open doorway she saw Joe working at his desk, head bent over a stack of papers as he leafed through them and made comments into the phone. Shirley looked up as she came in.

"Good *afternoon*," she said, her tone on the edge of sarcastic. "Over slept, did we?"

Emily ignored her, continuing through to the door of Joe's office. "He's on the phone," said the secretary, hustling from the chair to intercept her progress.

Joe rose from behind his desk. "It's okay, Shirley. I'll call you back," he said abruptly into the phone and tossed it into its cradle. "Close the door, Emily."

Shirley backed slowly from the room and Joe reached a long arm to finish shutting the door.

He surveyed her for a moment, then moved to tuck a lock of honey-coloured hair behind her ear. "So..."

Emily stood silent.

"Well, what did the doctor say?"

She looked away. "Inconclusive."

He waited, the sweat beginning under his arms but that was obviously all she was willing to give him. "Inconclusive? I thought these tests were pretty definitive. I mean, either you're pregnant or you're not. Right?" He linked his arms loosely around the small of her back and leaned down to peer into her face.

"That's what I thought, too." Her voice was faint. "But he wasn't confident of the accuracy of the test." His arms tightened reflexively and she looked up at him. "So they've sent a sample off. It will take a few days at the lab."

His heart pounded in his chest like a live thing trying to escape confinement. The doctor wasn't sure. So it wasn't 'no'! That's all he heard. She might be pregnant. She couldn't get away now. He'd have the time he needed to woo her, make her realize they belonged together. Make her realize he was the right man for her, the right father for her little boy. And the new baby.

He strangled at the thought, forcing himself to loosen his grip. When he spoke his voice had a strained sound to it. "So he thinks you're pregnant."

She shook her head. "No, he didn't really say that. Just that the test looked inconclusive but he'd seen them be wrong before so he wanted to check. He did an internal exam but that wasn't conclusive either."

He winced at the thought. "An internal, huh?" His voice went hoarse. "Emily, come here a minute." He backed around his desk, holding her against him. Sitting in his big office chair he drew her down onto his knee. "Listen to me, sweetheart. We don't want to wait too long and put ourselves in that position. And we don't want people to think we jumped into getting married just because we had to. This is a small city and you know how people love to talk."

She focused on his mouth, watching his lips move.

"Let's just announce we're getting married. We'll set a date for four weeks, a month from now, and just do it. Andrew will be fine, you two can move down here to the big house, and when the new baby comes we'll be ready for it. And people won't be counting on their fingers. I know it doesn't matter what people say but I'm trying to think of you."

She watched his fingers move back and forth across the

back of her hand and avoided looking at him. He closed his hand around hers and shook it to get her attention. "Don't you think it makes sense to set the date and just get moving on it? We could be married by this time next month and the fuss would all be over with."

That shocked her into action. "Joe, we don't have to rush. It'll only take a little while…" She trailed off at the expression on his face, then plunged on again. "He took the test, it has to go to the lab, and then there's the weekend. He thought he'd know Monday, Tuesday at the latest."

Joe nodded. "Okay," he said. "Okay." Then he kissed her, because he had to taste her again, feel her soft lips and smooth skin.

~~~

Emily wondered why she always made arrangements to meet at the food court. It wasn't very private, and certainly not quiet. Maybe that was why. She didn't feel cornered. Nor did she give out the signal that she was trying to hide, to shield her meetings from the public view.

She picked a table off to the side and sat with her tea steeping in a paper cup. The tea certainly wasn't as nice here, paper cups ensured that. Maybe it was time to quit worrying about appearances and start pampering herself.

She turned her head toward the entrance and scanned the area. Not very busy right now. She should be able to spot Russell before he saw her.

"There you are," a voice suddenly spoke on her other side. She jumped, hastily shaking the scalding liquid off her hand that had spilled from her cup.

Russ eased onto the chair beside her and grabbed her wrist to examine it. "Ouch. Sorry. Did I startle you?" His eyes looked guilelessly into hers. "I didn't mean to."

"It's fine," she said and drew her hand back, cradling her brewing tea.

He gave her a slow once over with his eyes, studying her fitted top and short skirt. "You certainly look fine." There was just the slightest hint of innuendo in his tone.

She ignored it.

"How's life treating you?"

"Fine, thank you, Russell." Emily sipped her tea and waited.

"Well, this is almost like old times." He looked around, then grimaced. "Not exactly. I doubt if we ever met in a food court."

She nearly laughed. The last place they would ever have met was a food court. A bar or lounge, yes. An expensive restaurant, no question. Maybe that's why she'd chosen this place. To keep from dredging up old memories.

Russell's gaze moved back to her face. "Listen, Emily. I want your help. I've got a deal going and I need you to do something for me."

Emily kept her face bland. "Why would I do something for you, Russ?"

"Russ. Ah, that's better. You've been calling me 'Russell'. So formal," he admonished.

Emily stared back at him, stone faced. "Russell," she said with intended emphasis, "why would I help you? We're not partners, we're not in a deal together. You'll have to get your own people to do things for you. Because I won't. I think I've made that very clear."

Russell nodded. "You've been very clear. But I have some argument on my side as well. You know I do, Emily. You have my child, a two year old boy who I've never even heard about. I didn't know he existed until I showed up at your house. Granted, I'd heard from your tenants that you and your baby moved up to Bonnie but I didn't know he was mine. Mine! Now that's going to be very hard to explain, isn't it? Not only have I had no visitation, no access to this child. I didn't even know he existed!" His eyes were hard.

"I'd hate to have to embarrass you publicly like that, Emily. I'd hate to do it. Then we'd be in court for weeks, arguing about DNA, the willful withholding of information, access to the child, who gets custody. It gets ugly, doesn't it? You don't look quite so lily white when stuff like that comes out. Don't look quite the responsible, reliable lawyer, do you? What happens to your future then? But more importantly, what kind of access will I get and what will I do with it?" He leaned back comfortably in the stiff little food court chair and stretched out his legs. He looked calmly around, then finally back to her.

"Nothing to say?" He waited. "Well, here's the deal. I don't need to ask for custody, not even access. I need to get this deal done. With your help, everything will go much more smoothly. What do you say?"

Emily's jaw was aching and she tried to relax the muscles in her neck. She sipped her tea again, lukewarm now and nearly tasteless, then pushed it aside.

"What kind of deal, Russ?"

He grinned determinedly, a mere rictus of his lips. "There we go. That's the Emily I know and love." He leaned forward, his face menacing. "Listen carefully. I'm not going to repeat this. And you'd better cooperate with me or you know what will happen."

She moved back, feeling overwhelmingly threatened. "Russell, slow down."

"Slow down? You've been dragging your feet and I won't put up with it." His voice was a low growl and his hand clenched into a fist on the table top.

"What's going on?" The mild tone of voice was out of sync with the hard expression on Steve Alexander's face. He had just appeared out of nowhere, standing beside their food court table, his eyes fixed on Emily. "You okay?"

Emily jumped in surprise and Russell whipped his head around and glared at the intruder. "What business is it of yours?" he gritted.

Grasping the opportunity, Emily rose from her chair. "Steve, just in time. I was getting ready to go, anyway." She grabbed her purse and took his arm, urging him down the aisle to the walkway and out the doors of the mall. The feeling of relief was overwhelming and she could feel Russ's glare burning like a laser beam into the back of her jacket.

"What's going on, Emily? Was that guy threatening you?"

She shrugged, feeling like a fraud. "It *was* getting uncomfortable. I'm glad you interrupted."

"Huh." Hands on hips, he looked thoughtfully down at her. "Who was he?"

"It doesn't matter." Legs trembling, she checked the time on her cell phone. She had fifteen minutes before Rumpelstiltskin closed. "Thanks Steve, I have to get the baby from daycare now."

As she walked away, she felt a wave of fatigue wash over her. She felt wasted. How could she manage, juggling all the balls that seemed to be in the air around her? What would happen if she just sat down and stopped trying? She was scared.

~~~

Emily was working in the kitchen, stirring a pot on the stove when a knock sounded on the glass kitchen door. Andrew ran over and slapped his hands against the panes. "Joe," he shouted through the glass. "Hi."

Joe cautiously slid the door wider and Andrew ran to the opening to press his face there and peer out at him, grinning.

"Hi, there, little guy. How are you?" He slid the door further, swung Andrew into his arms and stepped through. Looking over he examined her where she stood at the counter. "What are you up to?"

"Just making some tomato soup," she gestured at the pot on the stove. "I thought it sounded good but now I'm not sure." He moved nearer and reached out to massage the back of her neck.

"Not sure, eh?" He kissed her temple and peered into the pot. "It smells good."

She shook her head. "It did smell good, but now it doesn't."

"I see." He gave her a long look, then led her over to the overstuffed chair and sat her down, Andrew still on his arm. "Where's Verna?"

"She's gone down to Victoria, visiting her daughter this

weekend. Just Andrew and me here." She smiled up at him.

"Well, I had an idea. I wondered if you and Andrew would like to go out on the boat with me. It's pretty calm out there and Mia packed a picnic lunch for us. There's even iced tea."

She looked doubtfully up at him, then her gaze dropped to her son as he carefully removed everything from Joe's shirt pocket and examined it. "Look out. He'll rob you blind."

Laughing, he glanced down. "There isn't anything there he can't have. Oh, except that. Don't want ink all over my shirt." He retrieved his pen and slid it into his pants pocket. "He can play with the rest." He looked back down at her wan face. "What do you think? Do you want to try the boat?"

She slowly shook her head. "I'm afraid to. I often get motion sickness anyway, so with how I'm feeling right now..." She let it trail off.

Joe nodded. "Right. Well, how about coming down to the gym for a while? We can do a bit of a work out, and still have the picnic. Even Andrew can work out." Andrew kicked his heels in excitement and Joe quickly caught his foot as it connected perilously close to his groin.

She laughed lightly. "You'll soon discover how dangerous he can be."

He grinned and put his hand on her hair. "It's nice to see you laugh. Shall we go?"

~~~

Next day she stopped at Jon's Bookstore to browse. Her appointment with the doctor wasn't until later and she simply didn't feel like going into work. She'd always been stern with herself about going to the office and staying there till the work was done. But there weren't too many issues waiting for her attention today. And she felt too tired to deal with it.

She didn't want to read the questions in Joe's eyes or deal with Shirley's sniping. She'd decided not to go in. She phoned in to tell Shirley that she had other meetings and would see everyone tomorrow. Shirley had tried to question her further and for once she simply hung up without answering.

Now she stepped inside the door and inhaled the slightly

musty old leather smell of books. Jon was nowhere in sight but the attendant behind the desk smiled a greeting. Emily moved forward into the stacks and browsed for a mystery to keep her busy till she saw the doctor. She found something for herself and walked over to peruse the children's section, finally spotting an interactive book about Noah's Ark with pictures that popped up as the page was opened.

"That's a really cute one, Natalie's kids have it and they love to read it." Emily turned around to find Jon smiling at her from the cash desk and the girl nowhere in sight.

"I didn't see you when I came in, there was someone else behind the desk."

He nodded. "I know, I was just out for lunch. Now Joyce has gone for her break. Come and have a cup of tea with me, it's ready." He gestured to a couple of chairs set in the corner with a pot and cups on the side table. All the furniture in the store was old, even antique, except for the bookcases themselves, and some of them looked pretty weathered. Emily smiled and gratefully lowered herself into one of the chairs with a sigh.

"Thank you, that's so kind. I could do with a cup of tea just now."

Jonathan tested the handle of the pot with his hand then grabbed the tea cozy to use as a padded glove while he poured. "What have you got there?" He nodded at the books in her hand.

"Oh, just something to read while I wait for the doctor. I have an appointment and it always takes so long. I'm getting this mystery for Verna, she likes them. I find them too grisly, they're usually about children who have been murdered and it's too tough a read for me."

Jon nodded and sipped his tea. "I've read a few and they're really good but you're right, they are pretty grisly. Are you sick, is that why you're seeing the doctor?" He looked concerned. "I can drive you over there if you like and wait while you see him, especially if you don't feel well. Joyce should be back soon."

"Oh, Jon. That's so nice of you." Her voice broke as she leaned forward and began to cry. She tried to hold it in but the tears leaked between her fingers, dripping onto her lap. "I'm so sorry. I don't know what's wrong with me. I'm just tired, I think. That trip really took it out of me. Sorry, Jon." She took the Kleenex he offered and mopped her face, heaving a big sigh. "Well, that was dignified. You'll probably be very wary of inviting me for tea again if that's how I react." She gave a wobbly smile.

"That's okay, I've been known to lose control myself, not quite in that way maybe but in other equally impressive ways. Like simply not showing up for family events when I can't bear to be grilled by my folks about how I'm doing. So, how are you doing?" He bent a keen gaze on her.

Emily laughed silently. "Nice segue, Jon. What do you mean, how am I doing?"

"I just heard some things and wondered if I could help." He looked determinedly back at her. "I heard that you and Joe had a pretty successful trip in Portugal, came back with some contracts signed and a big part of the business expansion plan in place."

She sighed and rested against the back of the chair, the warm cup cradled between her hands. "Yes, that's true, we did. It went really well and we found some fine products to bring in. Wait until you see them, they're lovely. Your brother's a clever businessman."

"Well, don't let that fool you, Emily. Joe hides most of his emotions under that 'businessman' façade but he's just as vulnerable as the next guy. He took a lot of shit from our folks growing up, he more or less shouldered it for all of us. We hid behind him to be honest, he had the broadest shoulders. But he needs the same things we all do, love and kindness, a home, a family of his own."

Emily felt warm, and set her cup down. "Are you giving me a lecture or are you promoting your brother's attributes as a possible mate?" she said sharply.

"Well, neither. I'm trying to tell you that Joe is more than he appears. I think he cares about you a great deal and I wanted you to know that means a lot. He doesn't enter into relationships lightly."

"I don't believe it." Emily shook her head, feeling anger stir in her belly. "What do you mean, relationships? What relationship? Are you talking about Margaret, now?"

"Margaret?" He looked dumbfounded. "Margaret, from Toronto? She's long gone. She's been out of the picture for literally months."

"You must be joking." Her chin came up. "Margaret dropped in for a visit just before we left for Portugal, not more than two weeks ago. And she stayed the night at the house, according to Shirley. So, not so long gone."

Jon's eyes crinkled sympathetically. "Yeah, I heard about that. We gave Joe a real razzing because he ended things with her shortly after you came to work at *Tanner Enterprises*. And no, she didn't stay the night. Joe drove her into Bonnie to a hotel and left her there." He shook his head. "You know you can't listen to Shirley."

Emily held his gaze for a moment, then looked away. "True," she murmured. She should have learned that lesson by now.

Jon went on doggedly. "Emily, we aren't blind, any of us, and as a family we care for each other. The talk has been going around the siblings about you and Joe. Not the folks, so you can relax there. However, they aren't blind either and Dad's like a bloodhound when he's on a scent, so be warned. But I've seen Joe's interest in you. And I heard you were unwell on the trip. Joe's been to see me since you got back and he happened to mention it because he was worried about you." He paused, took in her glare, but fearlessly plunged onward.

"You mustn't think we just talk to gossip. We love Joe and we think you'd be good for him. Anything we can do to help, we'll do it. If you're not feeling well, I'll drive you to your doctor's appointment and wait until you're ready to go home."

Emily dropped her head forward and took a deep breath, trying to think. "Thank you, Jon. You're a good man, anyone would be lucky to have a brother like you." There were tears in her eyes again, tears brought on by the thought of even having a brother, so she averted her face. She was way out of her depth today, tired and afraid and ill.

## CHAPTER TWENTY

When Emily got home, Verna told her Joe had called and was waiting at the big house. She snuggled with Andrew for a bit. When she'd gotten back from Portugal, he'd been angry with her for leaving for so long. It took a few days for him to recover and then he'd become clingy.

She talked with him and cuddled, then tucked him into bed before she went to change. As she moved about her room, she paused as the little copper fruit on her dresser caught her eye. They were so pretty. There was an apple painted a sunny red with a green leaf hanging off the stem. A pear, beautiful yellows and oranges. A peach rosy and luscious. And they all opened to display an enticing hidden sanctuary inside.

Joe had given them to her when they arrived back from the Portugal trip, he'd gotten them from Peralta before they left Sintra. She rubbed her fingers across the cool smooth surface of the apple and fingered the little leaf, thinking about him. He was very good to her, didn't manipulate like Russ had, didn't play games. If anything he was so serious he scared her. But that was mostly because his seriousness was focused and she was the focus. He was always doing things before she knew she wanted or needed them.

Shaking her head, she sat down to phone the Tanner house. He answered on the first ring.

"It's Emily. Can I come down and talk with you?"

"That would be great." His voice was husky. "I'll walk up and meet you."

He met her part way down the path. The weather was so warm he was wearing a short sleeved shirt. Emily had on a light jacket against the coming chill of evening and she shivered from nerves. Joe took her in head to toe before gingerly putting an arm around her shoulders to warm her. She didn't pull away and he tugged her closer.

"Do you want to sit outside on the patio, or inside? It's a little cool but really nice out right now. You can see the bay through the trees but it'll be dark soon."

Dark sounded good, so she said, "The patio would be great. Maybe you can lend me a blanket."

"Sure, I'll get you one." He seated her in one of the lounge chairs and headed inside. When he returned he had a jacket for around her shoulders and a lap rug. He'd put on a sweater and offered her a glass. "It's just iced tea but I can get something hot if you'd like."

"Does this mean I'm not allowed any alcohol?" She looked over at him in the gloom to gauge his reaction. His hand paused mid-air, then he set his glass carefully on the low table in front of him.

"No, no. I just didn't know… I mean, you can have a drink if you like. What would you like?"

Emily gave a wobbly chuckle and said, "I was teasing, Joe. Sorry."

He shook his head. "Don't tease. I'm a nervous wreck already. I don't know what to expect. Why don't you just tell me?"

She nodded and took a deep breath, letting it out slowly. "The doctor said the test was positive. I'm pregnant. We don't have a date yet, that'll come later. For now, it's just early in the pregnancy."

There, it was said, lying out there on the table. She heard

Joe give a low grunt as if he'd taken a blow to the chest. She glanced over at him. His eyes were riveted to her face.

"So, does that mean we're getting married?" he finally asked. "If so, I have to tell you I'm a very happy man."

Emily burst into tears. "This isn't a happy thing! This is a disaster. Simply a disaster! I can't just marry you, I can't and Andrew is… I'm stuck, I'm caught!" She buried her face in her hands. Joe seemed frozen in his chair, but only for a moment.

She felt him pull gently at her wrists and looked over them to find him kneeling on the paving stones beside her. "Emily, this is no disaster. A disaster is when a child is conceived and neither of the parents cares or wants it. A disaster is when you have nothing to eat and your children are starving too. This is the beginning of a wonderful life that we can share if we choose to. I'm hoping you'll choose to share it with me. I love you, Emily. I'm not sure you'll believe me right now but it's true. And if there's to be a baby, then there's even more to love. I'll love little Andrew too. Please consider my offer. I want to marry you." He kissed her fingers and pressed her palms to his mouth.

"It's not that easy. It's complicated. I don't know what to do…"

"Tell me. Tell me what's complicated. You said before that you're afraid, but I don't know what you're afraid of. If you're afraid I won't look after you or won't treat you right or Andrew, then…"

"No, Joe. It isn't that. It's never been that." She stared off into the gathering darkness, shivering uncontrollably. She was at a crossroads and knew she had to decide which road to take.

"What then? Tell me what you're afraid of. Tell me so I can help."

"I don't think you can help. I don't think anyone can help." She looked at him with desperation, then whispered, "I'll tell you, maybe you deserve to know." She took a shuddering breath and Joe handed her the glass. She glanced at him with thanks and took a sip. It tasted good and soothed her stomach. "You see, Andrew's father is in Victoria."

He nodded encouragingly. "Yes, so?"

"Well, he doesn't know Andrew is his, that is, not for sure. He suspects but that's all. And I've denied it."

Joe's face darkened. Even in the dim light she saw it and charged ahead before he could judge the situation and find her wanting. "I never told him. Mostly because he left town and I didn't know until after he was gone that I was going to have a baby. That was part of it. And he stayed away for years. I never saw him again. The other part is he's a user, he manipulates people. I knew he was like that and I let him manipulate me."

She traced the condensation on her glass with the tip of her finger as her voice became softer. "The truth is, I wanted a baby. I felt very alone and I wanted someone who was just for me. So I wasn't careful and I got pregnant."

She began to cry again. Joe stood and pulled her up. Then he took her place on the chair and tugged her back down onto his lap. He just sat there with his arms around her until she sank against him weeping into his neck. His arms tightened and she could feel him pressing kisses into her hair. She sobbed harder.

Finally it was all out there for him to see. What a relief. He could decide what he wanted to do now, knowing the whole story. He might think he wanted nothing more to do with her. Her heart was breaking.

"It's okay, Emily. Sweetheart, it's okay. Don't cry any more. Please don't cry." He whispered into her hair, rocking her in his arms until her sobs abated. Then they just sat there rocking softly in silence.

~~~

Finally Joe pulled back and said, "Can we move inside and sit on the sofa?"

She laughed through her tears and struggled to her feet. "Yes, let's go in."

Joe led the way through the glass doors and got her seated.

"I gather the iced tea wasn't a hit, so what would you like?" He looked down at her, smiling slightly.

"Oh, the iced tea was good. It sits well on my stomach, I'll have that please. I was just nervous I guess."

Joe fetched the tea, setting it on the table in front of them, then seated himself beside her. He put his arm around her shoulders. "You couldn't have been more nervous than I've been in the last weeks. I've been walking on a bed of nails with bare feet, that's what it felt like." Gently he ran a fingertip up her arm and goose bumps broke out where he touched.

"You don't have to be nervous about what I might think of you. You're magnificent. There's no other word for it." He kissed her softly on her upturned mouth.

"Now, tell me. Andrew has a father but the father doesn't know about Andrew. The father left town and you never saw him again. But he's in Victoria. Does the father have a name?"

Emily looked at him fearfully, then let out a breath. "His name is Russ, Russell Barrie. He's blond like Andrew. He's from Victoria and left town suddenly because the police wanted to question him in connection with a land deal." She paused, but Joe continued to look quizzical so she continued. "The land deal actually went through a couple of people, so they were never able to pin down just who did what. Someone sold a house that wasn't theirs. That person pretended to be the owner and sold through a second party to a third person. The police think that first person was Russ."

She gasped a breath and pressed her hand to her chest. "By the time the real owners of the house discovered what had happened, their house had been legally transferred to someone else. The buyer acted in good faith, but Russ, if it was him, and at least two other people didn't. It's a very hard thing to prove and our land law is fuzzy on what happens then. I mean, if you hold the title as it's registered at Land Titles Office, you own the land. But the person who now owned the title wasn't the true owner. Very convoluted and clever. No one ever said Russ was dumb."

"So Russ is a crook and he's Andrew's father. Why is he back in town, and how do you know he's back?"

"André told me. Russ started calling the office in Victoria to talk to me just before we moved up here." Emily began to shake, clasping her hands stiffly in her lap. "André promised he'd simply have the staff take messages and pass them on to me. Shortly after we moved, he told me Russ had called the office quite a lot and I finally phoned him on my cell phone. I told him that I didn't have any interest in resuming our relationship."

Joe's face had been getting more flushed the longer she spoke and now looked like a thunder cloud, but Emily gazed at him apprehensively and plunged on. "I said I didn't want to hear from him again."

His arms were like steel bands around her and she struggled to loosen his grip. "Sorry," he said. "I just don't like situations like this. Someone should take the guy out and pound him a few times."

Emily gave a tense laugh, her voice wobbled. "That's one reason why I hesitated to tell you. You can't go and have him beaten up because you don't like him talking to me."

He tightened his grip again. "I know, I know. So when was this, how long ago?"

"It was the day we had lunch here and the afternoon meeting with Geoff about the Presentation Dinner. André told me that Russ had been calling three or four times a day. I called him when I got home that evening. I thought he'd gotten the message and gone away after that first conversation. Or at least, I hoped he had." She shivered.

"But then he dropped in at my house here. He'd been watching. He must have been, because he waited until just after Verna left to knock on the door. He came in and that's when he saw Andrew. He asked if that was his son. Andrew is so much blonder than I am. He's a lot like Russ."

"Andrew has your eyes."

She turned her head and smiled at him, thinking what a nice thing to say. "Yes. But he has Russell's coloring. I told him a lie, that Andrew wasn't even two yet and I'd have had to be pregnant for a year for him to be Russ's child."

Joe pressed his cheek against her hair. "Is that it? How did he find you up here?"

"He dropped in at my house in Victoria, talked to the tenants. They gave him my address. And no, that isn't all. He called again just before we left for Portugal, got me on my home phone because Shirley had given him the number. He said he had a business proposition."

Joe swore, and she put her fingers over his mouth. "I told him not a chance, and I didn't want to hear from him again."

She paused to get her breath, and just sat there for a minute. This was the hardest part to divulge. Then she looked him in the eye. "He hasn't gone away. Fathers have rights, Joe, and he'll find out quickly enough what they are. It's not that I think he'll want to take Andrew away from me, although it gives me nightmares just thinking about it. It's that he'll use that hold on me any way he can."

She fell silent. Joe watched her face intently for the space of a few moments. "Do you still love him?" His mouth was grim.

She glanced up quickly, startled by his rough tone. "I don't love him. I don't know if I ever loved him. I was just infatuated. He was charming and paid attention to me."

Joe's eyes searched her face, but he nodded and said, "I don't know what we can do about Russ right now. I have to think about this and what it means. It puts everything into a different perspective, doesn't it? It makes an even stronger argument for settling something between us." He caressed her arm and drew a deep breath. "Emily, do you think you can see your way to marry me?"

"Joe, I just don't know…"

He talked over her objections. "It makes more sense than ever. Andrew might be safer if you're married than if you're a single mum, no matter how well employed. You have to think about that."

She looked deeply into his eyes. "Do you really want to marry me because I'm pregnant with your child, Joe? Surely there has to be more to a marriage than that."

"I think there's more to us than that." His voice dropped low. "You can't forget how this child was conceived. I'm hoping there'll be more of that. Aren't you?"

She flushed, and her gaze dropped to her hands twisting in her lap, her body heating under the intensity of his focus. "Yes, I'm hoping for more. I guess that's something to build on."

His gaze became fierce. "That isn't all we have, but it's a pretty important part of it." His mouth descended on hers. Emily barely caught her breath before he had her down on the sofa, hard and heavy, pressing her into the cushions. His hands stroked her, not rough but taking, possessing. She felt herself melt at his touch.

"Joe." She pushed her fingers through his hair. "I don't know if I want to make love right now. I'm not ready."

"I didn't say we had to make love." He pushed her sweater up and pulled her bra cup down so it cradled her breast. His mouth descended on her nipple and she arched up off the sofa at the sensation.

"Oh," she sucked in her breath. "Go easy. They're really sensitive."

Joe jerked back, a picture of shock. "I'm sorry. Do they hurt? Oh my God! I'm sorry."

"It's okay," she laughed weakly. "I'm just a bit tender, they get very sensitive, and you can't... I mean, you can, but just gently."

Joe looked down at her nipple, then licked her carefully with the tip of his tongue. She hummed. He blew on the damp peak. "You'll have to tell me all these things," he murmured. "I don't know anything about pregnant women. I've never been with one."

He looked so serious, she puffed out a laugh. "That's a good thing, isn't it? I'd wonder what you were doing with a pregnant woman, given that you aren't a father."

He grinned and covered her breast with his hand, gently massaging her. "Does this mean we can't make love for a while? For a few days, for a week, for a month, what? I need to have some idea. I'm not sure how much longer I can wait but I'll do whatever I have to." He lowered his mouth to nuzzle her throat, his hand roaming lower and sliding under the waistband of her jeans.

She put her hands on his head, rubbing his thick black hair and lifted her mouth for his kiss. "We could make love now," she breathed. "I guess I'm ready, after all."

He searched her face. "You'd better not be teasing."

Her eyes felt huge in her face. "I'm not teasing."

He looked at her again, then suddenly heaved himself off the sofa. "Okay, all right then." He bent down, scooped her into his arms and headed for the stairs.

"Joe, be careful. Joe!"

"I've got you, it's okay." He gave a shaky laugh. "I'm going to carry you so you don't change your mind and turn back before we get to the bed." She hung on tight, her head tucked against the side of his neck. She wasn't going to change her mind. She'd been waiting just as long as he had.

# CHAPTER TWENTY ONE

Joe laid her on the bed and began to unfasten her clothes, nudging her hands aside as she tried to help. "I'll do it," he said, his tone gruff and hands shaking at the rising tension. When the clothes had been stripped away in a progressively frantic manner and he was finally on her, in her, lodged inside, gently moving in her, he paused. He kissed her mouth, then bent his head to gently lave and suckle her breast. She moved impatiently but he stilled her with his hand. "We're just going to take it slow, I don't want to hurt you."

"You're not hurting me." And she lifted her hips, pressing harder against him.

Breathing heavily, he tightened his arm around her lower back to hold her in place, keep her pinned to the sheet. "We're just going to take it slow," he gasped, "so we don't go off like rockets."

"I like rockets," she murmured.

He moved again, pressing insistently and distracted her with a long slow kiss, then rolled to the side. "I don't mean to jump to conclusions, but does this mean you'll marry me?" His voice came out as a hoarse rasp. He didn't really want a discussion right now, he wanted to ravish her like he'd been driven to for the last month, but he needed to pin her down first. "Are you agreeing to marry me, Emily? Put me out of my misery, please."

She looked back at him with eyes that had glazed over. "I'll marry you, Joe," she whispered. Her skin was slick with sweat and she pulled herself up over him as he rolled, gently lowering herself again onto his rigid length. He gazed into her eyes, his chest heaving. "Good, that's good. Can we go slow this time?"

"Okay," she whispered, "maybe just slow."

"That's better." He moved in time to her beat until they were both heaving for breath. "That's it, that's the way, sweetheart. You're so good. Take your time, it just gets better." She rested her head on his shoulder. He kissed her hair and felt her breasts pressed to his chest as he made small movements to rub her sensitive tissue, placing his thumb down there to conduct a delicate massage, then removed it, then returned. Her heart beat frantically under his hand.

"Joe, oh Joe, I have to come now, I have to."

"Okay," he said, "come on baby, come to me." And she came in slow rolling contractions that went on and on. He increased his tempo, waiting for her to finish, then brought himself over the brink right behind her. Holding her tight in his arms, his heart pounded heavily against hers.

*I love you, Emily. I don't know how it happened this fast, but I love you so much it hurts.*

~~~

A while later she stirred languidly. Joe lifted his head to give her a slow wet kiss. "There you are," he said when he stopped for breath. "I wondered where that beautiful woman had gone, all soft skin and urgent emotion. I've missed you, baby."

She smiled up at him in a way that made his breath catch and his heart hurt and started him loving her all over again. His tender caresses with hand and mouth brought her finally to a long slow completion. He slid into her hot wet passage just as she crested, his smooth strokes building in power to take him over the edge.

A long time later, he brushed her skin with his hand, raising goose bumps where he stroked. She sat up slowly and reached for her clothes. "Would you like to relax in the hot tub, before you go back to your place?" he offered. "Come on, it's just down on the back patio. Dog will meet us, he loves it when I'm out there. Bring your clothes, there's a shower beside it."

She was shivering by the time she put a foot into the heated water. She slid in and lay back relaxing in the curved seat while Joe turned off the water at the shower and stepped in beside her. It felt like heaven.

"Isn`t this great? I love it out here at night when the sky is clear. The stars are so close and bright, you can see the silhouette of the trees down by the water. Can you smell the arbutus blossoms?" He pulled her onto his lap and gave her a gentle kiss. "How do you feel, sweetheart, do you still feel sick?"

"Sometimes, not tonight. I feel pretty relaxed, actually."

"Hmmm, I wonder why." His tone was dry.

She giggled. "Well that too, but it's a relief to get this business with Russ off my chest. I didn't know whether to tell you, or how to tell you. You must think I'm pretty awful for keeping Andrew from his father."

"No, I think mothers from time immemorial did what they had to do to protect their children. And half the time they had to protect them from the child's own father. That's what I think you were doing. We don't need to worry about Russ tonight. I'll think of something. We can handle Russ, don't worry."

Emily looked doubtfully up at him in the gloom but didn't reply. Joe tightened his arm and breathed in the perfume of her hair. "You have the best smelling hair. I always notice it, when I can get close enough, that is." He felt her smile against his shoulder.

"This last drought nearly did me in." He massaged her breast gently under the water, taking in the new firmness in the tissue and knew she felt his erection harden again beneath her thighs.

Dog trotted up, suddenly shoving his cold wet nose into the small space between them and they both laughed. "There you are, you roving beast. Out and about were you? I hope the sheep were safe, while you neglected your duties."

He reached up and ruffled the dog's head. Dog sat down, finally grunted and flopped on the patio stones to wait them out.

Joe walked her back down the path, Dog at his heels, and stopped at her door. He gave her a fierce look. "Sweetheart, thank you for agreeing to marry me. You don't know what it means to me." His voice got gruff and he cleared his throat. "I love you very much. I'll be a good husband."

Tears sprang into her eyes.

"No tears," he said. "No tears. I'll wait until you go in. I know you're tired. Have a good sleep."

He leaned down for a goodnight kiss that turned heavy enough to leave her propped back against the door as he pressed forward. He pulled himself upright with an effort, bracing himself on the frame with one hand, his eyes boring into hers. Finally he looked away. "Okay, see you in the office tomorrow. Don't come in too early. Thank you for a wonderful evening."

His eyes twinkled as he looked back at her. "Off you go," he warned, "before I come in with you."

She giggled shakily and hurried inside.

~~~

"Geoff, we need a pow wow. Maybe this evening if you can manage it. Yep. Get Jon, too. No, just you, me and Jon. We need to plan some strategy. Top secret. Don't even tell Vanessa, let alone Natalie or the folks. Okay, see you at Jon's place. We're less likely to be interrupted there."

Joe was just replacing the receiver when Shirley came in. "Emily just got here," she said, sounding concerned. "She's late again. I wonder what the problem could be. Maybe her little boy." She set his coffee on the desk and walked out.

Joe pondered her heavy backside. Yes, he'd certainly let

this situation get out of hand. He thought about what Emily had said, about Shirley standing outside her door listening in on her conversations. Not that Joe didn't want to know who Emily was talking to.

But that was a different issue altogether. He certainly wasn't going to ask Shirley.

It was way past time to do something about her. The new secretary, Anna, that Emily had hired to work with her seemed to be good and very professional. Joe hadn't had too much to do with her yet. She was part-time and working directly for the VP. But she got a lot done in the hours that she was in the office.

On the other hand, Shirley was having a really hard time with the new girl. She made oblique comments, something about Anna not knowing what she was doing, Anna getting in her way, Anna taking phone calls while Shirley was on coffee break.

He figured that was Anna's job. But she liked all calls to go through her. That way she kept a finger on the pulse of everything that happened in the office and knew what everyone was doing.

Now he said to her back, "Ask Emily to come in here for a minute, would you, Shirley? And find out what she wants to drink." Shirley shot him a sweet smile and glowered out into the hall as she thundered back to her desk.

A few minutes later, Emily walked into his office. As always she looked fabulous in a tight navy suit, the skirt short enough to get his heart moving faster. The jacket was open, revealing a sheer pale pink silk blouse with a lacy camisole beneath. His eyes riveted on her chest and his mouth went dry. She held a coffee cup and sheaf of papers.

"Joe, can we look at the contracts that we've gotten from that rug dealer in Greece before we move on to anything else? I need to make a response today but I'm not sure we want to go where he's trying to take us."

She looked up from the papers and he quickly glanced down at the notes on his desk to mask his expression. He was afraid he might have looked a bit intense just then.

She sank down into one of the chairs in front of his desk and he looked up as if noticing her for the first time. "Good morning, Emily. How are you this morning?"

She blushed.

He grinned and added, "I'm fine, by the way."

Her colour intensified and she hid her face behind the papers in her hand.

"Fine, too, are you? That's a relief."

His grin slid away as his expression sobered. "How do you feel, really? No sickness this morning?"

She shook her head. "No, not right now. I didn't feel too well when I woke up but I'm okay at the moment."

He nodded. "So, it comes and goes. Will you tell me when it comes, so I can help out? Maybe you could go over to the house and lie down, or get a cup of something that would settle your stomach. What do you do when it comes?"

She shrugged. "There's not much to do. Mostly don't eat something that might upset it, keep weak ginger tea around, dry crackers. If it's really bad, the doctor will give me something, but they don't like to. It's best to just wait it out. With Andrew..." She trailed off, her eyes darting to his face. "We'll just see how it goes."

He waited, but she didn't say more. "With Andrew, what happened? I want to know about him, you know. What happened with him?"

She gazed out the window when she answered. "With Andrew, it started kind of by the book at about four weeks and was gone by three and a half months. So if the same holds true..."

"You'll be feeling better by mid-August," he finished for her.

Her head came around and she nodded guardedly.

"I was hoping the wedding would be the end of July," he continued. "Do you think you can manage that? You may still be feeling badly."

She looked like a deer caught in the headlights.

"We were going to set a date, remember? The question is whether you want the pregnancy to be showing at the wedding or get married before that." He watched her watching him, then got up and went around his desk, reaching to close the door.

"Come sit over here on the couch. There. Now, it doesn't have to be a big wedding, but it can be if you want. What do you want, lots of people and a big production, small and intimate, do you want it here or in Victoria? Every woman thinks about what she'd like when she marries, doesn't she?" He smiled, watching the way her mouth curved upward. "Emily, what have you been thinking?"

She collapsed against his shoulder and he wrapped his arms around her. "I used to dream about it, Joe. But in the last few years I haven't thought about it at all. I don't have any family. Well, an uncle in Alberta with a couple of kids, my cousins. But I don't really know them."

"But you have the Dubuys, don't you? They're like family. And you have good friends. Shall we make this a real celebration and have everyone in who can come?"

~~~

She considered it, resting against him. She hadn't really thought of this as a celebration, more like another task that she had to perform. Her life had been full of them, tasks set up for her by her parents and later that she set up for herself. Finish school, be a good daughter, try not to cause trouble in the house of mourning.

Then university, and along the way the task became to bury her parents, settle the estate. Find law articles and then a job. Look after Andrew.

But, no. Andrew had been the one thing that wasn't a 'task'. He was her joy.

So she was supposed to view this wedding as a joy, too. Getting married seemed the best thing to do. She was still unsure. Joe was a very attractive package, she was fascinated with him. But she didn't *know* him, hadn't spent nearly enough time with him to know if he was the man she should marry

Well, she could do it. She knew from experience she could do most anything if she set her mind to it.

"We'll talk about it, Emily." Joe was speaking low in her ear. "Tomorrow we'll write up a list, all the things we have to decide. Then if it's too much, we just do a smaller wedding, till it isn't too much. If that means you, me and two witnesses, so be it. We'll still be married, won't we?"

She gave a choked laugh and leaned on his shoulder.

## CHAPTER TWENTY TWO

Jon led the way back to his kitchen. "What will you have?" He glanced at Joe. "There isn't much - beer, scotch, coffee. I have a bit of pop." The three brothers opted for beer and took it into the living room, settling on the sofa and chairs. "Cheers," said Jon.

Talk, as always, was related to business. Geoff and Jon had been working on a system to share a couple of staff between their stores, as Jon struggled with organizing a café to augment his bookshop enterprise

Jon finally looked at Joe. "So, what gives, bro?"

"Okay, guys," said Joe, "I asked you to meet me because I need some help." His brothers casually shared a glance before nodding and leaning forward to listen. Joe looked back and forth between them.

"Emily and I are getting married. She's agreed to be my wife."

They looked at him for a minute, then grinned at each other.

"What?" said Joe. "What's going on? Come on, you guys."

Geoff laughed. "We already guessed. Right Jon?"

Jon nodded.

"We just aren't sure why you need our help. To get married that is," Geoff continued. "We can tell you what we know about women but don't know if it will prove useful."

Jon yelped with laughter and the colour climbed Joe's face.

"But congratulations. We both like her a lot and couldn't be happier for you."

Red in the face, Joe grinned. Jon gave him a one-armed hug. "Good going, big bro. We're proud of you. How's she feeling?"

Geoff looked quizzical.

Joe's face got redder. "Fine, she's fine." He hesitated. "We've decided to get married within the month, we've set the date for four weeks from now. I'd like you both to stand up with me, if you would."

That prompted more barbed comments about rushing to the altar. "Afraid she'll change her mind, right? Mind you, as the older brother, I can see you'll do whatever you have to in order to be married before me." Geoff seemed to be on a roll with his comments.

Jon really laughed at that one, congratulated him on delivering a body blow.

Joe just sat bemused, then had to grin at the silliness. After a few more comments, he cleared his throat. "If you two are quite finished."

"Hell, no," said Jon. "We're just getting started, we've been saving it up for weeks. You don't think you took us by surprise, do you?"

Joe had to laugh. "I know. I know. Can't put much over on you two goons." He sobered suddenly. "See, the thing is, I have a problem. That is, Emily has a problem and so it's mine, too." He looked so serious, his brothers sat up and paid attention.

"Emily's little boy, Andrew, is the issue."

Jon scowled. "What do you mean, he's the issue? What's wrong with him? Don't tell me you don't want the little guy, because that's just ..."

"No, of course not. It isn't that. The problem is Andrew's father."

The men bristled. Geoff shifted his shoulders. "He won't allow his son to live with you two, once you're married?

That's the most ridiculous thing I've ever…"

"No. just listen. Andrew's father is a man named Russell Barrie. He suspects that Andrew is his son. Emily hasn't confirmed it for him."

At the incredulous look on both faces, Joe rushed to continue. "Before you condemn Emily over this, please let me explain. Barrie took off from Victoria before Emily knew she was pregnant. And the reason he took off so suddenly was because the police were looking for him." As he explained, the expressions around him grew grim.

"So, did the police catch him?"

"Not according to Emily. But she didn't see Barrie again until he started calling her law office in Victoria a few weeks before she moved up here. He managed to trace her here and started harassing her with phone calls and then visits."

"Shit." Jon stroked his jaw reflectively. "So now he wants the child and the mother back as well, I suppose."

Joe shook his head, his mouth grim. "Not quite. He says she doesn't have to come back to him, she just has to help him out in another real estate deal that he's trying to put together. She's a lawyer, she can notarize the signatures and that will get him off the hook with whoever might claim fraud or a scam after the fact. At least that's my guess."

Geoff frowned. "How did he get her phone number? I thought it was unlisted."

"No one says he's dumb. He went to the house she rented out in Victoria, and spun a line for the tenants. They gave him her new mailing address. Once he had that, he found *Tanner Enterprises* and called her at the office. Then Shirley gave him her home number."

"I told you!" Geoff leaped up. "I told you she was going to be trouble! Who would give out an unlisted home phone number, especially of the Vice President of the company? Is she nuts?"

"I know." Joe`s face was dark. "We've begun the process of getting rid of her, but that's not the point here tonight."

"Damn! You should have just fired her when Emily

started there. Joe, that shouldn't have happened!"

"I know!" Joe's glare could have peeled paint.

Jon made a shushing motion with his hand, easing them both back into their chairs.

"This is a mess." Geoff shook his head.

Jon stepped in. "There might be some way to halt this guy in his tracks, if it weren't for Andrew. Whatever we do we have to consider him. We could always notify the police of where he is and that we heard he's trying to conduct another scam. That might at least slow him down, especially if they began to harass him. Has he seen the baby?"

Joe looked down. "Yes, and asked if it's his child. First she told him that Andrew wasn't two yet, so he couldn't be his. But Andrew's very fair, his coloring is quite distinctive. And I guess Barrie looked like that as a kid."

"So not the fellow you saw her with in town," Jon muttered to Geoff.

Geoff looked uncomfortable.

"What fellow?" Joe leaned forward. "You saw her with someone? When?"

"A couple of times. Kind of a big guy, lean but strong looking, medium brown hair. Fairly tall, he's got a couple of inches and a few pounds on me. They were having lunch in the food court at the mall the first time I saw them."

Joe frowned ferociously. "When was this?"

"Before you went to Portugal. Well, a month before probably. The second time was shortly after that, just before you left."

"In the food court?"

"No, not the second time."

Joe glared at him.

Geoff shrugged. "The second time was at the Steakhouse. It was lunchtime, she was just leaving as I drove up with my manager. He escorted her to her car and gave her a kiss before she climbed in. He kissed her the first time too, if you really want to know."

He looked at Jon, avoiding Joe's gaze. "Look, I feel really

uncomfortable telling you this, but you weren't going with her then, not that I was aware. So I felt it wasn't any business of ours who she saw, okay?"

Joe averted his eyes, his jaw clamped.

Jon caught Geoff's gaze and raised his eyebrows. They waited.

"So," Jon finally put in, "that wasn't Russell Barrie the father. This is someone else. Does this new guy figure in here? We don't know."

Joe ground his hands together.

Jon heaved himself up and went for more beer.

Geoff huffed out a sigh. "I'm sorry, Joe. I never would have told you. But with this whole issue coming up now…"

Joe put up his hand to stop the flow of words. "It's okay. Maybe it isn't even my business. And I rely on you guys to be honest with me, just like I'm honest with you. I rely on it."

Geoff slapped him on the back and caught the beer Jon tossed his way. "Okay, then I'll tell you that I've probably seen Russell Barrie as well. Not so tall, but heavily muscled. Very light hair, almost white. She met him in the food court too, I saw them there two days ago."

Joe stared.

"He didn't kiss her," Geoff felted inclined to clarify.

Joe's face got darker.

"He was just getting up to leave when I went by. Emily was gathering her stuff together at the little table. I decided not to stop, I had a meeting with the mall council and was already late."

Joe blew out a breath. His eyes were hard as he looked from one brother to the other.

Geoff plowed on. "So, where are we on this? Does Russ Barrie want custody of Andrew?"

Joe shook his head, braced his hands on his thighs and blew out a pent up breath. "No, at least not so far. It was more in the manner of a veiled threat. If Emily doesn't do what he asks, there's always the child to negotiate with."

Jon shook his head. "She must be worried sick." He

looked over at Geoff. "What about that buddy of yours from school, the one who became a cop? Could we do something through him? Maybe make Barrie feel like it's too hot to stay around here?"

Geoff looked thoughtful. "That's an idea. But we need to find out more about him and what he's up to this time. Maybe hire a private investigator."

"What about Emily and Andrew? Are they in danger? Is he likely to snatch her or grab the baby to force her to act?"

Joe rubbed his eyes tiredly. "I don't know. I doubt it but there's always a chance, I suppose." He ploughed his hands through his hair. "We need a plan, I just don't know what."

"I have a suggestion." They both focused on Jon. He held up his hand, and counted off on his fingers.

"One, Geoff calls his buddy the cop and finds out all he can about the last suspected crime and what Barrie's part might have been. Also tips off the cop that Barrie's back in Victoria and trying to do a similar stunt again. Two, Joe gets any further information from Emily and takes steps for their physical safety, hers and Andrew's. Three, I do an internet search for information on Russell Barrie, see what I dig up." Jon was the nerd in the family, and if there was information to be had on Barrie, Jon would find it. They all nodded. "Then we meet up again and go from there."

"Thanks, guys." Joe blew out a breath. "That's a start, at least. And it gives me hope we can help nullify this man. I mean, at some point she's going to have to confirm that Andrew is his. But once that's done, we won't encourage him, that's for damn sure."

Jon lifted his fourth finger. "That could just be the ace in the hole. If Emily sues him for child support, he's looking at two years of back payments plus all the years ahead. That might just be enough to scare him off. She can always promise constant court appearances as long as he sticks around."

~~~

Joe stopped at Rumpelstiltskin and pulled his truck into

the parking lot. As he approached the door, it opened and a young mother emerged dragging a wailing toddler by the hand. Joe held the door as they noisily departed and let himself into the play-school.

He always had to grin at the organized chaos that he saw when he came here. Vanessa had talked about the `end of day` syndrome and this must be it. The caregivers were still trying to do some simple programme but the little kids were hyper as all get out. They knew they were going home soon, parents were arriving in ones and twos to pick them up, and the mood grew more and more frantic.

Andrew was running in a circle with two other boys until they were too dizzy to stand up. In the middle of the game he spotted Joe, and froze in place on his back on the floor. Joe peered down at him. "Are you ready to go, little guy?"

Andrew nodded solemnly, all the giggles magically gone.

"Okay. Well, come on." He reached down and tugged his hand. "Do you have a backpack? Where is it?"

"Hi, Joe." Vanessa walked over and took Andrew's other hand. "How are you? Is it your turn to pick up Andrew? This is looking pretty serious, if you're doing Dad-duty." She grinned at him impudently.

Joe grinned back. "You can't scare me. I can do Dad-duty as well as the next guy."

Vanessa laughed. "Good for you. When's the wedding? We haven't received an invitation, yet."

Joe ruffled the hair at the back of his head and blew out his cheeks. "Yeah, they're coming. We're a bit slow, but they're coming. The wedding's in three weeks, it's called a quick turnaround."

She grimaced slightly. "We should have done that. The planning is driving me nuts and my mother is so involved I feel like abandoning it and letting her carry on without me."

She looked down at Andrew. "He's been really good. I think he likes it here and he's made a little friend, haven't you, Andrew? You and Cammie are friends, right?"

Emily opened the door wide when Andrew knocked.

"Hello, you. What are you doing here all by yourself?" She looked up to see Joe right behind him.

He grinned. "He wanted to knock."

Emily smiled and pulled the little boy into her arms. "I see. So, how was playschool? Did you have fun? Was Cammie there?"

"When I got there, he and Cammie and another little guy were running in circles till they fell down," said Joe. "Looked like a lot of fun. I didn't try it, though."

She laughed.

He leaned into the doorway. "Would you like to go out for dinner this evening?" he asked softly. "I didn't get a chance to ask you earlier."

Emily pulled a face. "Can we do it tomorrow? Verna has gone out and I'm very tired. I was looking forward to an early night."

"Okay. That would be good. Tomorrow it is. I'll come up and see you to set a time, how's that?" He leaned in for a long kiss that got him all excited, holding her and Andrew in his arms and wishing for a whole lot more.

Things would be a great deal simpler once they were married. For one thing, he wouldn't have to try to maneuver time alone with her. They'd had that one night, the night she agreed to marry him and he hadn't had a sniff of her since. Five days of business, meetings, talks with his brothers but no time with his fiancée. It was maddening. It was driving him nuts.

He drove his truck down to the big house and parked it just long enough to change and make a phone call, then headed back out. He'd gotten a call to meet with someone Jon had found who might be able to help in this unnerving situation with Russell Barrie.

It was well after midnight when he returned and as he drove down the long driveway he saw all the lights were off in Emily's house. And there was a strange car in the parking space beside her garage door. He gritted his teeth, sincerely hoping it belonged to one of her girlfriends.

## CHAPTER TWENTY THREE

Emily tucked Andrew into bed and tidied up the kitchen. Verna would be home soon, so she left a light on in the living room. As she started up the stairs, tea cup in hand, the doorbell rang. Verna must have forgotten her key. Emily peeked through the viewfinder and whipped the door open.

"Don, what a surprise! Come in. What are you doing here?" She grabbed his arm and tugged him in.

"Hi Emily, how are you?" He leaned in to kiss her cheek. "I was just visiting my folks in Campbell River and heading down to Victoria, but it's a long drive. You on your way to bed?"

Emily looked blank for a minute. "Yes, I was…"

"The lights were going out as I walked up to the door."

She laughed. "It's been a very long week."

"No kidding, same here. Do you mind if I use your couch? I'm wiped and didn't want to keep driving."

"Sure. You don't have to sleep on the couch, we have a spare room now with a real bed. And we can visit in the morning."

~~~

When Joe walked around the back of the house to the patio late the next morning, it was to find Emily, Andrew and a man he didn't know relaxing around the remains of a large breakfast laid out on the umbrella table.

He pulled up short and felt a spurt of pure rage wash through his veins. He got so little time with her, yet here was this stranger staying the night and relaxing the next day with his feet under her breakfast table.

Emily saw him and leaped to her feet. "Joe!" She gave him a sweet smile, grabbed his arm and leaned in for a melting kiss. When she pulled back, her cheeks were pink. He felt the anger start to fade.

"Come and meet my friend, Don. Don this is Joe, President of *Tanner Enterprises* and my boss. Don is a very old friend. Doesn't he look old?" She flashed a teasing grin at the other man. "He's an actor and is just finishing a run of *The Sunshine Boys* at the Orpheum Theatre in Vancouver."

She tugged Joe over to a chair just as Verna emerged from the house with a fresh pot of coffee and an extra cup. He settled in for a visit with the group, all the while vowing that this situation could not end too soon. He had to get this wedding put together and over with. His nerves weren't going to survive. When Andrew crawled up into his lap, he felt himself relax a little more.

~~~

Emily arrived early into the daycare parking lot. Just as she turned off the ignition, the passenger door opened. She gaped as Russ climbed in and closed the door. "What are you doing here? Russell, get out of my car."

"No, no. Calm down. We need to talk and you don't seem to want to give me the time. I've been waiting for you. You don't always come yourself, eh? Got a few proxies going on." He gave a tight grin. "But we have to work something out, so listen. I need your cell phone number. We have to have an agreement or I won't hold back. I'll press my parental rights and everyone will know that you didn't even tell me I have a kid. You'll have to share him because I'll go for joint custody."

She stared at him, her lips clamped shut.

"Come on. You know we have to do a deal. I've got a proposition for you because really, you don't have a choice. I agree not to make any claim on the kid and you help me out. I think that's fair. We both get what we want. It's nothing illegal, I just need to make sure it's all done properly so it can't come back on me."

"What deal?" She wasn't looking at him, simply staring straight ahead through the windshield of her car. "I don't know what deal you're talking about."

"Yes, you do. It's simple. I have a fellow who's selling me his house and land. And I have a buyer for the property. I just need the documents that say he's selling of his own free will, with independent legal advice. You know what you have to do, notarize his signature, advise him of his rights, and get him to sign. I won't have any trouble like last time."

She finally looked at him. "Where is this property?"

"Ah, now we're getting somewhere. I could always scoop the kid, you know."

She blanched.

"I won't, of course, now that you're cooperating. As long as you're cooperating. Give me your cell number. We'll start there."

"You know, Russ," she said slowly, "I won't do a thing for you until you've signed your own notarized agreement. It'll say you give up all rights to the child and will never make any kind of claim or effort to approach him, no visitation and no contact. That's how it has to be."

He gave her a hard look.

"I mean it. No help from me until you agree. Give me your cell number and I need your current address, names and addresses of your next of kin. I'll call when the document's ready. We'll use one of the lawyers in Bonnie, we're doing this by the book. It has to be airtight. No way will I do anything for you if you don't agree with this."

Russell pursed his lips and gazed at the doorway to the daycare where parents were coming and going, picking up their children. He looked back at her. "Sure. No problem."

He smiled, and her blood ran cold.

~~~

Joe arrived back from Vancouver tired and a little cranky. Emily wasn't in the office, she had a meeting in Bonnie according to Anna. She wasn't answering her cell phone. He found the wedding planner's file on her desk, some of the forms filled out, others with questions on notes stuck to them. Her office was pretty, unlike when Dad was there. It even smelled like her.

There were flowers in a vase. The area rug she'd found was formal enough to be business-like but the colours added life and depth to the room. Her law books were all arranged on the book shelves at eye level, the Contracts Law volumes closest to her chair within easy reach.

There was a picture of Andrew on her desk. He sat in a little child's play chair, his shoulders hunched up near his ears and a huge grin on his face.

Joe picked it up and examined it. He must have been about a year and a half. He'd grown so much, even since then. Even since they'd moved up here. He sighed and put it back.

Where was she?

~~~

Emily drove home, her mind far from the task of keeping her car on the road. Russell had signed the agreement. The lawyer had been surprised at his willingness to do so and spent a fair amount of time cautioning him on his rights of access to his child.

He'd impatiently brushed the comments aside and presented his identification in order to sign. Emily did the same, and tucked a copy of the executed agreement into her handbag.

She felt slightly more in control, only slightly. She knew as well as anyone what the agreement was worth. Russ could suddenly have a total change of heart and most Judges would simply overturn the contract and allow him access to his child. Blood was thicker than water, even under the law.

But at least she had the document and the cautions given by the lawyer. It showed how much Russell Barrie valued his potential relationship with his son. She hoped it would have at least some persuasive power in an argument over custody and access to Andrew.

Now her task was to handle the job Russell was demanding she perform. Well, she had her own ideas about how that should go. She wouldn't be railroaded, not even by Russ.

When she got to the house, Verna was just finishing the last touches on a simple supper. Emily called to invite Joe to join them. He sounded gruff, said he'd already eaten but would be up in a half hour. By the time he arrived, Verna was going out the door.

"Oops," Joe backed up in the entry. "In a hurry?"

Verna laughed. "I've got a yoga class in twenty-five minutes. Do you think I can make it into town in time?"

He pulled a face. "Don't speed. There was a cop at the highway turn off when I came by earlier."

"He wasn't there when I came home," called Emily. "But be careful anyway, Verna."

She smiled at Joe, feeling shy, and pulled him into the living room. "We've finished dinner but there's some left if you're hungry."

Andrew was still in his highchair, banging his spoon into an empty bowl. Bits of noodle were spread over his tray and in a half circle on the floor around his chair. He threw his spoon just as Joe walked into the kitchen, catching him on the leg.

"Andrew!" Emily reached to grab the bowl before it followed the spoon. "That's enough." There was a tug of war over the bowl before she won.

Andrew convulsed into howls, his open mouth ringed with tomato sauce.

"I'm sorry, Joe. He's a bit cranky tonight."

"Join the club," he said. Emily raised her eyebrows at him and reached for a damp cloth to wipe the baby down. It was a battle but she got most of the sauce off his hands and face, then pulled him out of the chair.

"Are you cranky, too?" she asked.

"Just a little. Where did you go this afternoon?"

Emily turned to face him. "Why? Did you miss me?"

He glowered. "Well, I didn't know what kind of meeting you had in Bonnie and you didn't leave any information."

She scooped her bawling son off the floor. "So now I have to report to you where I'm going and who I'm seeing, is that it?" She gazed calmly back at his frowning face, then headed for the stairs, Andrew wiggling wildly under one arm, crying loudly. Joe reached to take the squirming youngster and followed her the rest of the way up the steps.

She cracked the water taps in the bathtub, adjusted it for temperature and turned back to him, talking over the child's cries. She was starting to feel a bit cranky herself. "Well? Is that what you think?" she demanded.

She tugged one shoe off Andrew followed by the sock. Joe caught the other one. Between them, they got his shirt off, and Emily whipped his trousers down, tossing a couple of toys into the water. Joe lowered him slowly into the tub and the howls stopped. Andrew's red face showed a frown, then finally a look of contented concentration as he splashed and chased the floating ducks across the water surface.

He glanced back at Emily and shook his head. "No, that's not what I think. And that's not what I meant. You don't have to justify yourself to me. Other than at work, your time is your own. But if we're to have any kind of meaningful relationship, don't you think it makes sense to share with each other?"

Her cheeks flushed.

Joe plunged on. "You know where I am. You know who I'm meeting."

He rolled up his sleeves, knelt and picked up a face cloth. "Does he use special soap? Which soap is his?" He looked up to catch a baffled expression on her face. She pointed to the white bar. Grabbing it up, he lathered the face cloth.

"Joe, you don't have to do that. I can do it." She anxiously reached for the cloth but he gave her a pointed look and scrubbed one little arm and then the other, carefully navigating into the armpit and across the fragile white chest. He rinsed carefully.

When Andrew was tucked into his crib, still talking quietly to himself, she drew Joe down the hall. Opening the door to her room, she pushed him inside. "Take off your clothes. We have an hour before Verna's back."

"Are you seducing me so you don't have to tell me where you were?" He looked half serious.

"No, but if you want me to, I will." She smirked at the expression on his face.

He huffed out a laugh. "Please do." His clothes were slung eagerly to the floor and she was still giggling and struggling with her sweater when he grabbed her and dumped her onto the bed. Her clothes melted away and his hands began their journey over her with great care and tender purpose.

~~~

"Joe?"

"What?" he said, distracted. His gaze was on her breast, watching his hand gently reshape her. "Can I use my mouth on you? Are you tender?"

"You make me tender," she murmured.

He looked up questioningly.

"You undo me, you soften me. I was at a lawyer's office in town."

His hand stilled.

"I met Russell there. We signed an agreement."

His face hardened. "Why didn't you tell me? Am I not to have any part in your life?"

He thought of the private get-together that he'd had with his brothers. He had another meeting later tonight that he really didn't want to describe to her in detail. But he mentally put that aside. His activity was for her protection. He didn't know the purpose of her meetings.

But it was writhing under his skin, these reports of Emily

meeting different men in town. At least two different men, according to Geoff. And his brother certainly hadn't seen her every time she went to town, it was just fluke that he knew as much as he did.

He focused on her face. "What kind of an agreement?"

She bracketed his lean cheeks with her palms. "I'm sorry, Joe. I didn't think about that. It's always been my issue, my problem. And I was trying to solve it. I should have told you."

His mouth softened. "What kind of an agreement?" he asked again.

"A custody and access agreement. Russ signed away his rights. In exchange I gave up child maintenance payments. If he ever comes back to challenge it, he's agreed that he'll owe maintenance from the day Andrew was born."

Joe considered her for a moment, then fell back on the bed in surrender. "And what did you agree to do in exchange for it?"

She was silent for so long, he raised his head to catch her eye. "He must have gotten something from you. Because last week he was threatening to sue for access if you didn't help him with some deal."

She sighed. "I agreed to meet his client and do the legal cautioning for him. I think I've figured out how to do it. Once we meet, I'll tell the client what I think the market value of his property is, and it won't be what Russ is telling him. And then he won't sign. The caution will have done its job, made the seller rethink his decision."

Joe tugged on a lock of her hair. "And you think that will be enough to make Russ back off? It didn't sound like that's what he had in mind as your role. Don't you think he'll come after you again?"

She looked doubtful. "I figured at that point, I'd have all the information I needed to tell the police what he's up to. Till now I've had nothing to give them. But I'll have the name of the seller, the address of the property, the proposed sell price. It should be enough to stop him. He'll just move on. I hope."

Joe gazed into her eyes. "Emily, you're a brave woman. But could you consider talking to me? Could you think about sharing some of this stuff so I can add my two cents worth?"

She nodded. "I'm sorry. Really, I am." She laid her hand on his chest. "I'll try not to shut you out again."

He closed his eyes and held his breath as her hand moved lower. "Baby, you just light me on fire." His palm grazed her nipples, stroked her belly. "And we only have an hour. Let's not waste it."

She giggled. "I like your time management skills."

"Damn right," he said.

## CHAPTER TWENTY FOUR

Jon closed the door and led the way into his living room. "Geoff just called, he's on his way." He pointed to a frosted beer on the coffee table.

Joe sat down and snapped the tab on the can. "Okay, let's wait for him. Will he be long?"

Jon tilted his head. "I think that's him, now." They both heard the door open and Jon went for another beer. When he came back, Geoff was tossing his coat on a chair.

"I'll start," said Joe. "Emily met with Barrie today and got him to sign a custody and access agreement. He's agreed that, in exchange for her not asking for any child support, he'll give up all claims to Andrew. She got him to sign in front of a lawyer who cautioned him against giving up his rights. She says that makes it stronger but not foolproof. But it's something, and she thinks the persuasive quality is that if he's willing to give up those rights, he doesn't have much interest in the wellbeing of the child. If he comes back later for some claim it'll go against him that he got bought off that way."

"Well," said Jon. "That was pretty gutsy of her. Just up and said, sign on the dotted line, big boy. Or there'll be no cooperation. Pretty good." He shook his head in admiration. "What did she have to promise him?"

Joe snorted. "Exactly. She's promised to meet his client and give him a legal caution, notarize signatures, etc. That's the next issue. She's promised to meet with Barrie on Thursday and go to Campbell River to meet the seller. She's meeting him at noon at the entrance to the food court, seems like her favourite spot." Joe made a face. "Geoff, no reason you couldn't spot them there, and let us know when they meet."

"True. So what else have we got?"

Jon pulled up a sheaf of paper. "I've got some info on Barrie. He has a short record. Nothing violent, thank God. Mostly petty stuff when he was younger. Fraud. Not outright theft but sly stuff. But when I got into the police website, there were a lot more events where he was a person of interest. These were bigger scenarios with more money involved. I found that real estate deal in Victoria. It's still an open file but no recent action on it. There was a similar deal in Saskatchewan since then, where his name was involved. I imagine the police would be glad to get something on him."

"Okay, here's what my cop buddy had to say." Geoff took a swallow of beer. "He finally dug out the details of that case you're talking about, Jon. He says it would take some real evidence to make it active again. I said the guy might be working on a similar deal at the moment near here. He said, bring him the evidence."

"Yeah, that's what I got too." Jon nodded. "So I sent Joe to see this investigator I know. How'd it go, Joe?"

"Not bad. The guy said he'd spend a few hours finding Barrie and digging up what info he could. I'm seeing him tomorrow morning. He's working tonight or I would've brought him along."

The men looked at each other.

"Huh, not much." Geoff shook his head in disgust. "Where do we go from here? We can't just let Emily ride up to Campbell River with Barrie to meet his client."

"No way," said Joe. "No way is she getting in his car. I've already talked to her about it. I'm adamant. She thinks I'm being over-protective."

His brothers looked at him in astonishment.

"Are you kidding?" Geoff shook his head."

"So," said Jon. "We've got three days to figure something out. I don't know what more we can do if the investigator doesn't find anything. We could hire someone to tail Barrie full time between now and then. It's possible he'll pay a visit to his property seller to prepare the way for Emily's arrival." They all looked sombre.

Joe drained his beer and got to his feet. "I'll give you both a call, let you know what I learn tomorrow. I'm meeting him at his office at nine."

As Joe's truck rolled down the drive to stop in front of his garage door, he looked in his rear view mirror at the house where Emily slept. All the lights were out. He wanted in there, wanted the right to be there. He imagined her sleeping in his bed, warm and loose under the covers. This wedding couldn't happen soon enough for him.

~~~

Joe walked into the small older well-maintained building. Not his idea of what a private investigator's office would look like. There was a main reception area with a desk and set of phones. The young woman on duty took his name and made a call, then directed him up the stairs to the second floor. Joe found the right door and knocked.

Younger than Jon, the private investigator rose from behind the desk in the large single office and moved forward to shake his hand. "You must be Joe Tanner. I'm Dean Lowe. Glad to meet you. Have a chair."

Joe eyed him. Part Asian, he thought. No accent. Dressed casually but neatly in chinos and a blue shirt, sleeves rolled to the elbow. Seemed competent, perhaps a bit tired.

Well, he wasn't sleeping all that well himself. After his meeting with his brothers, he'd gone home to roll around in his solitary bed, consumed with worry and longing.

Was she genuinely willing to let him into her life? He really hoped so. He wanted to believe her. And he missed her. He wanted her in that bed with him, not up the hill in the other house which might just as well be across town. By the time they were married he felt like he'd be an old man.

Dean pulled a file from his desk drawer and laid it on the blotter. "I've done some work on Mr. Russell Barrie. You might be interested in what I have. He lives in a small apartment in Victoria in VicWest near the Railyards. He lives alone. He drives a late model Ford truck, club cab. It's not registered in his name, however. It's registered to a woman named Vi LeBlanc. She lives in Victoria as well. I'm not sure yet what the relationship is between them."

Joe liked the sound of `yet`. It implied he had confidence he'd know soon.

"He hasn't visited her while we were working him. No visible means of support." Dean paused. "I know you're worried about his relationship with Ms Emily Drury. They've met on three occasions since we started with him. They met in the food court and had a conversation, maybe twelve minutes, that was three days ago. They met at the Rumpelstiltskin Play School the next day. He was waiting for her and climbed into her car when she arrived. That conversation took about eight minutes.

"They also met yesterday afternoon. She got into his car and they went to a professional building here in Bonnie. They were in there for more than an hour. When they emerged, he drove her back to the same mall where she picked up her car." He just looked at Joe and waited.

Joe looked down, tapping his fingers together and trying his damnedest to contain his anger. Every time he learned something new, he could feel the rage building. He'd talk himself out of it, or tell himself he'd think about it later. But it was building to some kind of crescendo. He wasn't entirely sure who it was aimed at. Not entirely. And that just added to the uncertainty of what happened if and when it was set loose.

On the other hand, this young man was good. If he told him what was going on, he could possibly help them a lot more. He looked back up. "Are you bonded?" he asked.

Lowe looked startled for a minute, then smiled. "Yes, I

am."

"Do you keep information confidential?"

Lowe eyed him momentarily, that small smile still in place. "Absolutely. If I didn't, I'd be out of business in weeks. Of course I do."

Joe nodded. "Okay. Good. Well, here's what I know."

Lowe listened intently, occasionally making a note. He maintained eye contact the whole time, concentrating. When Joe stopped, he continued looking at him for a few minutes. Then, "Well here's what I think. This man has no history of violence. That's an important point, it downgrades the threat. He deals in fraud. That is, he works by deceit. If he's exposed, there's no more deceit so his purpose fails before it can get off the ground. Therefore if the property seller is informed of any true property value as Ms Drury intends, we assume his deal goes south. That could put him out of business around here.

"And from what you've just told me, he needs a use for his child before he's interested in him. Right now he's using him to get Ms. Drury to cooperate with him. If she refuses, I don't know what his reaction is. I'd be inclined to keep the child very safe for the next week."

Joe nodded, his jaw tight.

Lowe continued. "I think I should continue surveillance. Given we now have a timeframe for his operation, why not keep him under observation until it's over? Before Thursday we may find his seller, maybe even his buyer. Then we'll know what we're dealing with. It gives us a lot more flexibility in how we handle it. And if we've got the seller, we don't need to wait for Thursday. We can pre-empt Barrie."

~~~

Emily manoeuvred the tight corner near the mall and slid into the last parking spot at Rumpelstiltskin Playschool. Thank heavens, a parking space. Sometimes it was really hard to find one. In the past she'd had to park in the mall across the street and get Andrew back to the car through four lanes of traffic.

She rested her head on the steering wheel. She couldn't wait for this week to be over. The tension was killing her. Her shoulders ached, her back was sore. Breathing became difficult every time she thought about having to accompany Russell to see his client and tell him the news about the value of the property. She wouldn't know the real value of course, but she'd ask to see the assessment and had already spoken to a real estate appraiser in Nanaimo who covered that area. He'd promised to give her a ballpark figure over the phone once she found out what this was all about.

Unsnapping her seatbelt, she opened the door and swung her legs out of the car. Andrew would be glad to see her. This was his third day in daycare this week, something he definitely wasn't used to. He'd been tired and cranky last night, tonight would be no different.

The children were playing 'ring around the roses' when she arrived, opening the door in time to see them all fall down to shrieks of laughter. Vanessa wasn't there and another couple of workers were herding some of the children toward their coats and backpacks.

By the time she got him into his jacket, he was whining. She struggled out the heavy door, child under one arm, backpack slung on the other shoulder. Getting him into the car seat was another struggle. He bellowed and bucked against the straps as she bit back some rough words at a torn fingernail. Finally she managed to snap his seatbelt closed.

Tomorrow was going to be hard enough, but at least Andrew didn't have to go to daycare. He'd be home with Verna having a quiet day.

She slid into the driver's seat just as the passenger door opened. Russell climbed in and slammed the door. Emily gaped at him.

"Russell," she began and heard the car doors lock. She glanced back at her door as he casually snatched the car keys from her hand.

"Nice to see you, Emily. I'm going to get out and you're going to climb over the console into the passenger seat." He got out and walked around the car, opening her door.

"Over you go," he said.

She stared at him. "What are you doing?"

"We're going for a ride. Get over."

"I don't have to. Give me the keys or I'll scream."

"If you scream, I'll drag you out of the car and drive away. With my son," he added in a silky voice.

She scrambled into the passenger seat and Russell slid into the driver's seat right behind her.

"Good girl." He started the engine with a twist of the key and shot the gearshift into reverse. "Put on your seatbelt, you might need it."

They were on the highway in minutes, travelling right at the speed limit heading north. Andrew had stopped crying at the change of drivers and was silent in the back. When she looked over her shoulder, his fearful gaze was riveted to her face.

"Russell, talk to me." Emily had trouble keeping the tremble out of her voice. "What are you doing?"

He glanced at her but continued driving.

"Russell, please. Where are we going?"

"We're going to see my client."

Her mouth fell open. "You said that was tomorrow. We were to do that tomorrow."

His smile was like a knife in the ribs. "Emily, I'm just being cautious. Tomorrow is a long time from now, why put off what you can do today?"

"But we've got Andrew with us. He's going to be in the way and he's hungry. Let me take him home, please." There were tears in her voice. "Please Russell. I don't mind going tonight if that's what you want, but not with Andrew."

"I want Andrew with us," he replied, gearing down for a sharp turn. "He makes you easier to deal with."

Her gaze moved back to the road in despair, watching the end of day traffic coming at them in a steady stream. She didn't even know where they were going. Her hand fell to her purse and she felt around in desperation until she found the shape of her cell phone, pulling it into her lap without looking down. She'd just hold it and when she had a chance…

Russell reached over and took it right out of her hand. With the flick of a button the window slid down and as she grabbed madly for his arm, she saw her phone sail out into the middle of the line of oncoming cars. There was a screech of tires as it bounced off the windshield of a pickup truck and flew into the air before smashing somewhere on the pavement behind them.

As he drove, she grappled with her predicament. They were set up for tomorrow. She was to meet Russ at the mall and leave her car there. Russ would drive her to Campbell River and the home of his client. She'd give him independent legal advice and everyone would know where she was.

Joe had hired someone to follow Russell's truck. They had activated the gps locator on her cell phone, there was a voice transmitter hidden in the jacket she planned to wear. Now she didn't have any of that.

Andrew began to fuss as they drew close to the outskirts of the city of Nanaimo. "He needs something to eat, Russ. He'll cry if we don't feed him."

"Fine, we can stop at a grocery and you go in to get him something."

"Why don't you go in?"

"And leave you with him in the car?" His face showed open mockery. "Not on your life, sunshine."

"I'll go in if I can take him with me."

"No chance," his jaw tightened. There was silence between them as Andrew became louder in the back seat. Emily searched in her purse from something to eat, then found a small bag of nuts in the side pocket of the car door. She opened it and handed them back to Andrew as Russ drove on.

As it grew dark, Emily began to despair. How could she let anyone know where they were if they didn't stop? She leaned over to look at the gas gauge, but she'd just filled it up this morning after dropping Andrew off. They had lots of gas.

"I need something to drink," she said.

Russ grunted.

"So does the baby."

"Emily, don't make a fuss."

"I'm not. But we both need something to eat and a drink. You have to stop."

He slowed the car and pulled over on the side of the highway, turning to face her in the light of the dash. "How do you want to play this?" His gaze burned into hers. "We can stop at a drive through. That's the only thing I'll consider."

Okay, how could she use this?

He smiled, and the sight of it chilled her to the bone. "Forget it, Emily. I'll be driving, we'll decide what we're having and I'll order it. If you open your mouth, I'll drive away and we won't stop again. This is your only chance."

He looked like he meant it. She wasn't used to this Russell Barrie. He'd used that dead look on other people but never on her. She believed him this time. For Andrew's sake, she'd be quiet.

Emily spent the next few miles in the back seat helping Andrew with his dinner of chips and chicken pieces. He fell asleep as soon as he'd had his fill and she sat trembling beside him, brushing the soft blond curls away from his forehead. Once they got out of this predicament, he would turn out to be nothing like his father, she vowed. Nothing like him.

It was close to midnight when they approached the town of Campbell River. The signs at the side of the road grew in size and number as they got closer. Russell slowed, looking at the street names. When they got to the steep hill down into town, he took a sharp left and took off along a two lane paved road that wound through the forest. Andrew lolled over to the side and she wedged a rolled up sweater beside his head to keep it from banging on the car seat.

Russell pulled to the side of the tree lined road at a farmer's gate standing open and put the car in neutral. He turned his head to look at her. "This is where he lives."

## CHAPTER TWENTY FIVE

"What do you mean, you've lost him? You were tailing him!" Joe's voice had risen and Jon looked up from ringing in a book sale. He turned away and lowered his voice. "Where'd he go?"

"I don't know." The private investigator's voice sounded tinny on the phone. "He left his truck and walked into the mall. One of my men was following him and lost him in the mall. So my guy went back to Barrie's truck but he hasn't returned. It's still parked in the lot."

Joe pulled his hair in frustration. "So we don't know where he went?" He watched Jon bag the purchase and escort his customer out of the store. Then he turned the sign to 'closed' and engaged the lock on the front door of the bookstore.

"Well, we know he went to the battery shop and men's outerwear, and then we lost him. He probably left through another door."

"Yeah." He blew out a breath. "I'll call you back."

Emily didn't answer her phone and he looked at his watch. She should be home by now. He called the house and Verna answered.

"No she's not here, Joe. Should be home any minute, or else she'll call."

"I just called her cell but she's not answering."

There was silence. "That's unusual," Verna said.

An alarm went off in his head. "Unusual? She always answers her cell?"

"Yes. Always keeps it on."

"Can you call the daycare, see if she picked Andrew up?"

"Sure, I'll try the number. But they're probably closed by now."

Two minutes later she called him back. "She picked Andrew up an hour ago, I caught the supervisor as she was locking up. And Emily's not answering, I called her just now."

"Thanks, Verna. Let me know if you hear from her."

He quickly dialled Dean Lowe. "Emily's missing. She's not answering her phone."

"Okay, hang on." Joe heard computer keys tapping. "Her cell says she is on the highway just south of Nanaimo. But she's not moving."

"I think Barrie has her." Joe thought his jaw would snap, it was so tight. He rubbed a hand up his face as he watched Jon shrug into his jacket and get his keys out of the cash drawer. His brother stood waiting, tapping the keys on his thigh before he reached for his own phone.

Lowe's grunt of acknowledgement came through loud and clear. "Barrie's phone says he's in the parking lot at the mall, probably in his truck."

"Fuck!"

Dean ploughed on. "The locator on Ms Drury's car says she's above Courtenay and travelling north. They must be in her vehicle. We'll call the police." Joe heard Jon mutter a message to Geoff and click his phone off.

"I'm leaving now, with my guy. We'll be on the road in five minutes. We'll head straight up island and wait for a call from the cops." Dean Lowe must have heard the panic in Joe's voice, because he added, "Remember, he's not shown himself as a violent man."

Joe's fingers cracked as they held the phone to his ear in a vice grip. "Yes, but he's got her and the baby. We don't know what he'll do."

~~~

Emily unclipped Andrew's seatbelt and caught the baby in her arms as he slumped over. She struggled out of the back seat, nudging the door closed with her hip. "We're not leaving him in the car. And you aren't going to take him." Her glare was defiant. "I'm not going anywhere without him. Live with it."

Following Russ, she walked up an overgrown pathway onto a dark sagging front porch. Russell hammered on the door. It was finally opened and held wide by the thick arm of an elderly man in an old battered wheel chair. He flipped a switch by the door and the porch lit up.

"Hi there, Gregor." Russ stepped forward with his hand outstretched. "We're here, the whole family."

Gregor was a burly man, heavy in the shoulders and chest. His head was bald, a small fringe of white hair visible against his tanned skin. He waved them in and turned his chair to wheel back down the hall ahead of them.

In the small living room, he spun around to face them and pointed to a concave couch. "Have a seat. Who are you?" He fixed Emily with a bright blue stare.

"Sorry, Gregor." Russ stepped forward to take Andrew and Emily gave him up with ill grace when it looked like it would end up in a physical struggle over the baby. "This is Emily Drury. She's a lawyer. Works out of Victoria and Bonnie, she's well acquainted with land law." He laid Andrew on the couch and the little boy snuggled in, popping his thumb into his mouth.

Emily shook the man's hand. "Nice to meet you, Gregor. You have a last name, I imagine?"

Gregor grinned, a smile full of large white teeth, obviously false. "Downs," he said, "Gregor Downs."

Russell stepped in. "We're here to get the papers signed, Gregor. I know you're ready to sign but we want to do this right. That's where Emily comes in. She's here for your protection."

"Protection from what?" Gregor looked belligerent. "Who are you protecting me from, young lady? I can sell my property if I want to."

"You're absolutely right." Emily pulled a chair closer to him and sat down. She leaned forward. "You can sell any time to anyone, for any price. But the law does say that if you have been fooled into selling below the value of the property, you have recourse against the purchaser. That's the reason for independent legal advice. Russell wants to make sure you don't change your mind later and tell the court you were hoodwinked."

"Hoodwinked?" Gregor grinned. "I suppose that's worthwhile. It's hard to hoodwink an old logger on some things, but land isn't my specialty. This is the only land I've ever owned. My wife and I bought it years ago when the boys were just small." His wave encompassed the small rooms. "We raised our boys here and they've all flown the coop."

"How many boys did you have, Gregor?"

"Eh? Three, we had three. Good boys, well most of the time." He chuckled. "They got into a few scrapes, but who doesn't? One of them didn't make it. But the other two are grown. Fine men, they turned out."

Emily could see Russell getting impatient. He paced to the door and back, then walked down the hall to the kitchen.

"Are you alone here, Gregor? Do you live alone or does someone else live here?"

"Not since the missus died," he said. "Three years ago now. Been alone since then."

"Do you have a phone?"

"Sure." He gave her a quizzical look.

"Where is it?"

"In the hall." He pointed toward the kitchen at the back of the house.

"Okay, I might need to use it later."

He nodded.

Russell came back into the room with a glass of water in

his hand. "Can we get on with this?"

He took a long drink, eyeing her above the rim of the glass. "We don't want to keep the youngster from his bed." The look he gave her was hard and her stomach jumped with nerves. She checked her son on the couch. He was sleeping soundly.

"Russell, you can't be present while I caution Gregor. You'll have to wait outside."

"Okay. You've got five minutes."

"You don't decide how long it will take." She opened her purse and pulled out a sheaf of papers. "It usually takes a half hour. Make yourself comfortable out there."

"Don't try anything." His hiss was meant for her ears alone but she saw the surprised look on Gregor Downs's face as he narrowed his eyes at Russell.

"What's going on?" He looked back and forth between them.

"Russell's in a hurry. And this takes time. He'll just have to be patient."

Russ opened the door and stepped outside. Emily heard the door close behind him. This might be her best chance, maybe her only chance. "I'm going to use your phone now, Mr. Downs. I'll just be a moment."

Walking quickly down the hall, she picked up the receiver of the ancient black phone hanging on the wall. A rotary dial stared back at her. It must be the original phone from when the house was first built. She pulled down the 'nine', waited while it chugged back to position. Pulled the 'one', waited.

Her finger was in the hole to dial 'one' again when she heard the front door slam open. She pulled frantically on the dial, but Russell was upon her. She screamed as he tore the receiver out of her hand and yanked the cord right out of the phone. Then he calmly hung it back up and slapped his hand over her mouth to shut her up.

~~~

Joe rubbed his hands up his face and back through his hair. He shifted irritably under the seatbelt of Jon's van. "I can't take much more of this," he grumbled.

Jon glanced at him then back to the road. "We're almost there." They could both hear Geoff on the phone with Dean Lowe getting directions from the locator device he had on Emily's car.

"Turn left at Frank's Winder road, just past this light," he called from the back seat. "Go slow, it's a narrow road. Looks like they're about five miles in from the highway."

It took forever to navigate their way through the tree lined lane to the farm gate where Dean Lowe's car was pulled half off the road in a slot between a couple of trees. He and his employee opened their doors to get out, but their lights didn't go on. Joe realized they needed to do the same

It was pitch black but they could see the lights of a house dimly through the trees.

"Do we wait for the cops?"

Lowe turned his head toward them but it was so dark Joe couldn't see his eyes. "Yes and no," he said.

~~~

"Your time's up." She'd never seen that steel gaze that made her tremble or the angry flush on his cheeks. "Go in there and caution the man," Russell hissed. "Sign the documents. I have no more patience."

He twisted her arm up between her shoulder blades and pointed her down the hall toward the living room door. "There's more where that came from." He jerked her arm higher and she couldn't suppress a moan between her teeth. "Get this done, Emily. Your son's life is at stake."

"Okay. All right, Russ. Calm down." She panted as Russ relaxed his grip and the pressure eased on her burning shoulder.

"I am calm. You're the one having a heart attack. Think how Andrew will feel."

Her heart stuttered. "I'll cooperate, Russ. I promise. Let go of my arm."

"Fine." He dropped her wrist and pushed her through the door with a firm hand on her back.

"Here we are, Gregor. Sorry about that. Emily dropped the phone. She's ready to go now."

Russ dragged an end table over beside Gregor's chair and pushed Emily into the other one. "Sit. That's right. Now read him his caution."

"Of course." Emily picked up her scattered notes from the floor with fumbling fingers and sorted through them. "Here we are. Gregor, there are a number of things to consider. Have you had an appraisal done of the property?"

"A what?" Gregor looked confused.

"An appraisal. That's where a licensed appraiser looks at your property and others like it. He then tells you what your property will sell for."

Gregor looked up as Russ reached for a stack of papers on the coffee table. "It's right here, Gregor. Remember, the document that told us what the property was worth."

"Sure, sure." He nodded at Emily and gave a little grin. "We did that."

"Okay. Who got the appraisal done for you?"

"I did," Russ barked. "Who do you think?"

She didn't acknowledge him. "You need your own appraiser to give you that information, Gregor. Russell's man isn't necessarily a disinterested party."

Gregor gave her an intent look. Then he blinked. "What else?" he asked.

"Are there any fees involved?"

"Sure, there are always fees." Gregor pulled the documents out of Russ's grip and leafed through the pages. "Right here. Seller's agent, that's Russ. Buyer's agent, that's Russ as well. Registration fees at land titles office. Legal fees. Property transfer tax. They're all right here."

Emily took the paper and held it in her hand. She didn't even need to read it. She knew now how Russell worked.

"Mr. Downs," she said. "You don't have to pay all those fees. Russ is making money on the purchase and sale of the land. He can rightfully levy fees for that. But the registration and legal fees are paid by the buyer. What else is here?"

Before her eyes could focus, Russ snatched the paper from her hand. "Get on with it, Emily. Gregor doesn't mind paying those fees. He's fine with that."

"Let me see it, Russell."

His face went florid and he moved back a few steps. "Emily, this is going to get difficult if you don't get it done."

She turned back to Gregor. "How many dollars in fees, Mr. Downs?"

"About eighty thousand. I know what it's like these days, what things cost. Not like what it used to be."

Emily turned a shocked face to Russell then stared in growing alarm. "What are you doing?"

He stood from the couch, Andrew in his arms. The baby's eyes had opened and a look of shock appeared on his round face. "Get it done, Emily. We'll be outside."

"No!" She leaped from her chair. "Stop that!"

Lunging at him, she managed to grab his arm and hang on. "Russell, let him go."

He yanked the baby away and Andrew began to cry, a trembling sob that broke her heart as he held out his arms to her.

Russell stepped back and held the little boy tight. "Do you want him, Emily? Then sign the documents."

Andrew's cries became louder, his screams rising above their voices. "Russell. Please. Let me have him. I'll do it, just give him to me."

"No," he roared. "I've had enough! Sign the damned documents."

"Russ, please. You're holding him too tight, let go." She made a grab for her son as she tried to hold back her sobs. Then she couldn't help it, her eyes opened wide in amazement at the sight of Gregor Downs rearing up behind him. Russell Barrie turned to see what had put that expression of shock on her face just as Gregor slammed the fireplace poker into the side of his head.

## CHAPTER TWENTY SIX

Joe walked up and down with Andrew in his arms, comforting the crying child. "Could you turn the sirens off?" he gritted at the nearest police officer. "No one needs them now."

The officer bobbed his head and went outside, tramping down the front step. In a few minutes the sound stopped and the light strobes flashed silently from the tops of the cars.

Emily was sequestered in the kitchen surrounded by police, being questioned while the medics worked on the body on the floor. Gregor Downs was guarded by two cops as he sat in his wheelchair off to the side of the living room.

Joe moved over and pulled up a chair beside him, Andrew now lax and slumbering on his shoulder. "How are you doing?"

"I'm okay."

"Did you know Russell Barrie well?"

"What? No, not well. He dropped in one day to talk about property and said he wanted to make an offer."

"Were you willing to sell?"

The bright blue eyes looked straight into Joe's. "My wife is gone, the boys aren't interested in the land. I can live somewhere more comfortable, can't I?"

"Yeah, I imagine so."

The ambulance attendants settled Barrie onto a stretcher and strapped him in. Lifting together, they carried him through the door and down the hall to the front step.

"I wonder if he'll live," Joe murmured.

Gregor looked up at the cop who was watching the action, then back at Joe. "I'm stronger than I look," he muttered. "Everyone thinks because I'm in a wheelchair that I can't get around. I'm just unsteady on my feet. I was a logger for forty years, why would I be weak?"

Joe put his hand on the thick shoulder and squeezed. "Good thing you aren't. That's all I can say."

Gregor gave him a gratified look. "That's what I thought, too."

~~~

It was dawn before the police let them leave. That was when they discovered the keys to Emily's car had departed in Russell's pocket to the hospital. A scramble ensued. Finally Joe left with her and the baby in Jon's van. Dean Lowe would drive to the hospital and get the keys, bring Jon and Geoff back to pick up her car.

She dozed for most of the drive home. Andrew woke and cried a few times, and she climbed in the back seat to be near him. They were all hungry but he was too upset to sit in a restaurant so they cancelled their order and got back in the van. Five minutes later they pulled out of a drive through with lunch in a bag.

At Nanaimo the little boy was sleeping again and Emily crept back to the front passenger seat.

"Hi." Joe's slow smile went straight to her stomach or somewhere lower.

"Hi, yourself."

He slowed his speed and reached to take her hand. "You okay?"

"I think so."

"That was some ordeal you two went through.

Tears glittered in her eyes and she clung to his hand. "Yes, it was. I didn't know if we'd survive. I've never seen him like that." She fell silent, watching the scenery as it passed.

"Jon called. Russell's in surgery, he has a severe concussion."

"Oh." Her shrug was noncommittal.

"Are you worried about him?"

She shook her head. "No. but if he dies it might go hard on Mr. Downs."

Joe grunted. "Downs seems able to look after himself. I think he'll be all right." His thumb stroked the backs of her fingers. "I was scared stiff."

She glanced at him, and her gaze stayed, pinned to his face. "Me too. I didn't know that side of him, didn't know he could be like that." Sighing, she glanced behind at her sleeping son. "I never want to be in that position again. Ever. If I have to move to another country or change my name and disappear, I'll do it if it means I don't have to deal with Russell."

He squeezed her fingers. "I don't know what we can do but whatever that is, we'll do it. We'll keep you and Andrew safe from him."

She shivered in delayed reaction. "What must your brothers think? That your fiancée should be connected with someone like that. It's deplorable."

Joe put on the signal and took the left hand turn that would lead them off the highway to the road to Arbutus Bay. "They're just glad we managed to find you. That locator on your phone really threw us for a loop. It was stuck on the Island Highway near Nanaimo. We couldn't figure out what had happened. Lucky we did double service and put one on your car."

"I didn't know you'd done that. I thought I was alone and no one knew where we were. It was terrifying."

"I did it the night before." His voice was guarded. "Dean Lowe said we needed to cover all the bases and there wasn't time to discuss it with you. I just slapped it on your bumper when I came home that night."

She gave the ghost of a smile, just grateful help had

arrived. "Thank you, Joe."

He scrutinized her face carefully, slowing the van for the turn down the long drive. "You're welcome. Emily, your lights were out when I came home so I couldn't tell you about it. I promised to talk to you about issues that come up and I'll keep my word."

She nodded, rubbing her cheek against his shoulder. "I will too."

## CHAPTER TWENTY SEVEN

Joe stood under the awning and watched his bride appear at the end of the aisle between banks of chairs arranged on his sunny front lawn. Two of her friends had walked single file before her and now she came slowly, holding Andrew's hand in hers.

Her dress was pale green, matching her clear eyed gaze, the small sleeves like butterfly wings on her shoulders. The waist was cinched high and tight beneath her beautiful breasts, panels of gauzy fabric falling in a jagged line to her ankles. Her baby bulge was just beginning to show but it wasn`t noticeable under the gown. Her gold earrings glittered with green stones.

Andrew wore a little jacket with brass buttons on the pockets and a small bowtie attached to his shirt collar. He ginned excitedly when he spotted Joe and let go of Emily's hand to torpedo towards him. Joe squatted to give him a hug and grab him up in his arms. Then Verna reached to take the baby as Emily arrived at his side.

His chest was tight and his heart hurt. Breath came shallowly in his lungs as he took her hand and gazed into her eyes. Today had finally arrived. He felt like he'd been waiting forever for her.

Perhaps he had. It seemed that with her presence in his life, she answered some question that he'd asked long ago and had never found the key.

As the ceremony ended, he turned to the small crowd of family and friends behind them and presented his wife. They clapped and cheered, rising from their seats to come forward with words of congratulations. André Dubuy and his wife had come, along with three of their children and their families.

Natalie and Ken with their two offspring along with Geoff, Vanessa, and Jon were present. His parents were proudly promoting the champagne chilling on ice under the catering tent. Numerous friends were here, and Emily's gang that had been up to visit so often put on quite a showing.

He didn't know how many people had come. Verna said there were seventy confirmed but it seemed like more from where he stood. He glanced at his wife standing nearby talking with his sister Natalie. He loved that woman and needed her in every facet of his life. She looked beautiful, feminine and helpless, yet he knew that was far from the truth. Even so, she needed him almost as much as he needed her.

If he had anything to say about it, their life would be loving and full.

Taking her hand, he pulled her away from the throng, leading her past the play area where Andrew was being organized into a game of tug of war by his niece. Her big sober gaze always intimidated the little boy into doing whatever she told him.

He led her around to the red brick patio. It was empty. The guests were still milling in the front yard where tables were being set up for dinner.

He drew her into his arms. "Marry me, Emily."

She gazed at him, eyes brimming with mirth. "I'll think about it."

He laughed and laid his mouth on hers. The connection was instantaneous. She lit him up so fast, it made him gasp for breath. He hugged her tight, feeling her shape, her breasts pressed to his chest, her hips under his hands. This was his woman.

"Dance with me," he said as the band began to play.

Sylvie Grayson's next book from Great Western Publishing
to be released in 2015.

# *Earth Quake*

*When Chloe Bowman's husband disappears, the police think she is involved. But she is as confused as everyone else. One minute he's there, the next he's gone. It is as if the earth has moved under her feet, and she's been left to pick up the pieces. As she struggles to put her life back together, she begins to learn more than she ever wanted to know about her husband's life - a life that was entirely hidden from her.*

*Ross Cullen is lead detective on the case, and although he's drawn to the grieving widow, he also knows that when one member of a family disappears, the first place to look for the villain is among the other family members. And Chloe is the closest one.*

*But his attraction to her is dangerous for his career. And when he gets too close, he could get burned.*


*... an intriguing sneak preview of Sylvie Grayson's next book from Great Western Publishing*
to be released in early 2015



*Well, he's gone. I don't know where he went, but he isn't coming back today.*

The tears welled in her eyes, and she blinked fiercely. *I'm not going to cry, I'm just not. I've been doing that for weeks.*

Before the crying started, she'd just been numb, too numb to feel anything. The tears wouldn't come then because she simply couldn't believe that he wasn't there. Now they wouldn't stop.

Chloe looked over at Davey. He'd fallen asleep on the patio, lying beside Plutie on his dog bed. Plutie saw her look, and gave his skinny white tail a thump but didn't move. *He is committed to Davey. That's a nice thing in a dog friend.*

She should pick her son up but she didn't have the energy. *He might get fleas lying there.* But she didn't move. Her gaze rested on his still face and the half moon crescents of his dark blond lashes. Not as fair as his father, but his blond hair showed strong red highlights in the sun. His chubby hands were half curled in sleep.

She still thought she saw Jeff sometimes, driving past in a pickup truck or walking down the street ahead of her. She'd catch a glimpse of a tall redheaded man and some tilt of his head, some angle of his jaw would start her heart leaping in her chest before she got a clearer view. Then she'd have to stop for a minute, catch her breath, allow her heart to slow down. It might be the height of him, the breadth of the shoulder, that certain shade of brown of his leather jacket.

It wasn't that she was still looking for him. And yet somewhere beneath conscious thought, her mind and her body were yearning toward him. And so she'd see him in the back of every tall redheaded man, in the side of every tanned facial plane, in the brightness of every brilliant blue eye. It was exhausting.

She looked out over the yard. The lawn looked like a golf green, it was so smooth and perfect. Funny about that. She'd tried to cancel the installation of the lawn, she'd simply run out of money. But they said, no, the bill had already been paid when the order was placed. An underground sprinkler system was part of the deal.

She shrugged. The installers had done a great job, the lawn looked wonderful. Same thing when she went to pay the property taxes on the house and land. They'd already been paid. It was nice, because she'd been getting short of cash. But puzzling. Jeff was obviously a better detail person than she'd given him credit for, that these bills had been paid before they were due.

She still had some tradesmen coming around. With a new house, there were always a lot of last minute details to take care of. The fireplace mantels went in last week. Again, it had been booked and prepaid some time ago. They looked great. Chloe had been wondering how she'd finish off those fireplaces, but she needn't have worried. She was getting used to this.

Bees buzzed around the flowers in her flowerpots on the patio, lightly touching every bloom. The tomato shrubs gave off a strong herbal scent in the heat. It was so quiet she could hear the dragonflies as they patrolled the yard like small aircraft across the expanse, searching out insects. They looked like prehistoric creatures in a modern world.

Dog Two prowled the shade over by the workshop, now and then stopping to listen, then moved methodically along with his nose to the ground or watched the drive with expectancy in his pose. Overhead the red tailed hawks circled. There were three today. *They must have their baby out with them, training it to hunt. Even the hawks had a partner to raise their baby wit*h.

She wouldn't cry, she just wouldn't.

Chloe looked down at the pad of paper on her lap, and tapped the pen against her thigh. Now what? She'd promised herself she'd make a decision today. Some kind of decision, any decision. It had been three months, with no word, no clue of where her husband had gone. Ninety-two days.

This limbo didn't work and things were starting to fall down around them. She didn't have any cash flow, the debts were mounting, and people were calling her daily to sort something out, to pay an overdue bill. She had to make a decision, she needed to start somewhere.

She'd been waiting all this time for Jeff to come back, for him to walk in the door and take up the reins of their life again. He'd have some outlandish explanation for why he'd been gone, something unreasonable that would make her so angry, but oh, so relieved that he was home. They'd have a huge fight, and then begin their lives again, together. That's what she'd been waiting for.

But it never happened. No matter how much she longed for it, how often she prayed, how fiercely she ignored her circumstances, it didn't happen. She was going to have to take up the reins herself.

First the vehicles, there were three. At least there were two here at the house. Jeff's Mercedes had disappeared along with Jeff. But his pickup truck and her convertible were both still here. She had loved that little convertible when he bought it for her.

"No," she said, slightly aghast, "we can't afford that, at least not right now when we're building a house and everything."

But Jeff had laughed and handed her the keys. "Try it out," he said. "You'll change your mind, I guarantee it. It rides like a dream."

They laughed together and jumped into the car like two kids, Chloe taking the driver's seat. It did ride like a dream, so much power she could pass any other car on the road. Never mind that it had no back seat for Davey, or trunk space for groceries or luggage. That was just like Jeff, so generous, so impractical. He never consulted her about it, he just did it.

Tears welled again, but she impatiently brushed them away.

So, she had these two vehicles to work with, and she could only afford one. She'd sell the convertible. That would bring in a lump sum that would carry them for more than a few months for mortgage payments and expenses while she figured out what to do. The truck was fine, almost new. Jeff only had the best. It had a club cab, which meant Davey's car seat fit perfectly behind the front seats, and there was still enough room for four other people if she needed that much space, or loads of groceries and hauling.

Besides, the convertible was in her name so she could sell it. The truck wasn't, so she couldn't. It was as simple as that.

And if Jeff came home and was outraged that she'd sold the car that he bought for her, that she'd loved from the moment she drove it, she'd just give him a piece of her mind for leaving her alone like this with all this mess on her hands and no information, no resources, no tools, no.... no nothing!

Tears dripped onto the paper.

She took a deep breath. She couldn't keep breaking down like this.

Eyes still leaking, she turned the damp page and wrote out a car advertisement for the internet. She'd do a search and find out what they were selling for. Summer was the perfect time to sell a convertible, before the winter rains came and people stopped thinking about travelling around with the top down.

Then she stared at her list again. It was very short.

Her boarder was coming soon. Amanda was the daughter of her mother's friend and Vivienne had talked her into the arrangement. Amanda was just eighteen, coming to Victoria to go into first year at University, and very shy apparently. Vivienne had offered Chloe's house for room and board to help Amanda get started.

At first Chloe had been furious. She already had enough to deal with, Jeff had just disappeared. The police were not helpful, in fact acted as if she were part of it, as if she were deceiving them. She was convinced they never looked for him, never conducted a proper search. Everyone else was pelting her with questions and requests, and in the middle of all the chaos Vivienne phoned with a boarder for her, the very last thing she wanted.

Well, now it didn't seem such a bad idea. She could use the money.

She tapped the paper again with the end of the pen. Maybe she should take a bunch of boarders, students needing a place to stay. If she got four or five, she could pay her mortgage with the board money. She doodled some numbers on her pad. That could actually work.

Now she had two things on her list, 'sell the car', 'prepare for the boarder'. She added another item, 'look for more boarders'. Maybe she'd let Amanda help her out there. It would work best if her first boarder got along with the other people, maybe friends of hers from school. But, if she was as shy as Vivienne said, she might not have any friends.

Chloe made a note to herself to search the internet for information on boarding for students. She'd stick with university students. They were less work than high school students, more independent, didn't need ferrying places or babysitting.

She looked around her yard. She could try to grow something edible. It wasn't anything that her mother had ever done. But her neighbour, Mrs. Farrell had lots of things growing in her garden. Maybe she could ask her about it. Late summer, it might not be the best time to start. She could find out.

She added 'grow garden' to her list. Mrs. Farrell, Jayde as she insisted Chloe call her, had been a Godsend. She talked Chloe into growing dahlias. Her new yard had been all grass, with an empty swath down one side set apart for gardens. But Chloe didn't know the first thing about gardening, hadn't a clue what to plant.

Jayde said, "Then grow dahlias. Come on, there'll be a big sale at the church in Brentwood Bay, and they always have a huge dahlia section. You can't go wrong."

Jayde dragged her off to the sale, and picked out dozens of tubers, telling her she could thank her later. And she did thank her. The dahlias were blooming now and it looked like they'd keep blooming well into fall. She loved them.

As her wandering gaze landed on the building across the yard, her hands stilled. That workshop and all the locks on the door. There had only been one lock there when it was first built and they moved into the suite in the upstairs of the little building while the house was still under construction. There were two heavy locks on the door now, and she couldn't get into it. She made another note, 'get a locksmith'. She'd have a new lock put on so she'd have a key.

Dog Two sat beside the workshop door. He was there all day, every day. He must be in mourning just like she was. He let her feed him, but he didn't seek her out. Only when someone came down the drive did he leave his post. First, he'd go on alert and the hair on the back of his neck would rise. Then she'd hear a low growl. It had alarmed her initially, she'd be working in the garden when she'd hear that growl and jerk to attention.

Usually it would be a car slowing down at the curve. If it carried on down the road, that was all that happened and Dog Two would lie down on the grass or go back to patrolling the yard. But if the car came into the drive, Dog Two would give a couple of short barks and leap to the gate, waiting at attention with the hair lifted all along his back.

She didn't know if he was waiting in eagerness for his master to come home, or on guard to protect them from whatever intruders were hoving into view.

She'd wondered if she should get rid of the dog. But it was Jeff's dog, and Dog One had disappeared with Jeff. The dogs grew up together, were from the same litter. Now that Dog One was gone, Two seemed almost lost. So she'd gone out of her way to try to befriend him. It didn't take long.

The two dogs had always been very protective of Jeff, and by definition, protective of anyone in Jeff's life. So although Chloe wouldn't let Davey play with the dog, she was thankful for its presence. She slept better knowing Two was patrolling her yard.

Just then her phone rang and Two stopped his pacing round the yard, going on alert. Chloe snatched the phone up from the wicker table in front of her, her heart thumping. But the call display showed that it was her mother. Not who she hoped. Not Jeff.

~~~

Ross shifted on the seat of his truck and cranked his neck sideways to snap the stiffness out of it. This was why he didn't do surveillance police work anymore. This sit still and do nothing, this hurry up and wait, was hard to put up with. He was sergeant now, and had made detective more than a year ago. He didn't have to do a lot of the grunt work.

But he'd wanted this case, it was different. And he'd had Jeff Sanderson in his sights for more than a year. There'd been a woman, who contacted the detachment nine months ago to complain that she'd been swindled. Ross was convinced Jeff Sanderson had been involved. She was out thirty thousand dollars and didn't know where it had gone.

She'd thought she was buying into an investment. The man she was dealing with, Tom McLean, had been selling a part ownership in an apartment building. She was introduced to the man who did the management of the building, a guy named Monty. Yet, when the dust settled, Tom McLean was gone, her money was gone, she couldn't find Monty, and the building was owned by someone else, someone she'd never heard of, let alone met.

She couldn't give them Monty's last name, of course, because it was obviously an alias but the description was too close. Sanderson was an easy guy to profile, six foot three, broad shoulders and lean, erect bearing, with bright red hair and blue eyes. He was a handsome man, most women thought so, and this woman was no exception. She'd been impressed with his looks and gave a very thorough description.

Mrs. Brandon didn't want to go public. Her former husband had given her the money as part settlement of her divorce. She was afraid he wouldn't hand over the rest of the money without a fight if he found out she'd lost the first lot on a scam.

Sanderson had already been a person of interest when this information came into the detachment. Ross had his men following a small money trail and it seemed to lead to Sanderson. Then a few months later the Missing Persons Notice crossed his desk, filed by Sanderson's wife. It all seemed too convenient.

He kept up-to-date on the police search but felt the wife

had to be in on it, whatever 'it' was. This was just too slick. After the husband disappeared, the house got finished, the lawn went in. The property taxes were paid on the property. He knew because he'd checked. Now, how did she have the money to do all that, if the husband took off without warning, leaving her high and dry?

The story was way too smooth. Sanderson took his share of the proceeds on the divorced woman apartment building rip-off, and disappeared? He didn't buy it. Thirty thousand dollars wasn't enough to disappear with. There simply had to be more to this story, a lot more.

It was his day off today and he didn't have to be here. There was no reason to keep the wife under surveillance. But now and then Ross liked to come out here and park, keeping an eye on the yard. Dan might be right, he had too much time on his hands. Dan Parker was the Constable that had drawn surveillance duty on the wife, right after she laid her Missing Persons information. He had lots to say about her, constant comments about how she went around her yard with very few clothes on. It kept him on the edge of his seat, he claimed.

Ross thought he'd been joking, but from where he sat, Chloe Bowman was wearing a tight camisole and not much else. Well, maybe a pair of panties if he looked hard and squinted his eyes. Good God, didn't she have neighbours? He panned the area with his binoculars, but really, no one could look into her yard. She had a lot of privacy. And she took advantage of it.

She looked darned good too, at least from this distance. She had an impressive chest that he'd already heard about from Parker, and he hadn't been exaggerating. If he was Jeff Sanderson, he wouldn't just take off and leave her here. What if she got tired of waiting? That idea would certainly keep him up at night, if he were the husband.

The house was situated in a grove of tall evergreens, with a big yard of lawn and gardens stretched out to the south. There was a second smaller building, that he understood to be a tool room or workshop on the lower floor with an apartment built above. Even that was far enough away so it didn't impinge on her privacy, and the windows of the apartment were on the other side of the building, affording the Sanderson yard and grounds a lot of seclusion.

If he hadn't found this old logging road on the hill behind the property, and tucked his truck in behind a few firs, he wouldn't be looking into her yard either. The house was set on eight acres, partly treed, part cleared. It had been farmed at one time, but the field now looked like pasture. There were two sheep inside the fence, he'd seen them as he drove slowly past this morning.

There was also the dog. He'd spotted the animal, a serious looking beast, as he walked down the road the other day. It had kept its eyes on him the whole time he sauntered past, growled low when he paused at the side of the road. Then it followed him to the edge of the yard as he walked on. That was a trained animal. It looked part German Shepherd. Ross would have serious hesitations about entering that yard at night without an invitation.

He'd seen the tapes of Chloe Bowman's interview at the police station. She'd first made a Missing Persons report on the thirtieth of April and a few days later, when nothing had come to light, she'd been asked to come in and answer some questions. Her brother, John, had come with her into the interview room.

At one point, he objected to the tone the officer was taking, and asked if she was under suspicion because her husband had taken off. Chloe had burst into tears and the officer told him that he didn't need to be there, it was Chloe Bowman they were interested in talking to. Bowman had stated, while leaning over the table into the officer's face, that when he left, Chloe left.

The confrontation had sparked police interest in the brother and his possible connection to Sanderson. After some fairly extensive and unfruitful sifting of information, they'd found nothing to connect him to the case other than the sibling relationship.

But Chloe herself had been impressive on the tape. She'd obviously been shaken. She looked tenuous but dogged as she recounted everything she claimed she knew about her husband's last days in Victoria. Her husband was gone, his laptop, his cell phone, his dog called Dog One and his car were all gone. She'd answered the same questions over and over as they were put to her different ways, until she sagged back in her chair in exhaustion.

"Well," she said. "I've had enough. If there's anything else you want to ask, then please ask. Otherwise I'm going home now."

She stood, looking down at the officer who sat with his finger on the page and a surprised look on his face. "I'm tired. Now, you've had my cooperation, and I want yours. Find my husband. Quit beating about the bush, quit dragging your feet, quite pretending he ran off on his own and find him!"

She'd turned her back and headed for the exit, followed closely by her brother. The officer at the door looked past her to see what his instructions were, then opened the door and escorted them out.

It was Ross's opinion that Chloe Bowman and her brother John were two of a kind, cut from the same cloth. Chloe was just younger and hid her steel under her feminine nature. But she was just as tough in her own way and just as determined.

And beautiful. He'd been fascinated by her dark glossy curls and fair skin, the large liquid eyes. He'd watched the recording more than once and it irked him to know that it was as much to look at her as to analyze the information.

He watched now as Ms Bowman called across the yard to her little white dog and leaned down to ruffle his ears. Ross slowly panned the binoculars over her form, feeling his temperature rise. Maybe this kind of surveillance wasn't healthy. He might get a fever just watching her.

# Suspended Animation

*by Sylvie Grayson*

*Be careful who you trust...*
Katy Dalton worked hard to save her money. And working with her friend Bruno to invest it seemed like a safe bet. But her job disappears and she needs her money back, everything Bruno has already loaned to Rome Trucking. When Katy insists he return her money, Bruno stops answering his phone and bad things start to happen.

Brett Rome is frustrated. The last thing he wants to do is leave a promising career in hockey to come home and run his ailing father's trucking company. What he discovers is not the successful business that he remembers, but one that is teetering on the very edge of bankruptcy and a young woman demanding the return of the money she invested.

With the company in chaos, Brett hires her. But danger lurks in the form of Bruno's dubious associates. What secret are they hiding and why is Katy in trouble? Can Brett put this broken picture back together, and is Katy part of the solution or the problem?

*A thrilling roller coaster of a story...*
*Sylvie Grayson has found her niche, you'll love this book...*

**see more at her website**
**www.sylviegrayson.com**

## ABOUT THE AUTHOR

Sylvie Grayson was born in British Columbia, Canada. She has lived most of her life in that province in spots ranging from Vancouver Island on the west coast to the North Peace River country and the Kootenays in the beautiful interior. She spent a one year sojourn in Tokyo Japan.

She has been an English language instructor, a nightclub manager, an auto shop bookkeeper and many other professions. She found her niche at university and completed degrees in Sociology and Law. Now she works part time as the owner of a small company, and writes when she finds the space and energy.

She still loves to travel, having recently completed a trip to Singapore, Thailand, Viet Nam and Hong Kong. She lives on the coast of the Pacific Ocean with her husband on a small patch of land near the sea that they call home.

If you enjoyed this book, please consider giving a review.

Sylvie loves to hear from her readers. You can visit her at her website –

**www.sylviegrayson.com.**

Made in the USA
Charleston, SC
09 January 2015